"What is it?"
moving as cl...

"Aileas, tell me. Do y...
not be troubled with...

Against his lackadaisical manner, she was unmovable. Against his sarcasm, she was silent. But now, when he sounded so kind and sincerely concerned, she answered honestly. "I don't understand why *you* would want *me*."

He reached out and took her chin gently in his hand, his blue eyes gazing at her with serious intensity. "Do you not?"

She shook her head. "I am not like other women."

His smile made her heart race. "Exactly, Aileas," he murmured. "You are not like other women." Then he pulled her into his strong, encircling arms and pressed his lips down upon hers....

Dear Reader,

Harlequin Historical author Margaret Moore began her popular WARRIOR SERIES with the publication of her very first book, *A Warrior's Heart,* during our premier March Madness promotion in 1992. Now, sixteen titles and seven Warrior books later, the series is still going strong, as you will discover with this month's *A Warrior's Bride.* Don't miss this wonderful tale of a peace-loving knight and a fiery noblewoman who make an unlikely match in a stormy marriage of convenience.

We are very pleased to have *USA Today* bestselling author Merline Lovelace back in our midst with her new Western, *Countess in Buckskin,* the passionate story of a Russian countess who falls in love with the rough-hewn American lieutenant who has been forced to escort her through the untamed mountains of California, as well as a ranch story from Cassandra Austin, *Hero of the Flint Hills,* about a woman who is engaged to an aspiring politician, but finds herself drawn to his rugged half brother.

And in *A Wish for Nicholas* by Jackie Manning, a young woman who has been draining the income from her profitable land to improve the lives of the crofters must protect her secret, and her heart, from the dashing naval war hero who has been given her estate as a prize.

Whatever your tastes in reading, we hope you enjoy all four books this month.

Sincerely,

Tracy Farrell
Senior Editor

A Warrior's Bride

Margaret Moore

Harlequin Books

TORONTO • NEW YORK • LONDON
AMSTERDAM • PARIS • SYDNEY • HAMBURG
STOCKHOLM • ATHENS • TOKYO • MILAN
MADRID • WARSAW • BUDAPEST • AUCKLAND

ISBN 0-373-28995-2

A WARRIOR'S BRIDE

Copyright © 1998 by Margaret Wilkins

Printed in U.S.A.

Books by Margaret Moore

Harlequin Historicals

* *A Warrior's Heart* #118
China Blossom #149
* *A Warrior's Quest* #175
† *The Viking* #200
* *A Warrior's Way* #224
Vows #248
† *The Saxon* #268
* *The Welshman's Way* #295
* *The Norman's Heart* #311
* *The Baron's Quest* #328
‡ *The Wastrel* #344
‡ *The Dark Duke* #364
‡ *The Rogue's Return* #376
Δ *The Knights of Christmas* #387
* *A Warrior's Bride* #395

* Warrior Series
† The Viking Series
Δ In-line Christmas Collection
‡ Most Unsuitable...

Harlequin Books

Mistletoe Marriages
"Christmas in the Valley"

MARGARET MOORE

confesses that her first "crush" was Errol Flynn. The second was "Mr. Spock." She thinks that it explains why her heroes tend to be either charming rogues or lean, inscrutable tough guys.

Margaret lives in Scarborough, Ontario, with her husband, two children and two cats. She used to sew and read for reasons other than research.

To Alice Lanning of Peggy's Cove, Nova Scotia.
A delightful, inspiring lady.

Chapter One

England, 1227

Sir George de Gramercie halted his horse on the mud-slicked road and cocked his head. He had heard colorful curses before, but nothing quite like the stream of invective coming from the other side of the hedge-row.

However, it was not his appreciation for the eloquence of the curses nor his wish to be of service that brought the wry, sardonic smile to his handsome face or caused him to signal his column to halt.

He did so because the husky, angry and intriguing voice of the person who had obviously been thrown and abandoned by their mount belonged to a young woman.

The steward, a thickset man of personable countenance and graying hair, shrouded in a dove-gray cloak, ceased his account of the business he intended to transact in London, nudged his horse closer to his tall, elegant lord and eyed him expectantly. The other men, attired in tunics of scarlet and green, waited patiently

behind, their horses shifting and snorting in the cool
spring morning.

The grassy verge shimmered with droplets, and
nearby, the trees budded with the first tender shoots
of green and rust. Catkins had appeared on the surrounding alder trees, and the pale yellow coltsfoot
peeked out of the taller grass. Beyond, in the valley,
a light mist rose, softening the landscape and momentarily obscuring the sight of Dugall Castle.

George didn't respond to his steward immediately,
for a young woman's head suddenly appeared in a
hole in the hedge, popping out like a badger startled
by the noise of the men and horses. As this interesting,
unkempt personage ran a slow, appraising and inscrutable gaze over George, then his steward, he was getting an equally good look at her—at least her
face.

She was, he surmised, rather well past her girlhood,
with extremely disheveled, curly chestnut-colored hair
tied back in a thick braid from which tendrils of hair
had escaped. Several freckles were scattered across her
cheeks, and brown eyes beneath brows lowered in suspicion watched him warily. He could see the top of
her clothing, which was made of simple homespun and
looked to be some kind of tunic with a plain shift or
shirt underneath. His gaze traveled lower, enough to
see the swell of her breasts and to realize that the
bodice of her tunic was held together by one thin lace.
He could see no further because of the hedge.

George rode closer to the gap. "That mouth is much
too pretty to be sullied by cursing," he noted calmly.

The young woman did not reply to his criticism in
words. She scowled.

George did not appreciate being scowled at, even

by so pretty a young woman. Nevertheless, he easily managed to hide his annoyance. "Have I found a damsel in distress?" he asked lightly.

Still no response, just impertinent, sullen silence. A rather familiar sullen silence, George realized. His expression altered ever so slightly, although his voice remained as unconcerned as ever. "Or are you, perchance, a horse thief?"

The woman made a sniff of derision.

"Ah, I have it!" he cried, suddenly triumphant, and he saw her eyes widen with surprise and dismay before he continued with mock seriousness. "You came here for a secret rendezvous!"

"How dare you say such a thing, you—" she declared indignantly, her brown eyes full of angry scorn.

The steward moved his mount closer. "Have a care, wench," he warned. "Don't you know to whom—"

"Richard, please!" George interrupted calmly. "It doesn't do to frighten the peasants."

"No, it don't," the young woman confirmed, a slight hint of a smile playing about her lips, while the expression in her eyes turned distinctly mischievous.

The steward gave the woman a disapproving look before he moved his horse back.

"Tell me," George asked in his most charming tone of voice, "is it much farther to Sir Thomas Dugall's castle?"

"'Bout a mile," the wench replied with an unexpectedly graceful shrug of her shoulders.

"Do you belong to the castle?"

"Aye, me lord."

"And your horse has abandoned you, not a lover?"

"Aye, me lord. He run off. I'll catch him soon enough. Good day, me lord."

Clearly, she assumed he would accept that as a dismissal.

But George didn't like being dismissed, by anyone. "Would you care for assistance?"

She met his magnanimous offer with a burst of hearty, throaty laughter. It was by far the most robust laugh George had ever heard a female make, and its sheer pleasure made him smile in response, although he felt frustrated more than anything.

"I take it that's a refusal," he observed.

"Oh, aye, me lord," the wench confirmed after she had stopped laughing. "He'll go home right enough."

George was tempted to think of some excuse to continue this conversation, but the impatient movement of his troops behind him was not encouraging. Besides, he would be seeing this unusual young woman soon enough, anyway.

"Very well, then, since you are not in distress, I bid you good-day." He bowed politely and noticed with a pleasure he did not reveal that she bobbed a curtsy. Then he signaled his men to continue on their way.

As they did so, he noticed that the young woman grinned slyly before her head disappeared back through the hedge.

The steward drew beside him. "Gracious God, Sir George," Sir Richard Jolliet said. "What a saucy wench! She had to know she was talking to a nobleman." He nodded toward the pennant snapping in the breeze, carried by a nearby soldier. "And she says she belongs to Dugall Castle? I could more easily believe she spends all her time tending sheep. Alone."

Sir George smiled at his retainer. "Oh, come now, Richard. Her manner was impertinent, but let us consider the household."

"Indeed," Richard agreed.

It was well known that Sir Thomas Dugall's household was lacking in a woman's gentle touch. His wife had died years ago, after the birth of their only daughter. Since that time, the household had consisted almost entirely of men, and that included not just Sir Thomas and his six sons, but the servants, as well.

"A pretty creature, for all that," Richard mused aloud.

"I suppose, if one could see beyond the dirt," George replied with a purposefully cavalier tone.

Inwardly, however, he was quite astonished at how much he had enjoyed his unexpected encounter. It was not in his common experience to be spoken to in so blunt a manner, and he found it rather refreshing.

"Well, I thank the Lord we have no such impertinent wenches at Ravensloft."

With a wry smile, George looked at his steward. "I would take care how you speak of that young woman when we get to Dugall Castle," he said. "Despite her clever playacting, she is not a peasant. That was Aileas, Sir Thomas's daughter."

Richard's jaw dropped. "That...that...*she*, Sir Thomas's daughter?"

"I am absolutely certain of it," George replied evenly. "To be sure, she is much grown from the last time I saw her, but I recognized her eyes nearly at once."

Indeed, how could he forget those flashing brown eyes? It had been years, but he would never forget Aileas Dugall's eyes as long as he lived.

"That is the woman your father wanted you to marry?"

"Yes."

"That creature—when surely he knew that Sir Thomas Dugall is not a man to part with so much as an acre of land? What possible reason could a man have to take her?"

"Perhaps because he enjoys a challenge?" George offered noncommittally.

"I think she would certainly prove to be that," the steward acknowledged pensively.

"It's not as if Aileas Dugall is a complete stranger to me," George observed. "I knew her when we were children."

"Yet you rarely went to Dugall Castle, my lord," Richard remarked. "And they never came to Ravensloft." The steward frowned in puzzlement. "Why would she pretend to be a peasant?"

"Her idea of a jest, I suppose," George said with a shrug of his broad shoulders. "I wonder if she recognized me, too?"

"She must have, by the pennants."

"Yes, yes, of course," George murmured. And if she did, he thought, what did she think of me?

Although he did not believe he had acquitted himself poorly in their recent conversation, he had planned that this reunion of sorts be conducted with the utmost courtesy and formality—not an impromptu conversation through a hedge.

What other young woman of his acquaintance could swear like the most battle-hardened foot soldier? What other marriageable noblewoman would be riding about the countryside alone, her hair as wild as a bird's nest? Who else would pretend to be a peasant when meeting the man who was quite possibly going to be her future husband?

"But, my lord—if you will forgive my saying

so—why should you marry *her?* You can have your choice of several eligible young ladies of good family and fortune.''

''My father thought an alliance with Sir Thomas and his sons a good idea, since they are a fractious bunch. If we are not allied, who knows what they might decide to do, once freed of their father's restraining hand?'' Indeed, he recalled Aileas's brothers as a brood of rambunctious, combative louts seemingly bent on breaking one another's bones.

Sir Richard shifted uncomfortably in his saddle. ''Surely they would never attack you!''

''I doubt it, but since no particular young lady has captured my fancy, why not pay Sir Thomas a visit? There seems little harm in it.''

''Or any great good, either,'' Richard noted bluntly. He caught George's eye and spoke with more deference. ''Forgive me for asking this, my lord, but since your father is deceased, why...'' He faltered and stopped.

''Now that my father is dead, why should I honor his wishes after having avoided the marital state and ignored his suggestion for nearly fifteen years?'' George asked for him.

''Well, my lord, yes.''

''Perhaps to fulfill his dying wish,'' George replied truthfully. Then, because he disliked any conversation that threatened to become maudlin or sentimental, he grinned. ''Nothing has been confirmed or signed. This is merely a neighborly sojourn.''

''If I were not your steward, but a friend, I would urge you to use caution in the matter of this proposed marriage,'' Richard said quietly.

''You are my friend as well as my steward,''

George replied sincerely. "And believe me, Richard, I shall be as cautious as I can."

"I am glad to hear it."

"The mist is clearing," George noted. "We should be at the fork for the London road soon. You think you can conclude the matter of the taxes with dispatch?"

"I believe so, my lord."

"Good. Otherwise, I shall be forced to take my estate's business matters into my own hands, which will be most tedious." He gave his steward a grin, and the man smiled in response.

As they continued on their way in companionable silence, George thought of his recent encounter with the woman his father had wanted to be his wife. He knew little about Aileas, but he should have expected the unexpected. She had never been like other girls he had known.

Maybe she had been too embarrassed by her appearance to admit who she was.

Somehow, though, he doubted it, to judge by that secretive, mischievous grin. Besides, he had never seen Aileas embarrassed, not even that memorable day when he chased her for throwing apples at him and her skirt had gotten caught on a low branch. She had ripped her skirt to get away, revealing her long, bare legs.

Were her legs still that long and slim? Was she still as fleet of foot as a deer?

If she was, she was probably already home by now, announcing his arrival.

George ran a hand through his rather too long hair. If Aileas wasn't embarrassed by an unkempt appearance, *he* was. He had no desire to look anything re-

motely like a pauper when he reached Dugall Castle
and once again faced Sir Thomas. For this reason—
and only this reason, he told himself—he wore his
finest scarlet tunic, his cloak trimmed with ermine, and
had selected his best soldiers as his guard.

They reached a fork in the road with a white cross
marking the way to London. Once again George signaled the column to halt. "Well, Richard, here we
must bid you adieu."

"Yes, my lord," the steward acknowledged.

"Godspeed."

"God go with you, my lord," Sir Richard said, and
he smiled warmly. "Since you are so kind as to call
me friend, let me give you some friendly advice. Make
no hasty decisions regarding a marriage."

George chuckled ruefully. "I have managed thus far
without being chained in wedlock," he said. "Trust
me, then, when I tell you it will take more than my
father's wish to compel me to make such a momentous
decision."

Sir Richard nodded and, with an escort of ten men,
turned down the road for London, while Sir George
de Gramercie headed for the large, imposing edifice
rising out of the mist.

Aileas skittered down the embankment and splashed
her way across the ford. She scrambled up the other
side and then dashed through the wood, along the path
leading to the village outside her father's castle. The
grass was wet and slippery, so she could not run quite
as quickly as she would have liked. Still, taking this
route, she would easily be home before Sir George had
even reached the mill.

As she lightly leapt a fallen tree branch, she remembered the other well-dressed fellow's face when she'd stuck her head through the hedge, and laughed out loud. How surprised he had looked!

Hurrying on, she easily brushed aside the wet branches of oak and chestnut and beech, pausing in her swift progress only once to tuck her skirt, which she had hiked up the moment she had left the hedge-row, into the thick leather belt around her waist again. Then she was off, paying no heed to the mud coating her boots or the state of her clothes as she thought about her encounter with the man her father thought she should marry.

George de Gramercie had not looked surprised when she stuck her head out of that hedgerow. Amused, perhaps, but not surprised. She had recognized him at once, of course, with his waving fair hair, bemused blue eyes and charming smile, although he was, in some ways, quite different from the youth she remembered.

His face had grown thinner, more angled and less rounded. His body, too, was decidedly more muscular. Nevertheless, if she had not seen him, she would have known him by his voice, which was now more deeply masculine, yet still melodious, and always so very polite.

Indeed, in manner, he didn't appear to have changed very much. He had always been courteous, even to peasants, and so neatly attired that the few times he had come to Dugall Castle with his father, she had been so tempted to spoil his clothes that once she had thrown rotten apples at him until he had finally chased her out of the orchard.

How angry he had been—so angry that she had actually been afraid of him and had torn her dress rather than face his wrath when he caught her.

But he never had, and the next time she had seen him, he had acted as if nothing at all had happened.

Today, he mustn't have guessed who she was, or he would have addressed her properly and asked about her father. If he had known he was speaking to Sir Thomas Dugall's daughter, he would not have dared to suggest she had been left by a lover.

On the other hand, she had never been able to tell what George de Gramercie was thinking.

Nearly at the village, she pushed through some underbrush and stepped onto the main road. She quickly untucked her skirt and surveyed the muddy road, smiling when she saw the hoofprints. Demon had passed this way recently, making his way for home after throwing her.

She never should have taken it into her head to try to catch sight of Sir George de Gramercie before he arrived at Dugall Castle, or at least not with Demon, who hated the wet. He had been feisty and skittish the whole ride, and had balked at a low jump near the hedgerow, sending her tumbling.

She hurried along the road, drawing a few glances from the villagers, but they were used to seeing Aileas alone and barely paused in their tasks. From habit, she surveyed the walls and towers of her father's castle, making sure the sentries were in their places. Although it had been years since her family's estate had suffered an armed attack, her father insisted that everything be maintained in a battle-ready state.

He had also been improving the fortifications for years. Until he took possession of it, Dugall Castle had been little more than a lone, round stone keep with a

chapel added at one end. Sir Thomas had enclosed a
large area with a series of defensive walls and circular
towers. Besides the hall and chapel, the inner ward
now housed stables and barracks, armory and mews
and an expanded kitchen, which he had the masons
attach to the keep by a long corridor. Guest quarters,
also attached to the keep by means of a stone stairway,
were the latest addition.

The guards at the gatehouse saluted as they stood
aside to let her pass. "Have you seen my—" she began, but the watchman was already nodding.

"Aye, Lady Aileas. He's in the stable already."

"Good," she said, knowing the groom would attend
to Demon, so she was free to find Rufus.

Hurrying past the corner towers, she reached the
wide, flat, grassy area where her father's men usually
trained. She easily spotted Sir Rufus Hamerton's red-
haired head among all the other men and called his
name.

With a broad smile, Rufus detached himself from
his fellows, who barely acknowledged the familiar
sight of their lord's daughter, and strode across the
damp grass toward her, his hair ruffling in the breeze
so that it looked even redder. His cheeks were likewise
red from physical exertion, and he wore only breeches
and boots, his leather tunic slung over his muscular
shoulder. Sweat dripped off his massive chest, and as
he approached, she could tell by the stench wafting
toward her that he had indeed been working hard.

"God's wounds, I'm tired," he announced in a
deep, resonant voice as he casually scratched himself.
"And parched. And if I don't get to the garderobe
soon, I'm going to burst." He started to walk to the
men's barracks. "What brings you here in such a

hurry, Aileas?" he asked jovially. "Are we under attack?"

"No," she replied, "not exactly."

He gave her a curious look.

"We're going to have visitors in a little while."

"Oh?" Rufus halted and put on his tunic before smiling down at the shorter Aileas. "Who?"

"Sir George de Gramercie."

It was obvious Rufus didn't remember the name, for he shrugged and resumed walking, picking up his pace so that she had to trot to keep up with him.

"Our neighbor's son who's been roving all over the country for the last ten years like a traveling minstrel," she reminded him. "Now that his father has died, he's come home at last."

Rufus's response was a desultory grunt.

They had reached the outskirts of the barracks, a large wattle and daub, timbered structure near the stables and armory. Rufus obviously couldn't wait to get to the garderobe, for he turned down the small alley between the stable and armory and sighed as he relieved himself.

"God's holy rood, that's better," he said when he returned and began walking toward the barracks again. "So what's all the fuss?" he asked, gazing at her with puzzlement. "Lots of visitors come here."

She couldn't believe Rufus had forgotten about Sir George. "He's the man my father wants me to marry!"

Rufus barked a laugh as he shoved open the barracks' heavy wooden door. "Isn't he the one you said spends more on his clothes than his armor?"

"Yes," she said, catching the door before it hit her, then following him inside the large and chilly room, whose only furnishings were straw pallets covered with rough woolen blankets, a table with one basin and ewer and wooden chests—one per knight, squire or page. There were hooks on the wall, upon which hung an assortment of clothing, armor and weapons. In one corner was a battered chamber pot.

Several men were also there, resting after their duties or before their watch. They called out greetings and nodded to Aileas. "Seems we're about to have a popinjay in our midst, men!" Rufus declared. "Get out the feather beds and clean sheets!"

Aileas smiled at Rufus's sarcastic remarks. Surely once he saw Sir George, he would realize that she could never marry a man like that. Why, besides being vain, he was too thin, with no stomach at all to speak of. Surely he couldn't fight worth a fig. And while his family was rich, he was probably lazy and derelict in his duties as the lord of an estate.

Nevertheless, she didn't want to talk about her future with an audience, so she lifted her brows and said, "Is it not nearly time for the changing of the guard? And should not some of you be cleaning your weapons? If my father sees even a hint of rust…"

She did not have to say more, for the men quickly grabbed their accoutrements and went out, bowing their farewells.

"I'm thinking of having my old blade mended instead of going to the expense of a new sword," Rufus said meditatively as he hung his sword belt on a peg.

"What?" Aileas cried, her hands on her hips. "That's stupid! It's been mended so much, it's sure to snap any day now."

"It's expensive to have a new sword made. Besides, the handle of my old one fits my hand perfectly."

Aileas realized she didn't want to get involved in a discussion on the merits of new weapons versus old, familiar ones. "What about Sir George? What if my father insists that I marry him?"

Rufus threw himself down on the first straw pallet he spied and gave her a quizzical look. "Isn't he the one been neglecting his duties all these years?"

"Yes!"

"Then why would your father want you to marry a reckless puppy like that?"

"Because our lands join."

"Well," Rufus said, making a pillow of his hands and lying back so that he was looking at the beams in the ceiling, "you would be the lady of a great estate. You could do much worse."

For a moment, Aileas was very tempted to kick him. Didn't he realize she thought *he* was the perfect man, the perfect warrior? He would be the perfect husband, too.

How blind could a grown man be?

"I saw him. On the road," she revealed scornfully as she sat cross-legged on a nearby pallet. "I'm sure he's as vain as ever. You should see his tunic. It's *embroidered*. He probably cries if he spills anything on it."

Rufus chuckled companionably. "I can hardly wait to meet him."

Aileas could hardly wait for Rufus to meet him, too.

Then he would see that she could never marry a man like Sir George de Gramercie.

Chapter Two

As far as George could tell, nothing at all had changed at Dugall Castle in the years he had been away. The grimly gray stone walls were still thick and imposing, and the soldiers guarding the gates still numerous and watchful, as if a horde of enemies might suddenly sneak out of the moat and attack.

Inside, there was not an animal, bale of hay, barrel or stick out of place. Several men were engaged in swordplay or practising their technique with mace and chain. Even the servants seemed to bustle about in a curiously military manner, and not a one of them was female.

Far from making George feel secure and safe, it was as if the castle were under seige, with all the women safely sent away. Indeed, everything about Dugall Castle seemed to give the place a curious sense of tension and impending doom that George did not like.

The surrounding village also had this air of suppressed anticipation, which was quite unnecessary, given the general peace in the land and the amiability of Sir Thomas's neighbors.

As George dismounted and handed his reins to a

page who trotted out to meet them, he suddenly realized that he could feel insulted, or even threatened, by this castle's battle-ready state, until he considered the squalor of some noblemen's castles. Here, everything was neat and exactly where it should be, which was not usually George's experience of households where men were on their own, without women to organize their domestic comforts.

Sir Thomas himself marched out of the great hall almost at once. Though his neighbor's face was marked by several scars of battle and tournament, his bearing was still erect, and his gaze still as piercing as a hawk's. As usual, he wore a surcoat exactly like the one he had donned years ago when he went on Crusade.

In fact, as George noted the several clumsily mended rents and the distinctly gray tinge to the white fabric that comprised the majority of the overgarment, he realized that perhaps this was the very one. Under that was a coat of very fine chain mail, polished to gleaming perfection. Sir Thomas wore no gloves, despite the cold, exposing gnarled, chapped hands, which George didn't doubt could still level a man with one blow or maintain a grip on any weapon for hours.

He had always made George feel like a naughty little boy. Fifteen years, it seemed, were not enough to erase that sensation.

Sir Thomas halted and briskly took his guest by the shoulders to give him the kiss of greeting, his mail jingling slightly. "Welcome, Sir George," he said, eyeing George's soldiers over the younger man's shoulder even as he spoke. "It is good to see you again."

"And you, too, Sir Thomas," George replied, wondering if his men found favor with Sir Thomas, for the old man had a keen eye for a fine soldier. He subdued the urge to ask. After all, he was an overlord in his own right now.

"Come inside and have some wine. It's late in the day. You must have gone slowly, or else come by the north road," Sir Thomas noted, his voice slightly condemning, with the unspoken implication that unless George had taken the longer route, the lateness of his arrival meant that he was a lazy fellow.

George reminded himself that Sir Thomas thought everyone who didn't work as hard as he did or take his military and lordly duties as seriously must be a lazy fellow, a judgment that encompassed every other nobleman George knew.

Then he realized that Aileas must not have returned, or if she had, she had not mentioned their meeting on the southern road. Considering her own impertinent behavior, perhaps she had thought that the better course.

They entered the hall, a large, exceptionally cold room in which the vast hearth stood empty. The walls were free of tapestry or anything that could remotely be construed as decoration, and the furnishings old, worn and unembellished. There was not a single feminine attribute about the place, nor were there any soldiers or noble guests taking their ease inside.

Sir Thomas sat in the largest chair on the dais, a heavy oaken thing much carved, with no cushion upon the seat. He gestured for George to sit next to him in a chair of similar design. George complied, to his regret, for the seat was as hard, cold and comfortable as a boulder, and the carving in the back of the chair made it feel as if fifty dagger points were digging into his back.

"How is Lady Aileas?" George inquired politely, deciding that if she had not thought fit to mention their meeting, neither would he. "I had hoped to greet her when I arrived."

Sir Thomas made a dismissive grunt. "She's healthy as that horse of hers. Took him out for a gallop. They'll be back soon."

Although George knew Sir Thomas was not a man given to emotional display—or, indeed, display of any kind—the perfunctory tone of his reply startled him nonetheless, especially when George recalled that Aileas had apparently been riding alone. "She is a skilled horsewoman, I'm sure," he ventured.

"Best I ever saw. Taught her myself," Sir Thomas bragged. "Better even than her brothers, and they're excellent."

Not excellent enough to keep from getting thrown and abandoned, George thought. "I daresay she likes a lively horse."

A cowed-looking page boy appeared in a doorway George suspected led to the kitchen. "Wine!" Sir Thomas barked, and the lad quickly disappeared. "Lively, did you say?" his host continued. "That stallion of hers is the very devil of a horse. I told her she'll break her neck, but she won't listen to me. Too strong willed." For all the apparent condemnation of his words, his tone was distinctly boastful.

"She has an escort, I presume?" George asked, certain the answer would be no and beginning to wonder if Aileas had met with another accident on the journey home.

"Escort?" Sir Thomas replied with a harsh caw of

a laugh. "She'd lose 'em in a thunderclap if she did. Prefers to ride alone. Always has. As long as she stays on my land, she's safe."

"Of course," George said, not willing to point out that outlaws and brigands often didn't respect a lord's borders, and the sight of a young woman alone would be tempting for such men.

Sir Thomas continued to peer angrily at the kitchen doorway. "Where the devil's the wine?" he bellowed, then he turned his fierce gaze on George. "She's like her mother, that one. See this scar?" Sir Thomas pointed at a small, crescent-shaped mark on his forehead. "Her mother gave me this the first time I tried to kiss her." His bushy gray eyebrows lowered ominously while the rest of his face remained immobile. "Aileas would do worse to any man who took liberties."

"Naturally," George replied nonchalantly.

Sir Thomas leaned back in his chair. Undoubtedly chain mail made that possible. The page boy arrived with a carafe of wine and two plain silver goblets into which he poured the burgundy beverage, his hands trembling all the while. Sir Thomas said nothing, but George smiled with kindness when the boy glanced at him.

The boy finished his task without any response, then quickly moved to the side of the room, where he proceeded to stare at the men as they drank. George suspected that the lad had absolutely no interest in anything passing before him except the necessity of refilling the goblets when necessary.

"Pity about your father," Sir Thomas remarked after taking a gulp of wine.

George took a sip of the surprisingly fine wine and

steeled himself to discuss that particular subject. "Yes. He was a good man."

"A good neighbor. Little lax, perhaps, but good for all that."

George forced a smile onto his face.

"Sir Richard Jolliet still the estate steward?"

"Yes, and his brother, Herbert, is the household steward. Richard has just gone to London to answer some questions about the taxes on my property."

"Not trouble with the exchequer, I trust?" the old man asked suspiciously.

"Not a bit. I may have to pay a little more this year, that's all. My estate has been doing rather better than expected."

"Ah! Glad to hear it. It was a hard winter, but those of us who were prepared weathered it easily enough."

George nodded his agreement, although he doubted anybody would ever be as prepared as Sir Thomas for bad times. His father always said that Sir Thomas lived in anticipation of a repetition of the biblical seven years of famine.

"Good men, the Jolliets," Sir Thomas continued with a hint of approval. "Trustworthy."

"Absolutely," George agreed.

"No doubt your father's affairs were in excellent order."

"Yes, Sir Thomas."

"Too bad you couldn't get home sooner."

"I came as quickly as I could," George said. Then he chose the one excuse for his delayed arrival at his father's deathbed that Sir Thomas could understand, and that would surely put an end to this painful topic, which he had no desire to discuss with near strangers—or anyone else, for that matter. "I was duty-bound to stay with Baron DeGuerre until after Candlemas."

Sir Thomas nodded and took another gulp. "Still, a pity."

George sipped slowly and tried not to be annoyed by Sir Thomas's unforgiving, judgmental tone.

"So, you want to marry Aileas," Sir Thomas announced suddenly.

George nearly choked. "I have decided to marry," he replied truthfully.

"Why Aileas?"

It had not seemed to occur to Sir Thomas that there might be other ladies George could marry. "My father thought she would be a good choice for me," he answered honestly.

"She doesn't get any land when she marries," the older man declared.

"I would not ask you for any." *Knowing better,* he thought wryly.

"Good. She does get a dowry, of course. Movable goods."

"Delightful—but of course, the true prize will be Aileas herself."

Sir Thomas stared at George as if he had suddenly started to speak Greek. "Save that kind of nonsense for her, boy, although she'll probably laugh in your face," he growled. "She *is* a prize, as I well know. Especially if you're ever under seige. Give her a bow and send her to the battlements, and you'll be glad you did."

George prevented himself from saying that he would never, ever, send a woman to the battlements, and certainly not his wife. "I'm sure she is a worthy woman."

"Aye, she is." Sir Thomas leaned forward, his back still absolutely straight, and fixed his hawklike gaze on George. "I'll be honest with you, George, because I always liked your father. I hope she takes you, but if she says no, that'll be the end of it."

"I would not have any woman feel she is being compelled to marry me against her will," George replied, some of his annoyance creeping into his eloquent voice.

Then Aileas entered the hall. George was pleased to see her present and unharmed, although despite the presence of guests, her hair was just as disheveled and she wore the most bizarre combination of male and female clothing George had ever seen.

Her shirt beneath the short leather tunic was definitely rough homespun. The sleeves of her undergarment, from wrist to elbow, were wrapped in leather thongs of the type favored by archers. Her skirt was too short, revealing—to his astonishment—men's breeches, as well as boots thick with mud, which she took no pains to dislodge before marching toward them.

That was not all that made George stare at her. For one thing, although he thought he detected a sparkle of mischief in her eyes, she actually seemed subdued. Perhaps that was explained by the repressive presence of Sir Thomas.

Or that of the brawny brute of a fellow with a florid face and red hair accompanying her. He was the type of man, George thought, who probably subsisted entirely on ale and underdone beef.

Then he saw her cast a surreptitious glance at her companion and a secretive little smile played about her lips.

Could it be that she cared for this lout, who looked as if he were totally unacquainted with the concept of soap, let alone its use?

And who was also ignoring her, staring instead at her father's guest in a manner so blatantly rude, George was exceedingly tempted to draw his sword and show the oaf the error of his ways.

Reflecting that this might not endear him to Sir Thomas and Aileas, who were, regardless of whatever else they might become in future, his neighbors, he refrained and assumed his most cool, unruffled demeanor. If Aileas Dugall wanted this red-haired ruffian, he would gladly take his leave and search elsewhere for a bride.

"Daughter, this is Sir George de Gramercie," Sir Thomas announced. "Sir George, Lady Aileas."

"Welcome, Sir George," the young woman replied politely, with not one sign that they had met earlier that day. Nor did she curtsy, even when George bowed.

When he rose, he smiled at her with his most charming and meaningless smile, the one he usually reserved for empty-headed nobles in the royal court.

Her eyes narrowed ever so slightly as she straightened her shoulders defiantly. "This is Rufus Hamerton," she declared, pointing at the red-haired fellow, who managed something like a bow. "*Sir* Rufus Hamerton," she amended.

George smiled at him, too.

Aileas had never seen such a bland smile, so distinctly at odds with the shrewd intelligence burning in his blue eyes and the subtle derision there. Did he think her a fool that she wouldn't note the disparity?

And why did he say nothing about meeting her before? Surely he recognized her.

Was he being chivalrous, thinking her father would be angry at her little joke? She eyed Sir George again, suddenly certain she had not fooled him one bit, either here or on the road. He had known exactly to whom he was talking—and yet he had accused her of having a lover! How dare he, the vain, overdressed—

Rufus shifted beside her.

If Sir George had thought to say such an outrageous thing back on the road, shouldn't he be wondering about Rufus? she thought angrily. Shouldn't he be a little curious? Or did he assume she was sitting about like other useless young ladies of wealth and nobility, waiting for any knight capable of movement to offer marriage?

And how was it he seemed so lazy and strangely insipid here, compared to the gracious, yet masculine, warrior on the road?

"Fetch two more goblets," Sir Thomas ordered the page, who jumped to obey immediately. "Sit down, Rufus. Aileas, join us."

A silence ensued as the boy returned with the required goblets and nervously poured out the wine, then scurried back to a corner.

"You remember Sir George, Aileas?" Sir Thomas demanded.

"Yes, Father, I do," she replied. She gave their guest a sidelong glance and watched as he drank his wine elegantly, his long, slender fingers lightly holding the stem of the goblet. Every other man of her acquaintance clutched a goblet as he would a weapon.

"You've been gone a long time," Rufus observed

before reaching for his wine and downing a large gulp, his swallows distinctly audible.

"Yes. I've been serving the Baron DeGuerre," Sir George drawled languidly. "When I was called home, I had no idea my father's condition was so serious. He was ill quite often. Indeed, after he seemed to have passed away, I pressed my dagger to his fingertip just to ensure that the priest hadn't made a mistake. My father was, however, completely and utterly dead."

His tone was so matter-of-fact and his smile so continuously banal, Aileas didn't know what to make of him. Rufus simply stared at him, dumbfounded, and Sir Thomas's expression was nearly as stunned.

"I'm sure you will agree, Sir Thomas, that I would have been negligent in my duty to the baron if I came home too soon. You would not want your sons, whom I understand are all from home in the service of various and sundry noble lords, to rush to your bedside unless you were in imminent danger of dying."

Sir Thomas cleared his throat. "No, no, I wouldn't."

"I didn't think so. Now, if you will be so kind as to show me where I am to sleep, I believe I should retire and change for the evening meal, which I'm certain will be absolutely delightful." He ran an appraising gaze over Rufus. "And I think I should wash."

"Yes, yes, as you wish," Sir Thomas muttered. "You there!" He snapped his fingers at the page boy, who once again ran forward. "Take Sir George to the bedchamber in the west tower."

The boy nodded and bowed, and Sir George rose. "Separate sleeping quarters for guests?" he inquired lightly. "How modern." He made a deep and graceful obeisance. "Sir Thomas, I thank you for your kind

welcome. Sir Rufus, good day. Lady Aileas, a pleasure. I look forward to seeing you at supper.''

Aileas watched Sir George stroll away. The moment
he disappeared from sight up the curving stone stairway leading to the upper tower, she turned toward her
father. ''How could any man speak so of his father's
death?'' she demanded.

Sir Thomas didn't answer right away. Indeed,
Aileas suspected he, too, was wondering what kind of
man he had invited into his castle, for there was a
singularly incredulous look on his face. Then he
cleared his throat and his face resumed its usual stern
expression. ''He has been gone for many years. He
has indeed been in the service of Baron DeGuerre.''

Aileas was even more confused. She knew enough
of the baron to realize that he wouldn't countenance
having a buffoon in his company for long.

Rufus smirked at Aileas, then turned a carefully interested eye on her father. ''Who would condone having such a fool near him?'' he mused aloud.

''He was the best fighter to come out of this country, save for my sons, of course. Don't be deceived by
his lack of size. He's thin, but he's wiry—and quicker
on his feet than any man I've ever seen.''

''Quite frankly, Father, I find it difficult to believe
he was ever anything but what we have just seen.''

''That's where you'd be wrong,'' Sir Thomas
growled. ''George is no fool, whatever he may seem.''
Her father set down his wine. ''Rufus, see that the men
are told the watchword for tonight. It's *alliance*.''

Rufus rose and bowed to them both before striding
from the hall.

Aileas rose to leave, too, until her father ordered her

to sit back down and regarded her with a speculative gaze. "What do you think of him for a husband?"

"He will do very well—for someone else," Aileas replied bluntly.

"I want you to marry him." It was not a wish or an opinion. It was a command. "His lands border ours, and he is a great favorite of DeGuerre," her father reminded her unnecessarily and before she could speak. "He's a rich man, with powerful friends, despite what he seems."

Aileas's hands balled into fists and she raised her eyes defiantly. "Father, I just thought—"

"*You* just thought? Did I ask you what *you* just thought? Granted the fellow's gone a little soft, perhaps, but that can change. A few weeks here, and he'll be what he was."

"Yes, Father."

"It is up to *me* to decide who you will marry. Remember that, Aileas."

"Yes, Father."

"You will wear your best gown tonight, and you will accord Sir George the courtesy his rank deserves," Sir Thomas ordered.

"Yes, Father."

His tone softened ever so slightly as he said, "Now you may go."

Aileas gave no indication of her feelings as she left the hall, but she hurried to where Rufus would be speaking with the guards. She waited beside the gate until he came out of the gatehouse, then grabbed his arm and pulled him into the shadows. "He's ordered me to marry him!" she declared. "As if I were a child!"

Rufus looked down at the angry young woman and

suddenly realized that they were speaking of an event that was very likely to occur. What Sir Thomas ordered always came about.

Even his daughter's wedding, Rufus assumed.

It had to happen sometime, of course. He had known that for years, in an abstract sort of way, although he had never seriously considered the matter, just as he rarely even considered Aileas a woman. She was more like a squire or page to him than a woman.

Now that he was forced to think of her as a marriageable female, he realized that he would be very sorry to lose such a friend.

Aileas married. To that peacock Sir George.

"What do *you* think of him?" he asked quietly. It would be worse if she was forced to marry someone she couldn't even respect, let alone like.

"He's very well dressed," she said scornfully.

"Your father says he's a good fighter."

"I will believe that when I witness it for myself."

"He does have powerful friends."

"So do jesters."

"He's rich."

"He won't be for long if he continues to spend so much on his clothes."

"Do you truly believe your father will force you to marry him?"

Aileas's steadfast gaze did not falter. "Unless someone better asks for me first."

Chapter Three

Suddenly Rufus felt sick, for there could be no mistaking the significance of Aileas's words or the unexpected yearning in her eyes.

She wanted *him* to ask for her.

But he could never marry Aileas. Indeed, the idea had never occurred to him in all the years he had lived at Dugall Castle. If it had, it would have seemed preposterous. He would as soon consider marrying Sir Thomas as he would his daughter.

Rufus wanted a *womanly* woman, a soft, tenderhearted creature who would soothe his brow when he was anxious, not offer to wrestle. A woman who would serve him his food and drink and anxiously await his opinion on their merits, not someone who wolfed down bread, meat and ale like a starving foot soldier. A woman who could do her best to soften his anger, not tell him to stop acting like a spoiled brat. Who would defer to him as head of the household, not answer back impertinently. Who would be pliant and loving and welcoming in bed.

Aileas do any of those things? He couldn't even imagine it. And especially not in bed. Why, it would be like…like sleeping with a younger brother. At that thought, it was all he could do to keep the disgust from his face. "I…I have other duties to attend to," he stammered as he backed away, then turned and hurried off.

Leaving Aileas alone in the shadow of the wall.

George slowly surveyed the room in which he was to sleep. It was as bare and comfortable as that of a penitential priest, he thought glumly. No feather bed, only ropes slung across the bed frame for him to sleep upon. A bare minimum of blankets. No brazier. No tapestries. One stool. "Am I to be martyred for marriage?" he muttered aloud.

"I beg your pardon, my lord?" the page asked timidly behind him.

He had forgotten the boy was there. "Sir Thomas doesn't believe in luxury, does he?" he replied, turning toward the lad and grinning. "No matter. Knowing Sir Thomas as I do, I came prepared."

The boy's expression remained stoic, and George decided it would be better to send the lad back to his duties. "You may go."

The page did as he was told while George sighed and rubbed his arms for warmth, thankful he had thought to include his own feather bed, warm coverlet, brazier, coal and even a carpet in his baggage. He did not intend to wake up frozen to the bed, and wished Herbert Jolliet, his household steward, was here to see that George had not been foolish to bring such necessities.

He went to the narrow window and looked out over the castle walls, past the village to the hills and meadows beyond. On a very clear day, he could probably see his own castle from the battlements on the other side of the tower.

Ravensloft was not as massive as Sir Thomas's fortress, and no castle could ever really be called comfortable, but his hall was certainly more welcoming than this one.

What would Aileas Dugall make of his home? She would find it vastly different, but whether she would view it with approval or not, he couldn't say.

Just as he couldn't say how she would react to the suggestion that a bath and a decent gown might improve her appearance. She might even be quite pretty, properly groomed and attired. Moreover, there was a sparkle of alluring fire in her eyes and an uninhibited frankness in her manner that made her one of the more fascinating young women he had met in recent memory.

Why, he was actually getting aroused as he thought about her. George had never imagined Aileas Dugall could excite him as she was doing now—and she was not even in the room.

Maybe she was still in the hall with Sir Rufus Hamerton.

A rare scowl crossed George's face. Apparently she preferred a big, stocky, ill-mannered lout, who seemed oblivious to her regard, to a courteous, well-dressed gentleman. All Hamerton's attention had been focused on *him,* although George had seen no hint of envy or jealousy or even concern for Aileas in the oaf's manner. Hamerton's regard had been more a sense of one warrior determining the fighting capacity of another.

Let him speculate all he would, for George had no doubt that should they ever meet in combat or at a tournament, he would triumph. With his experience, he could easily guess the kind of fighter Rufus would be—the kind who thought brawn all that counted, who would use his size and his weight to good advantage, but who would be completely outdone by a more seasoned, quick-thinking, fast-moving opponent.

Poor Aileas, if she felt a regard that was not reciprocated, George mused. Unrequited love was a fool's game, and one he had never played himself. Indeed, he thought such a thing betrayed a most humiliating lack of self-respect and marveled that a woman of Aileas Dugall's impertinent pride could fall prey to it.

Especially since George was quite sure Rufus Hamerton was the type of fellow who thought a slap on a woman's rump and a "How about it?" all that was required when wooing.

Or perhaps they were just friends.

Catching a slight movement in the shadows below, George leaned forward to look out the window. Rufus Hamerton was striding away like a man on an important mission. A few moments later, Aileas appeared, hurrying in the opposite direction toward the castle's main gate.

What was this? A cozy little meeting between friends—or lovers? Perhaps he had been wrong about Rufus Hamerton's lack of affection for his lord's daughter, and the fellow was very clever at hiding it, as unlikely as that seemed. George ground his fist into his hand as he thought that perhaps he had not been so far off when he made his joke back there on the road about Aileas having a secret rendezvous.

Then he gripped his fist in sudden resolution and grinned. What was it he had said to Richard? That Aileas Dugall would attract a man who liked a challenge?

Normally, George preferred to leave the challenges to somebody else, but here, today, he recognized what he felt: the pleasing thrill of entering a contest he would undoubtedly win.

For he was going to show that overgrown, overbearing red-haired ruffian how a gentleman wooed a lady.

As always when Aileas was disturbed, she hurried to the apple orchard. Passing Sir George's soldiers as they unloaded his baggage cart, she noticed there were several chests and bundles, far more than she might have expected. How much clothing did one man need? she thought with a derisive sniff.

Rufus didn't care what he wore. In fact, he didn't seem to care about much of anything, beyond his weapons and fighting. And her. Despite his reaction there in the courtyard, she knew he cared about her.

Once in the orchard outside the castle, she climbed to the top of the tallest tree. Soon the apple trees would all be in snowy bloom, but for now, only the beginnings of green leaves were visible.

With a sigh, she surveyed the surrounding countryside, her gaze resting on the hill near Sir George's castle. On a clear day, it would be visible from here. If she were to marry him, she would be comfortably close to her home.

Rufus's family's estate lay far to the north and west, nearly at the border with Wales. She wouldn't like to be so far away.

The bark was damp and slightly slick, but this tree was as familiar to her as her bedchamber, and as comfortable. Easing herself onto the highest branch that would bear her weight, she stared glumly at the west tower.

Men! They were all unfathomable, including her father. Couldn't he see that she would sooner marry a peacock than Sir George de Gramercie? He was far from her ideal.

Rufus was her ideal. A bold, fierce warrior who treated her as he would a man. Or at least a squire, she admitted to herself. Still, that was better than being treated as if she were no more than a mere woman, a simpering, weak creature totally under a man's domination.

If that was what Sir George wanted in a bride, he had certainly come to the wrong castle!

Surely that was not what Rufus wanted.

She chewed her lower lip thoughtfully, recalling the change in his expression when she hinted that he should ask for her hand. He had been surprised and…and dismayed.

The surprise she could, perhaps, understand. This talk of weddings and marriage took her aback, too.

But why should he feel dismayed? It could not be that he didn't know the affection she felt for him. Did he think Sir George likely to stand a chance with her? Did he feel her father would favor Sir George over him? To be sure, the proximity of her father's land to that of Sir George was something in his favor, but when it came to the personal attributes of the men themselves…

Her gaze lit on the corner of the stone wall that surrounded the orchard, the precise spot where Sir George had been standing when she had hit him with the rotten apples.

His handsome face had twisted with rage. He had

looked so angry she had been afraid he would drag her out of the tree and pummel her within an inch of her life. Indeed, she had been so frightened she had jumped out of the tree and taken to her heels.

Her gaze followed her route. There had stood the holly bush, now gone, where she had torn her skirt. She had dashed over the low rise and into the castle, not stopping until she was in the farthest corner of the hayloft over the stables.

If she were Sir George's opponent on a field of battle and saw that expression on his face, she would surely fear for her life.

But that had been long ago. Perhaps he had lost that capacity for fire and bold action.

Aileas scowled. She dare not refuse her father's command directly, for she knew how he would react to that, and it wasn't good. No, she would have to be subtle. She would have to find a way to show him that Sir George simply would not suit.

Oh, what was the matter with Rufus? she thought as she laid her chin in her hand. She couldn't begin to count the happy times they had shared, riding or shooting. She had watched him practice his jousting and swordplay, and he had always respected her advice on how to improve.

They were always together, or at least most of the time. Even if he often seemed to forget she was there, like the times he and the other men talked about their jaunts into the village and to one establishment in particular.

When they talked about what they did with their women.

Her body began to grow warm as she tried to picture

herself doing some of the more interesting things they had described with Rufus. Somehow, that wasn't easy.

Now, Sir George, him she could see moving in such a manner, caressing a woman's naked body with slow and agonizing strokes until she begged for him. She could envision a woman sliding her tongue along his flesh, or nibbling lightly on his ear, or—

She shook her head to clear it. Just because Rufus did most things hastily didn't mean he would that, too.

The main thing to remember was that she and Rufus were comfortable together. Why, they had laughed and joked together a thousand times, as her brothers did together.

Brothers. He treated her as her brothers treated one another.

He didn't think of her as a woman! He thought of her as his squire, or his companion, not as a woman to be wooed.

Certain she had found the answer, Aileas smacked her hands together so suddenly she nearly fell out of the tree. A quick grab at an upper branch saved her from tumbling to her doom, but that was not why she was breathing so hard.

She glanced down at her clothes. The breeches beneath the skirt. The tunic that was her older brother's castoff. She lifted her hand to her hair in its untidy braid, then laid her palms against her sun-browned cheeks.

Her brow furrowed with thought. She would have to change. She would have to show Rufus that she was a woman. A woman fit to be his wife. Willing to be his wife. Anxious to be his wife.

A moment's doubt assailed her. What did she know of being a woman, beyond the most basic physical differences? She didn't know how to dress or arrange her hair, or how to walk the way the few women who visited Dugall Castle did. Indeed, she had often wondered what those women would do if a mad bull chased after them, since they seemed unable to walk quickly, let alone run.

Then her confidence returned. How hard could it be? She did own gowns, two of them. One she had possessed for years, and the other—the other her father had purchased for her last year. Had he been thinking of her marriage even then?

Well, the idea of marriage didn't disturb her in itself. She would simply have to ensure that she was married to the right man.

And that meant Rufus Hamerton.

Feeling better now that he had washed off the grime of the journey, and attired in a new scarlet tunic that brushed the top of his finest boots, George paused on the threshold of the hall and surveyed the gathering.

As was to be expected in Sir Thomas's hall, there were no ladies present.

What he did see were several men of Rufus's build and temperament, if not hair color, lounging about, waiting for the evening meal. Several were discussing the day's training exercise, and in one corner, there was a lively conversation concerning the swordplay to be done on the morrow.

Sir Thomas prided himself on his ability to find and train the finest fighting men in England, and although he was not the only lord with such aspirations, he was perhaps the most competitive in that regard. With excellent results, George thought. Every man here looked well able to defend himself.

It occurred to George that Aileas Dugall must have met many different men in the years of her growing up, for Sir Thomas had refused to send her away to be fostered. While that bespoke a tender sentiment not readily apparent in Sir Thomas, George couldn't help thinking it might have been better for her development if he had done so. Surely Aileas would have benefited from a woman's teaching.

It might be better just to forget the whole notion of wooing Aileas Dugall, he thought as he watched the men. If she wanted Rufus, let her have him. If he didn't want her, that was none of George's business.

Then, behind him, George heard the familiar rustle of a skirt. He turned to see Aileas poised on the steps behind him.

She wore a simple gown of dark green velvet that did not quite fit properly, for it hung far too loosely at the neckline, exposing the tops of her undoubtedly fine breasts, while the rest of her bodice clung to her slender, shapely waist. Long cuffs lined with paler green silk sarcenet fell nearly to the floor, while the skirt flared out from her narrow hips.

Her hair was dressed in the now familiar braid, a little tidier, and someone had attempted to entwine green ribbons in it, with somewhat less than satisfactory results. Several stray hairs had escaped to brush her glowing cheeks.

Then he noticed that she still wore the same mud-encrusted boots.

She smiled warmly, and he was pleased—until he realized she was not smiling at him but at Rufus Hamerton, who was in the midst of a particularly boisterous group of men standing near the hearth.

Subduing the urge to scowl, George approached her

and bowed. "How lovely you look," he whispered in a low, seductive voice, giving her the most charming smile he could muster. "That color suits you to perfection."

She flushed, the pink tinging her dusky cheeks, and his smile grew more sincere. "Indeed, I thought an angel had descended when I saw you."

Her brown eyes flashed with scorn and her lip curled up in a sneer. "Angels," she hissed, "wear white."

"Of course. My wits were addled by your beauty." She stared at him as if he were mad, but he ignored her expression. "My lady, allow me to escort you to your place at table," he said as he took her hand and placed it on his arm.

She flinched.

He put his other hand over top, trapping hers.

Then Rufus, his thick red brows furrowed, broke away from his group, which had fallen silent, and took a step toward them. "Aileas?"

"Good evening, Rufus," she said, pulling away from George. "Good evening," she said to the other men, some of whom were staring with open mouths.

"God's wounds, Aileas!" Rufus declared loudly, running his gaze over her in a manner that struck George as singularly impertinent. "I didn't know you owned a decent dress." He started to grin like a monkey and the other men chuckled quietly.

"As you can see, I do," she answered sullenly, picking at the sleeve. Obviously she was not aware that such a movement pushed her breasts together in a very fascinating way.

Then, to George's dismay, she slid a sly glance at him before addressing Rufus in a loud, conspiratorial whisper. "Although some might not agree, I think I look like a fool."

What was next between those two? Winking? Exchanging kisses in a dark corner?

Maybe they already had.

George felt himself flushing in anger and fought to keep his expression mundane as he strolled toward the high table and casually leaned against it, assuming a languid air. "I think it a very charming gown, although I must say I hope you do not catch a chill."

"What do you mean?" Aileas demanded, facing him as the men smothered their guffaws.

Then Sir Thomas marched into the hall, accompanied by a priest who looked as if he could wield a sword or mace as well as any man in the hall. Sir Thomas caught sight of his daughter and halted so abruptly the priest nearly collided with him. "Aileas?"

She spun on her heel to face him, and George watched her regain her composure with admirable swiftness. "Yes, Father?"

George was pleased to note that Sir Thomas could be momentarily dumbfounded. "Aileas, um, you have not seated our guest."

"Oh, yes." She turned to George, and he could detect the contempt in her eyes if not her words. "You are to sit on my father's right," Aileas commanded, pointing imperiously.

"Naturally," he drawled in response and without moving. She could not order him like a servant, not in the presence of these other men. Indeed, not ever. "And you sit...?"

"Beside you," she answered brusquely.

At once George straightened and went to his place,

courteously holding the chair out for Aileas to sit. She
marched around the table and slumped into her chair
like a peevish child, obviously unaware that her gaping bodice gave him an excellent view of her very
lovely breasts.

George swallowed hard while telling himself that,
although her petulance was not a good sign, the night
was yet young.

Rufus bowed briefly and retired to another table,
something George was pleased to see. He didn't think
he could bear to try to converse with the fellow during
the meal. It was going to be difficult enough to maintain an indifferent demeanor.

The priest said a brief grace, notable for its odd,
bloodthirsty tone as he called upon God to bless those
in the hall and smite their enemies. When he finished,
the hall immediately burst into cacophonous sound, as
if shouting were the preferred method of communi-
cation. Huge hounds rooted among the rushes, seeking
discarded food and the bones the men tossed away.
The rushlights, cheap and smoky, did little to lessen
the deepening gloom.

The food, while plain, was plentiful enough. No
doubt Sir Thomas realized men could not do battle on
empty stomachs, or train well, either. A page refilled
his goblet and quickly moved on.

Deciding that he would take the offensive, George
turned to Aileas. "Sir Rufus seems to admire you,"
he noted dispassionately as he bit into some meat that
made him wonder how long it had been cooked. "He
appeared very surprised when you entered, though, as
if he didn't think you could look so beautiful."

Aileas tore off a large chunk of bread from the nearest loaf and proceeded to push the entire piece into

her mouth, unknowingly dragging the cuffs of her gown through her trencher. It was all George could do to keep silent about that and not wince, especially when she apparently missed his criticism and turned to him with a delighted expression. "Do you think so?" she asked, her mouth full.

They both glanced at Red Rufus, who was now, he noted smugly, primarily interested in the food the servants served, as if he and the others at his table were engaged in a contest to see who could shove the most food into their mouths in the shortest time. Good for him.

"You and he have been friends for some time, I presume," he noted.

"He's been here ten years," Aileas replied before wiping her lips with the back of her hand and belching.

Surely no noblewoman could be that lacking in proper eating habits, George thought, masking his disgust as he carefully cut a slice of meat and set it in his trencher. Aileas glanced at him, another disdainful smile on her lips, then she turned away and—yes!—winked at Rufus.

Who did not wink back.

George smiled and leaned back in his chair. "I suppose a stout fellow like Sir Rufus is good at wrestling," he observed.

"Rufus is good at many things," Aileas replied, divesting a capon of its leg.

"I daresay. And fighting of any kind."

"Yes."

"Can he read?"

Aileas stopped chewing and looked at him incredulously. "Read?" she said, her mouth full of capon. "Why should he read? He's not a priest."

"Obviously," George replied lightly. "The rule of chastity would be quite beyond him, I'm sure. He's the sort of fellow that has a different woman every night of the week, provided he can pay them, of course."

Aileas's eyes narrowed as she kept chewing, regarding him suspiciously.

"Forgive me, Lady Aileas, for speaking of such things in front of a lady."

She glared at him even more suspiciously.

He held her gaze, regarding her steadily, and then he smiled very, very slowly.

Stunned by how warm Sir George's knowing smile and shrewd gaze made her feel, Aileas tried to swallow—and instead began to choke.

Instantly Sir George began to pat her back, and in a moment, she spit the offending piece of meat out and cursed softly.

"What the devil happened?" her father demanded, eyeing her crossly. He had been in the midst of discussing the seige of Acre with Father Denziel—again—and he was not happy to be interrupted.

"A piece of meat went down the wrong way," Aileas explained, all the while acutely aware that Sir George's hand was still on her back. Not moving. Just...there. Warm and strong, as it had been when he had held her hand to his muscular forearm. Again she caught that pleasing scent, a fruity and spicy aroma that reminded her of festive feasts and mulled wine.

It must be the herbs sprinkled on the rushes.

Her father returned his attention to the priest and Aileas moved her shoulders until her companion removed his hand. "I am quite all right, Sir George," she snapped, surprised to discover that she could still feel the pressure of his palm on her skin. Indeed, she felt as if she might as well be naked in front of him.

It had to be this damned gown, she thought, shivering. She was indeed naked beneath it, for while she did own two gowns, she had forgotten that she didn't have proper undergarments. Nor did she have a maid to help her get into it. She had done her best to tie the laces herself, yet she feared they might come undone any minute.

She grabbed the neck of her dress and tugged it up. It kept slipping lower. And as for the sleeves, she would have done well to hack them off before she had ventured downstairs.

No matter what her father wanted, she vowed, this would be the last time she dressed like this. Why, she had nearly tripped on the hem on the stairs. She could have broken her neck.

She wouldn't risk that, not even for the pleasantly complimentary look on Sir George's—Rufus's—face when she came into the hall.

But Rufus hadn't met her gaze since.

Why? Surely he knew that she preferred him to this perfumed, overdressed popinjay with his fine embroidered tunic who sat beside her, eating as daintily as a nun.

Could his deference be because Sir George was rich? Did Rufus feel that he didn't deserve her because his family lacked wealth?

Yet what was that if he cared for her as she did him? He must know that she had little regard for wealth or station; the man himself was all in all.

"I am glad you are quite recovered," Sir George said softly.

She risked a glance at his face, to find that he was smiling at her again, regarding her with his very astute eyes, so different from Rufus's amiable brown ones.

Which, come to think of it, were not unlike those of one of her father's hunting hounds.

She quickly turned her scrutiny to the hall and spotted Rufus, deep in conversation with the armorer. They were probably discussing the merits of buying a new sword rather than repairing his old one.

She wished she could join them. She wished Rufus would look at her and wave for her to come to their table. Indeed, she wished Rufus would just look at her.

Anything to turn her attention away from this man beside her, whom, she vowed, she would not like, no matter how he smiled at her.

Chapter Four

The next morning, Aileas, wearing her customary garments of shirt, shortened skirt, breeches and belted tunic, hurried up the narrow stairs leading to Sir George's bedchamber, a pile of clean linen in her hands. If anyone saw her, they would assume she was taking the linen to his room. While that was a servant's task, it would be at least some excuse for what she was about to do.

Which was sneak into his chamber and see what he had brought that could possibly require so much baggage. As for the reason behind her curiosity, she told herself she was searching for more reasons to prove his unsuitability as her husband.

She stifled a yawn. The sounds of loud laughter and male conversation from the hall had prevented her from falling asleep for a long time after she had retired. That and venturing below to see what all the noise was about. She had seen Sir George in the middle of a boisterous gaggle of soldiers, apparently regaling them with tales of his exploits at several tournaments.

It had not pleased her to see Rufus paying rapt attention.

It would have been better to have found him sulking in the corner, looking envious or angry. Instead, he had looked positively...admiring.

But then, Sir George was an easy man to admire when it came to storytelling. In his deep, mellifluous voice, he told his tales with droll, self-deprecating humor, not bragging bravado. A few simple words or actions sketched a person for his audience, and his plain recitation—so different from the flowery stories of minstrels—proved unusually fascinating. Even she had lingered and—

She had to find proof that while he might have participated in tournaments and apparently with some distinction, he was too used to soft living to suit her.

She reached his bedchamber and quickly slipped inside. She closed the door, then turned to look into the formerly barren room.

The sight that met her eyes made her lean back against the door and clutch the linen to her chest as she stared, openmouthed.

It was as if she had suddenly been transported to a sultan's palace. On top of the simple bedstead was the thickest, softest-looking feather bed Aileas had ever seen or imagined, covered with fine blankets and a fur coverlet, as well as several brightly colored cushions.

On the floor was a carpet, as colorful as any of the cushions, and so thick it seemed incredible that one was supposed to step on it. A bronze brazier, piled high with coals, stood in a corner. A small, finely carved table was by the window, and the basin and ewer her father had provided sat upon it. In another corner stood a large wooden tub.

He must have bathed yesterday, which would explain the unique, intriguing scent that had beguiled her nostrils all through dinner last night.

Her gaze returned to the transformed bed. What would it be like to sleep on such a soft thing, to sink into its depths and be as warm and snug as a baby wrapped in swaddling clothes?

Pressing her lips together, she reminded herself that she wasn't a baby, but a woman.

Skirting the carpet, Aileas went toward the table and caught that now familiar scent. She set down the linen on the stool and picked up something wrapped in a piece of cloth from which the scent seemed to emanate. She unwrapped the cloth to discover a small piece of scented soap, then lifted it to her nose. Yes, that was what *he* had smelled like last night, when he was beside her. He must have used this soap when he bathed. It had glided all over his naked, wet body....

She dropped the soap as if it were one of the hot coals from the brazier. Suddenly anxious to get out of this sinfully luxurious den of iniquity, she quickly wrapped the soap again, all the while trying not to actually touch it.

Then, from outside the tower, she heard shouts of encouragement and the familiar clang of sword on sword.

Practice time in the inner ward. She would go there and tell her father what she had seen.

She was quite sure he would share her less-than-flattering opinion of a man who surrounded himself with such opulent decadence.

Even if he did smell most pleasant.

Unfortunately, Sir Thomas was not in attendance at the sword practice today, as Aileas realized the moment she rounded the corner and saw the men in the inner ward. Cheering encouragement, they had gathered around two combatants circling each other.

A practice engagement. Her father allowed such things, for while it was enjoyable for the men watching, they also learned by example. A wry smile grew on her face, for she knew the soldiers well enough to guess that several wagers had probably already been made, as well.

Curious and wondering who she would bet on to win if she possessed any money, she ventured forward. The men who noticed her moved aside, until she could see who was fighting.

It was Rufus, stripped to the waist and sweating profusely, and an astonishingly composed, half-naked Sir George, whose well-made leather breeches clung to him like a second skin, although Aileas would have been hard-pressed to find any evidence of sweat on his body.

It was a surprisingly good body, too. Whoever would have guessed that beneath the sumptuous clothing were such broad, muscular shoulders, lean, sinewy arms, narrow waist and long, strong legs? He had to be stronger and in better condition than she had suspected, too, for while Rufus was panting and glazed with perspiration, Sir George didn't even look winded.

She also noticed that he made Rufus, who lifted a broadsword as another man would a dagger and who usually dispatched his opponents in minutes, look clumsy and sluggish. It didn't take her long to see why.

Sir George was so light on his feet, it was almost as if he were dancing with Rufus, not waiting for him to strike. When Rufus did bring down his weapon, Sir George was no longer where he had been moments before, but someplace else.

When Sir George lifted his own sword, he did so with a strength and dexterity Aileas would never have suspected he possessed. Then he grinned with what looked like amusement and swiftly moved away again with lithe, graceful steps.

He was a far better warrior than she ever would have given him credit for.

She came a little closer and watched more carefully to see that she hadn't been quite correct in her appraisal of Sir George's expression, for while a smile constantly lurked about his lips, there was a gleam of competitive determination in his eyes.

So, he did care if he triumphed or not, even if he masked his feelings very well—unlike Rufus, who at that very moment gave a shout of annoyed frustration and charged like a bear with a bur in its paw. As he swung wildly, Sir George twisted abruptly and stuck out his foot, an intricate maneuver that sent Rufus sprawling in the dirt.

Before he could get up, Sir George sheathed his sword and held out his hand to assist his opponent to his feet.

"I don't want your help," Rufus grumbled, staggering slowly upright. "Where did you learn that?"

"A friend of my father's taught me. Urien Fitzroy—perhaps you've heard of him?" Sir George replied with a smile and elegant shrug of his broad shoulders. "An amazing fellow and quite a teacher, I assure you."

Rufus grunted his acceptance of Sir George's appraisal.

Then Sir George caught sight of her.

"Lady Aileas!" he cried with what seemed genuine pleasure. "I didn't expect—" He glanced down self-consciously. "Excuse me," he muttered as he immediately went to retrieve his tunic.

"Aileas, did you get a look at that move?" Rufus demanded, panting, not a whit embarrassed by his half-naked state.

And why should he be? Aileas asked herself. She had watched him, and every other soldier here, practice similarly attired, or unattired, a thousand times. Besides, she had six older brothers, so surely she should be acquainted with the male body.

But why would Rufus not look directly at her?

"Show me how you did that," Rufus ordered, turning toward Sir George again without waiting for her to reply.

Sir George, now wearing his tunic, sauntered toward them, his sheathed sword and finely worked leather sword belt held loosely in his hand.

"Forgive me for appearing so poorly dressed, my lady," Sir George said when he joined them. He wrinkled his nose in distaste. "I should wash."

Aileas tried not to think about that soap. "In truth, I...I must not stay," she stammered, "I...I only came to..." She couldn't very well say she came to denounce Sir George's lavish bedchamber to her father. "I came to see if you would all care for some refreshment."

Rufus frowned. "It's early yet."

"Delightful suggestion," Sir George replied. "Provided you will join us, my lady." He raised his patrician eyebrows quizzically.

"We're supposed to practice until noon," Rufus reminded her.

Aileas colored, for he was quite right. Her father had very strict ideas about keeping to a regular training schedule.

Sir George gave Rufus a slightly condemning look. "It is very kind of her to offer refreshments to a *guest*, who surely is not bound by her father's strictures regarding how he spends his day. And to tell the truth, I am extremely—" he paused and smiled ever so slowly "—thirsty."

Aileas's mouth went as dry as a riverbed in a drought under the force of his gaze. "I...I should have remembered before. I have to speak with the falconer. One of the pages can get you some wine. I'm sure you'll find one in the hall. Or the kitchen. Just ask—" Aileas realized she was babbling and snapped her mouth shut before she made herself completely ridiculous. Mercifully, he stopped looking at her. She could think better when he wasn't.

"So you can show me that move," Rufus declared triumphantly.

"Gladly," Sir George replied gallantly, giving her another long, slow smile, his blue-eyed gaze as intense as ever.

Suddenly Aileas thought she should get away from Sir George de Gramercie at once. Maybe then she would stop thinking it was a pity he had put on his clothes.

"Since I am to be deprived of your company, I might as well show this simple little trick to your friend," he said with sincere disappointment. The look in his eyes changed ever so slightly, as if he were reaching in to touch her very heart—which began to beat faster in response.

"After the noon meal, we could go riding together, if you like, Sir George," she offered impetuously, then silently cursed herself for a fool. She shouldn't be alone with this man. Not today and not ever, with his blue eyes and his smiles and his handsome face and astonishingly fine body!

"I would like that very much, my lady." Then he spoke quietly, so that only she could hear. "So much, I can almost forgive Rufus for being so rude." Aileas realized with a barely perceptible start that she had forgotten all about Rufus. "Until later, my lady."

He strolled back to join the others and Aileas hurried away. She rounded the keep, then hesitated. After first ensuring nobody was nearby to see her, she peered around the building to watch the men again, her heart pounding and the blood throbbing in her ears.

Rufus was already on the ground. "Show me again," he demanded petulantly as he lumbered to his feet.

"It's quite simple, really," Sir George said, feinting with his sword, then kicking out and twisting with all the suppleness of an eel.

Rufus landed hard on his rear and let out a bellow of frustration. Sir George leaned over to help him to his feet, then whispered something in Rufus's ear. They both burst out laughing.

"I'm glad you are such fast friends," Aileas muttered as she turned on her heel and marched away, determined to find her father, tell him what she had seen, and even more determined to be quite cool and composed when she went riding with Sir George, for only a coward would run away and hide from an opponent.

Yes, Sir George was her enemy, for it was Rufus she wanted, despite Sir George's winning ways.

Having changed his less-than-pristine tunic for another in a more sombre shade of blue, George sauntered toward the stable, his mood quite pleasant. He had undoubtedly proved his prowess as a swordsman to Aileas that morning. Now she would know that while Rufus might have the advantage of size, *he* had the advantage of skill and experience.

Not that he need fear any competition from Rufus. Not anymore.

He smiled to himself as he thought of the pile of linen he had found on the stool in his bedchamber. Someone had been in his room, and he could guess who—someone who had apparently investigated his scented soap, a costly indulgence all the way from Constantinople.

Sir Thomas's cowed pages or any other servant would surely never dare to touch any of a guest's personal belongings, let alone unwrap one.

Aileas would face no such strictures. Indeed, he could believe she would disobey almost any rule that did not apply directly to her.

Therefore, Aileas had investigated his soap. Perhaps even lifted it gingerly to her shapely nose and smelled it.

He wondered if she liked the scent, then grinned. She had to, if for no other reason than it would be a most pleasant change from the host of unpleasant odors lingering in the hall, the result of too many unwashed bodies.

What else had she touched in his room? What did she think of the bed? Had it crossed her mind that she could share it with him? That together they could sink into its soft depths, while he kissed and caressed and made love with her?

God's holy rood, he had better get control of his thoughts, George thought wryly, or he was going to be most uncomfortable in the saddle!

He rounded the corner of the stable and saw Aileas already astride a huge black stallion. He quickened his pace and smiled when she spotted him. "Is that the beast that so callously abandoned you yesterday?" he asked jovially.

"This is Demon," she acknowledged, her expression inscrutable.

As if in answer to its name or to prove its worthiness, the horse started to prance impatiently.

George was very impressed with the ease with which Aileas maintained control over the animal. "We missed you at the noon meal."

"I wasn't hungry."

"Your father did not join us, either," he noted.

"No," she said with a frown. "Apparently he has gone after poachers. He won't be back until the evening."

"I pity the man who dares to poach on his lands."

"So you should," she answered coolly.

"If you excuse me, I'll fetch my horse." Before he could enter the stable, however, a groom came out leading his own stallion, a brown horse nearly a hand smaller than Demon. "This is Apollo," he said by way of introduction as he swung himself into the saddle. "Shall we?"

"By all means," Aileas replied, and then she

punched her heels into the sides of her horse, which leapt into a gallop.

George stared, dumbfounded, as she rode out of the gate at a breakneck pace, soldiers and servants scattering in her path. Then, with a determined expression, he urged his own horse forward, calling out his apologies to the people as he galloped after her.

Aileas led him a merry chase, first along the main road through the village, sending the villagers running as she had those in the castle, then across the muddy fields, where peasants were sowing the first crops, before galloping along a woodland path that bordered the river.

Despite her horse's speed and the rough course, she kept glancing over her shoulder, obviously seeing if he was keeping up. He was—barely.

They crossed a large meadow on the side of a hill where several sheep were grazing, until the progress of the two riders interrupted them. The animals bleated in alarm and scattered. A young shepherd, startled out of an afternoon's slumber, jumped to his feet and stared at them.

Aileas and her horse plunged into a wood at the top of the hill. As George and Apollo entered the sheltered gloom, George told himself this chase was madness. He was risking his horse and his neck following the headstrong Aileas, who obviously knew the terrain well. If she wanted to behave in such an immature way, he decided as he pulled his horse to a halt, let her. As for him, he was getting hot and upset, two states he deplored.

Then he saw Aileas's horse slow. She slipped from its back and, with a challenging glance, led it into a group of willow trees, beside a stream or creek, no doubt.

He was thirsty, he realized, and a cool drink would do wonders toward restoring his equanimity, so he, too, dismounted and followed her through the trees. There was indeed a babbling brook there, and he saw her horse drinking. Tethering Apollo to one of the willows where he could still reach the brook, George looked around for her.

"You ride well."

Startled by the voice coming from behind him, he turned to find her leaning against one of the willows, her face slightly hidden by the slender, budding branches, her arms crossed and her expression as disgruntled as her tone had been.

"So do you, but I don't think the guards, the villagers or the peasants trying to sow their crop would appreciate that fact."

She scowled as she pushed herself from the tree and came toward him, moving aside the curtain of branches. "I don't want to marry you," she announced.

"Really?" he replied with a calmness distinctly at odds with the way he felt.

"No, I don't," she said firmly, planting herself defiantly in front of him.

"Well, I certainly cannot accuse you of playing the flirtatious maid with me. Might I inquire why my proposal is to be rejected before I even make it?"

"Isn't it enough that I don't want you?"

He fought to subdue his anger at her sarcastic tone. "Your father approves of the match and there are certain facts in my favor," he remarked, turning away from her and going to the brook. He picked up some pebbles and tossed them into the water as he counted off the reasons why she should want him. "I am wealthy. I am generous. I would treat you well. I am on good terms with several powerful lords. I am not without some personal attributes that I have been told women find appealing."

"Don't forget vain and dissolute," she said with a sternness that would have done credit to her father as she came to stand beside him.

He raised his eyebrows in a gesture of surprise that masked his growing vexation. "These are serious charges, my lady. I suppose you think me vain because I like fine clothes, and dissolute because I prefer to make my surroundings as pleasing to the eye and comfortable to the body as possible. If your family prefers a spartan existence, that is their right, just as it is mine to spend my money how I choose.

"While I see no reason to justify how I spend my money to you if we are not to marry, I will say, in my defense, that I never exceed my income, I always pay whatever taxes my overlord and the king require of me, and I have never been in debt."

Her gaze faltered for the briefest of moments, then she raised her chin to glare at him again. "I think the way you waste your money is a *sin!*"

"Think what you will, my lady," he said, facing the defiant, passionate woman who did not want him. "But, pray tell me, what is it you do want in a husband? Breadth? Height? Arms as thick as tree trunks? The manners of a boar? Red hair?"

She sucked in her breath and crossed her arms defensively as he continued to stare at her. "I want a *man,* not a conceited clown!"

"I *am* a man."

She sniffed disdainfully. "I suppose you have the necessary physical attributes—but that is all."

"For most women, that and what I have said before, would be more than sufficient."

"Well, not for me! I want a man I can respect. A man I can admire. Why, I ride better than you, can surely loose an arrow better than you, and with more accuracy. I daresay I could even wrestle better than you, if I had to."

"That may be true, my lady," he replied coldly, "but I smell better than you."

She gaped at him in outraged shock.

He leaned his weight casually on one leg and surveyed her slowly. Impertinently. "Let me guess the kind of man you *think* you would like for a husband. He will be admirably strong and a champion in the manly arts, as long as brute force is the main requirement. Such force is what he will bring to everything he does, including the marriage bed. Force, not pleasure. Not tenderness.

"At first, you will indeed respect him, until you realize that he gives you the same respect he gives his horse or his dog." She looked about to speak, but he did not give her the chance. "I have seen what happens when a woman is forced into marriage too many times to wish to experience it myself. So calm yourself, my fiery Aileas. If you do not wish to marry me, simply tell your father so, and that will be the end of it.

"And as for that redheaded brute you seem to find so fascinating, I regret that the feeling is not reciprocated. He has left you."

"What?"

"He left Dugall Castle immediately after the noon

meal.'' With that, George marched to his horse and took hold of the reins. He glanced back to look at her once more.

She stood motionless, no longer defiant, her expression one of surprise and dismay.

A primitive urge unlike any he had ever felt enveloped him, and suddenly, George's veneer of elegance and breeding dissolved. He strode across the space between them and tugged Aileas into his arms, pressing a hot kiss onto her tempting lips.

Desire, raw and needy, coursed through his veins the moment he touched her, and when she seemed to melt into his arms, offering no resistance, he held her tighter, leaning into her and pushing his tongue into her yielding mouth.

But it was not George's way to take without asking, or to behave with callous disregard, whatever his emotions, so his kiss changed, became gentler, more tender, yet still with the promise of that more powerful passion waiting to be released again.

Her response startled and delighted him, for she began to return his passion, kissing him as if she desired him with a yearning equal to his own.

What was happening? He didn't know. He could barely think, for he was overwhelmed and uncertain—

He broke away and, using every ounce of self-control he possessed, put a casual expression on his face as he looked into her desire-darkened eyes while she gasped for breath. ''Go, Aileas, and tell your father that we shall not marry.''

She swallowed and backed away, nearly stumbling. Her fingertips touched her lips for a moment. Then she reached for her horse's reins and yanked the unwilling beast out of the water. Still without speaking, she mounted swiftly and kicked her horse into a gallop. In another moment, she was on the other side of the trees, and then she was gone.

George sighed and slumped onto the ground near the banks of the brook. What had just happened here? What had he done?

He had never experienced anything like the sudden, wild, passionate desire he had felt for Aileas Dugall, and he could no more have prevented himself from kissing her than he could hold his breath for a day.

To what end?

How could he force his kiss on her like the worst of brigands, he who knew the price such unthinking, intense actions could exact?

Surely it was just as well that she didn't want to be his wife. No other person had ever stripped away his self-control as she just had.

He would find someone else. Someone calm and pliant, who did not rouse him so. A gentle woman, who would not inflame him.

That was the kind of wife he needed.

Chapter Five

Aileas angrily swiped her eyes with the back of her hand, and then her nose. She wasn't going to cry. Not over anything Sir George de Gramercie had said to her. And not over Rufus, either, if he could leave without so much as a farewell.

She wrapped her arms tightly around the apple tree's slender trunk and pressed her face against the rough bark.

Why would he go, and so abruptly? Did her hint of marriage to him strike him with such abhorrence that he had to flee?

"Aileas! Get down from there, *now!*"

Aileas gasped and loosened her hold, looking down through the budding branches to see her father, who was standing at the base of the tree glaring at her, his hands on his hips, his gray brows lowered in annoyance and his lips turned down in a frown that always filled her with dread. He was rarely *this* angry, and it was very tempting to remain above him in the tree. "What is it, Father?"

"Get down!"

She dutifully obeyed, albeit slowly, and stood staring at the ground. One of the stable hands must have told him she had returned.

"What in God's name did you say to Sir George?" he demanded.

No, not a stable hand. Sir George had returned and spoken to her father. She should have expected that, if she had been able to think clearly and logically. However, since their meeting by the brook, all she had wanted to do was get away from him and try to figure out why Rufus had gone away. She had been trying not to think about Sir George's remarks or his astonishing, unexpected and completely overwhelming kiss.

It had not been easy.

"Well? Tell me—for he says that he doesn't think you two should be wed. God's holy heart, why not?"

"Did he give no reason?"

"No. He just smiled that damned smile of his and said I should talk to you."

It took some firmness of purpose to refuse one of her father's requests, but she was fast learning that Sir George was not all manners and charm.

No wonder her father was angry. Not only was his plan for her marriage being thwarted, but Sir George had refused to explain. That type of response always angered her father beyond measure.

"I suppose he feels we would not suit," she murmured, realizing that when it came to facing her father's wrath, she was not as brave as Sir George.

"Not suit? What kind of modern nonsense is this? It would be a good match for both of you, as any fool could see."

"But if he has second thoughts, should we not respect them? After all, he is not a boy who cannot be credited with knowing his own mind."

Her father's eyes narrowed shrewdly. "Nor is he a girl who doesn't understand what's best for her."

"Father, I—"

"He is rich, he has powerful friends, he has a fine estate and the best stewards in the south of England to run it." Her father made a slightly scornful face. "He is good-looking, as far as that goes. What more do you want?"

Aileas rubbed her toe in the dirt and shrugged sullenly.

Sir Thomas's expression softened a little. "Daughter, I know he is different from what you are used to, but so would be many another knight who asked for your hand. And those who have, have been a damned sight worse."

Aileas looked at him, dumbfounded. "Other men have asked for my hand in marriage?"

"One or two," he admitted gruffly.

"Was Rufus one of the few?" she asked, her heart beating fast with hope.

Her father eyed her warily. "No." Disappointment pricked her bubble of excited expectation, and then her father burst it. "Speaking of Rufus, before he left, he asked me to tell you that he was very sorry if he had led you to believe…" His expression grew more stern. "Have I anything to worry about, daughter?"

She knew what he meant and answered in a low, but firm, voice. "No." She was a virgin still.

"Good. Besides, even if he had asked, I would have refused him my permission."

"Why?" Aileas demanded, even more surprised.

"He's a good man and a fine soldier—and the kind of fellow who will always be seeking adventure. He will not be content to stay at home. He would leave you often, for long, lonely days."

While she could appreciate the truth of her father's words—more so than she could credit Sir George's description of the type of husband Rufus would make—she was not content to have him discounted as a possibility. "Sir George has traveled much," she reminded her father.

"But now he has come home, and means to stay. He has had his fill of adventure. Aileas, he will be a good husband, and I think he will make you happy." His countenance softened a little. "George may seem indolent and vain, and indeed, sometimes I think he is, but he's a good man, for all that, and one who will treat you well." Her father's stern gaze faltered for a moment. "And his land is close to ours. I have no wish to see you far away from me."

These tender words, so unexpected and so rare, made Aileas's eyes fill again with tears, but of a different sort.

"So what is it to be, daughter?" her father asked gently. "Yes or no?"

"Can I not have more time to decide?" she ventured. "I hardly know the man."

"No. His belongings are being packed even as we speak, for he vows he will not stay longer and waste our time." Her father emitted a sigh of frustration. "What more do you need to know of him? You played together as children."

Yes, as children, when she had watched him, her whole being filled with scorn at his neatness and politeness, until she couldn't resist pelting him with apples. It was hardly the way to get to know someone.

She stared at the damp grass beneath her feet and contemplated her future.

She loved Rufus. Didn't she?

He didn't love her. If he did, he wouldn't have left and given that message to her father. He would have fought for her.

Sir George didn't love her, and she didn't love him, yet that kiss seemed to promise...

Her father was an excellent judge of men; that was what made him such a good commander. Perhaps she had disregarded Sir George too quickly. "Tell him..."

"What?"

"Tell him not to go," she whispered, not meeting her father's gaze.

"Now you're being sensible," he said approvingly, "but *I* won't tell him. He might think I am forcing you into this marriage against your will, and he won't accept you if he thinks that."

"Did he say so?"

"He didn't have to. I knew his father. As alike as two peas out of the same pod, those two."

She regarded her father steadily. "And am I not being forced?"

"Aileas, if you truly don't want to marry the fellow, then say so at once and we'll put an end to this. But don't make the mistake of thinking there is only one kind of good man in the world. I don't think you could ask for a better husband, and I'm sure you could do worse."

"Must I decide today?"

"If he leaves, that will be the end of it. They are proud, the de Gramercies." To her surprise, her father gave one of his rare smiles. "They are conceited enough to believe that their brides should be eager, not just willing, to have them.''

"You speak of pride, Father," Aileas said. "If I ask him to stay, won't I be humbling myself? He already knows I don't favor the marriage."

Her father's brusque laugh filled the air. "This is one time being a girl will stand you in good stead," he observed wryly. "Women are changeable as weathercocks."

Aileas was about to protest that she knew her own mind well enough, when his countenance softened again.

"There is a time for humility, Aileas, and I think this is one of them, unless you would rather let Sir George go." Her father regarded her tenderly. "I do not want you miserably wed."

Aileas nodded slowly, trying to decide what to do.

It was very tempting to let Sir George leave, taking with him the troublesome notion of a marriage to him.

Yet what would be the consequences? The knowledge that other men had already asked for her hand had surprised her, especially since there had never been a man at her father's castle who had even made her think of marriage, except for Rufus.

Rufus, who had had plenty of opportunity to ask for her hand and had not. Who, when she had hinted that she wanted him to marry her, had remained silent. Who had even looked horrified at the notion. And who had then run away.

Who else might come to marry her? Someone she would finally have to accept or else be a spinster all her life? Someone like the kind of man Sir George had accused her of desiring, who would be a terrible husband?

Who would not kiss her with that exciting combination of fierce passion melting into wonderful tenderness, until her knees felt weak and her whole body throbbed.

She slowly turned on her heel and began to walk toward the castle.

"Well, Aileas?" her father demanded behind her. "What is it to be?"

"I am going to ask him to stay."

George tapped his foot impatiently as he watched his foot soldiers pick up the last of the bundles in the now barren bedchamber. It was the folded feather bed, which was to be taken to the stable and loaded on his baggage cart with the rest of his things. Then he would go while there was light enough to reach the inn halfway between Dugall Castle and his own.

He had no wish to remain here a moment longer than necessary, even though it seemed that Sir Thomas knew nothing of his daughter's reservations. Indeed, the older knight had been completely taken aback when George had returned and told him the outcome of his latest meeting with Aileas. He was quite adamant that Sir George must have been mistaken.

George had been in no humor to go into any details about his recent confrontation with Aileas; nevertheless, he had made his opinion perfectly plain. If he was not wanted as a suitor, he would go. Let the father find out anything more from his child. For his part, he would simply go, and gladly.

"Sir George?"

He turned at the unexpected sound of a timid female voice and was even more startled to see Aileas standing on the threshold, her head lowered demurely and her brown eyes regarding him warily. "Yes?" he demanded with no attempt at courtesy, which apparently was not appreciated here.

"You...you are leaving?"

"Obviously, my lady. I see no reason to remain where I am not wanted."

Aileas sidled into the room, her gaze roving over the walls, the window, the bare floor—everything but him. "I hope you are not offended by anything I have said."

He laughed out loud. "Offended?" he queried with scornful sarcasm. "Why should I take offense, just because the idea of being married to me is as welcome as being tortured?"

"I didn't mean to make it sound that way."

"Well, you did. Now, if you will excuse me, I had better see that my men haven't dropped my belongings into a puddle."

He took a step toward the door, but to his surprise, she moved to block his way, closing the door and bracing herself against it. She looked directly at him, her brown eyes once again flashing defiant fire, and he felt as if the true Aileas had appeared. "You have to stay," she said firmly.

He crossed his arms and regarded her coolly. "I am not your lackey."

"Please," she amended with no hint of contrition.

He raised one fair eyebrow quizzically. "Whence comes this change of heart, my lady? Are you your father's serjeant, relaying his command?"

"I would like you to stay, too," she said.

He passed in front of her, then turned on his heel to survey her slowly. "Well, well, well, what am I to make of this sudden change of heart?" He tapped his teeth with his forefinger as he regarded her pensively. "Has the young woman seen something of merit in me after all?"

"Do you doubt that possibility?" she asked, derisive mockery in her eyes.

"She does seem singularly blind to my charms," he continued, as if he thought her deaf, too. "Why else? To please her doting father?" Before she could respond, he shook his head briskly, like a dog just out of water. "No, that cannot be. Sir Thomas does not dote." He began to pace, pausing every so often to transfix her with a quizzical, blue-eyed gaze. "Why, my dear, why do you come so anxiously to my bedchamber and ask me to stay?"

Suddenly he halted, and his expression altered in a fraction of a moment to something hard and cold that made her feel as if she had underestimated the power inherent in the man before her. "Could Red Rufus's hasty departure be a cause?" he said, his voice as cold as ice on the millpond. "I do not take other men's leavings."

Shocked by the change in him, she could make no answer.

Then, so suddenly she had to wonder if her eyes had been playing tricks on her, his countenance resumed its usual calm and cool demeanor. "But he is gone away."

"He does not want me and I do not want him."

He continued to scrutinize her like a tutor examining a student. "Is that so?"

"Yes!" she cried, so fervently George wished he could believe her. Then she clasped her hands together tightly and looked at him. To his surprise, he saw a yearning that was both pleading and defiant and went straight to his lonely heart. He could guess what she was feeling: a need that she did not want to acknowledge, even to herself.

He knew that because he felt the same.

Her gaze faltered. "Please stay," she whispered, her voice as gentle and soft as any woman's could be.

"Why?" he asked again, doing all he could to keep his breathing steady and not take her in his arms to hold her against him and tell her that he understood.

"Because...because I ask you to."

At that moment, he would have done anything she asked of him, no matter what the price, even leaving her forever.

He turned on his heel and strode to the window, bunching his fists as he fought to regain mastery of himself.

What was she doing to him, this defiant, pleading woman who acted like no woman he had ever known, and yet who made him feel such need and desire it was as if every other feeling he had ever experienced had been but a pale shadow of those that filled him now?

But he knew, too well, what strong emotions could do, and he would dominate them.

Unfortunately, the longer she stayed in the bedchamber, the harder it was for him to force the memory of their shared kiss from his mind, or the remembrance of her yielding, and the more difficult it became to accept the notion that she did not want to be his wife.

When he could trust himself to speak calmly, he turned around and leaned against the sill of the window.

"While any better explanation you can offer for this

unforeseen request is sure to be fascinating, I do have duties I can be attending to at home. Forgive me if I astonish you with that idea, but it is so.''

She took a deep breath. ''Sir George,'' she began, her voice sounding reasonable, ''I fear I have been very discourteous. Please allow me to improve your impression. As for marriage, neither of us need make a decision in haste.''

''What else must I do to impress my worthiness upon you, my lady?'' he inquired. ''Slay a dragon, like my famous namesake? Perform a series of tasks like the labors of Hercules? Or perhaps you wish to see if I will perish in the attempt and so rid you of my troublesome presence?''

Aileas's lips twitched as if she would smile, but her voice was serious when she said, ''No, I have no desire to set you to impossible tasks.''

''Because I already have one, no doubt.''

''What is that?''

''To make you like me.''

Again her gaze faltered and she twisted her hands anxiously.

''What is it?'' he asked gently, moving as close to her as he dared. ''Aileas, tell me. Do you want me to go away so you will not be troubled with more talk of marriage?''

Against his lackadaisical manner, she was impervious. Against his sarcasm, she was silent. But now, when he sounded so kind and sincerely concerned, she answered honestly. ''I don't understand why *you* would want *me*.''

He reached out and took her chin in his hand, his blue eyes gazing at her with serious intensity. ''Do you not?''

She shook her head. "I am not like other women."

His smile made her heart race. "Exactly, Aileas," he murmured. "You are not like other women." Then he pulled her into his strong, encircling arms. "So I do want you," he whispered before his lips pressed down upon hers.

But not as before, in the wood. Here, he was gentle. Tender—and yet she could sense, beneath the tenderness, a passion as fierce as any she could hope for. It was only that Sir George was keeping it in check, for the moment.

A wild excitement swept through her, warming her blood and sending it throbbing throughout her suddenly weightless body.

Their kiss deepened, his lips moving now with a firm surety over hers. She felt his hands cup her buttocks and his hips ground into hers while a low moan escaped her lips.

When he pulled away, she almost cried out in protest.

"My first qualification to be your husband, my lady," George said softly, smiling down into her half-closed eyes. "I will be an excellent lover." He began to stroke her arms.

"I can tell," she breathed before he kissed her again, his passionate embrace urging her own willing response.

Then his lips left her mouth, trailing along her chin as he began to caress her back. "I will cherish you as few noblemen cherish their wives."

His mouth reached the top of her breasts while his fingers played with the plait of her hair, undoing the thong that tied it, then loosening the thick mass until it fell about her shoulders. "I will be a good father," he murmured.

She could only nod.

"There has been another man in your heart."

"Yes...no..." she confessed. Nobody else had ever made her feel this way. Had even so much as kissed her, let alone aroused such indescribable sensations.

"I will make you forget him, Aileas."

His hand moved up, cupping her breast as he continued to kiss the naked flesh of her neck. "Yes," she gasped.

"Marry me. Be my wife. Come to my bed."

"Yes," she sighed, helpless to refuse.

"Let the wedding be soon."

"Yes..."

"Very soon."

"Yes..."

Suddenly, he stopped and stepped back, leaving her breathless, stunned, staring. "I want you, Aileas," he reiterated firmly, and for a shocked moment, she could not believe he could sound so matter-of-fact after what he had been doing...making her feel...

Aileas forced herself to think, to let her mind move beyond the sensations that still raged within her aroused body. To do that, she had to look away from him, from the yearning expression in his eyes, the desire on his face, his sensual lips.

Her father thought Sir George was a good man and would be a good husband. Rufus didn't want her. But what really mattered, she knew, was *her* opinion of the man before her.

No man had ever made her feel as desired as Sir George did, and he was not the conceited, ineffective simpleton she had thought him. He was a fine fighter, a bold warrior, and handsome and elegant as few men were.

Taking a deep breath, Aileas made her decision. "I believe I would rather marry you than not."

"Hardly a vigorous approval, my lady," Sir George remarked calmly, although inwardly, he was anything but calm. He wanted to wed her very much—just how much was surprising even to himself. Truly, she was quite unlike any woman he had ever met, and the thought that this wild, untamed creature would come to him of her own volition was intensely thrilling.

Nevertheless, he dared not sound as if she could hurt him with a negative answer. His pride gave him the strength to sound cool and to mask his great pleasure that she had not refused.

"I believe you would make a good husband."

He had hoped for a less prosaic response. "Is there no other reason, my lady?" he asked, trying to make her acknowledge that primitive hunger they so evidently shared.

"No," she replied, but she blushed a bright red, and he knew that might be a more truthful response than anything she could say.

"You do like me, don't you?"

"Yes," she confessed, albeit reluctantly and still without looking at him. "I like you."

"I am very glad you have accepted me, Aileas."

"I...I shall tell my father what we have decided."

"And I will stay, but only for tonight, when I will sign the marriage contract," George replied, yearning to take her in his arms again, but wary of destroying what he had so far accomplished. She wanted him for her husband, and that had to be enough, for now. "I shall go home tomorrow to prepare for the wedding, and my bride.''

"Very well, Sir George," she replied softly. She went to the door and opened it, lingering a moment to look back at him with desire-darkened eyes.

After she left, George had to sit down until his equanimity was restored. Then, whistling, he went to find his men to have them bring back the feather bed.

Sir Thomas made the announcement of the betrothal of his daughter to Sir George de Gramercie in the hall that night. If he was surprised, no man could tell. As for his garrison, they appreciated the extra ration of wine while truly sorry for the loss of such a fine companion.

Aileas told herself she had made a wise decision, and Sir George, sitting beside her, so outwardly calm, envisioned his father smiling down on him with approval.

Some days later, Rufus heard about Aileas Dugall's impending marriage as he sat in his cousin's manor far from Dugall Castle.

He did not sleep that night.

Chapter Six

The moment Herbert Jolliet spotted his brother's entourage, he tried to kick his mare to a gallop. Unfortunately, the beast was unused to such a speed and only broke into a bone-jarring trot. Despite his discomfort, Herbert continued to urge it forward as fast as it would go.

"Brother!" Sir Richard cried, genuinely surprised at the appearance of his sibling, who was being jostled in his saddle like a bag of turnips because of his unaccustomed haste. His hair was disheveled, his cloak askew, and his mouth hung open. He looked disgraceful.

Whatever was wrong, surely there was no need for such a spectacle. Nevertheless, Richard put a welcoming smile on his face.

"What brings you out to meet me?" he asked jovially, pulling his horse to a halt in front of his escort.

Sir George's men, clad in their tunics of scarlet and green, also came to a stop behind him. They began to murmur their surprise and Richard wished his brother had fallen from his horse and broken his neck before he caused any speculation, unless he proved to have something truly important to relate.

Herbert likewise tugged on his horse's reins to halt the animal. "I have something of great import to tell you!" he declared breathlessly.

"I guessed as much from your unexpected appearance," Richard answered. His tone was civil, but he ran a disgusted gaze over his brother that the men behind him would not see. "Ride ahead with me, and you can tell me this important news as we continue toward Ravensloft."

Herbert nodded, then tried to turn his horse on the narrow roadway. He was no horseman, however, and finally Richard grabbed the reins and pulled the horse around. Then together they rode ahead at a more sedate and dignified pace.

When they were out of earshot of Sir George's soldiers, Richard scowled. "Can you never learn to be subtle, fool?" he demanded quietly. He glanced over his shoulder at his escort. "These men have no need to know our business."

"Everybody already knows what I am about to tell, except you," Herbert retorted. "Sir George is to be married."

Startled, Richard yanked on his reins, halting his horse so abruptly he almost fell off his saddle. Incredulous, he stared into the face that was like his own, except thinner and more sallow. "What?"

Herbert nodded. "To Aileas Dugall. Tomorrow!"

Richard punched the side of his horse, which began walking again. "That's impossible!"

"Is it?" Herbert demanded in a tone nearly as cynical as his brother's had been. "Then someone had better tell Sir George, because he's been preparing for it ever since he returned from Dugall Castle.''

"His father tried to get him married off for fifteen years. Why should he marry now that his father's dead?''

"How should I know?'' Herbert whined. "But he is.''

Richard stared at the road ahead. "I used to fear his father would take another wife,'' he murmured pensively. "I never thought *he*...''

"What are we going to do?'' Herbert asked. "A wife in Ravensloft is—''

"I know what it is,'' Richard growled. "It's trouble. Keep quiet while I think.''

Herbert obeyed, sullenly regarding his brother as he maneuvered his horse away from some underbrush that encroached on the road.

"What about Elma?'' Richard asked suddenly.

"She's going to be the new mistress's maidservant.''

"How did she manage that?''

"I don't know.''

"You don't know much, do you?'' Richard sneered. "I would have thought Aileas Dugall would be the last woman George would choose, if he did decide to wed. She's a barbarian, like her father.''

Herbert's eyes widened with interest. "What do you mean?''

"Sounds interesting, does she? Well, take care, dear brother. She's not soft, like Lisette. She's as hard as iron and probably as tough as old leather. We'll have to take care for the next little while, till we know the lay of the land. Do you understand me?''

Herbert nodded slowly.

"Tell Elma that, too. We must be cautious and do nothing that arouses suspicion, or we could all wind up with a noose around our necks."

Instinctively Herbert's hand went to his throat while Richard Jolliet, trusted steward to Sir George de Gramercie and friend to all, rode thoughtfully at his side.

George ran his hand through his hair and tried to make sense of the list of foodstuffs written on the parchment before him. Although it was early in the day, he was already seated at a large, dark table in his solar, a room more notable for its comfort than its size. The tapestries that usually covered the walls had been removed to be cleaned and, since George had ordered that those in the hall be done first, had yet to be replaced.

A thick carpet still covered the floor, however, and George's oak chair was made soft with cushions. The windows were large, curving at the top like those of a cathedral, so the room was bright and fragrant with spring breezes.

Unfortunately, George was in no humor to take pleasure in such comforts. He was trying to figure out what had gone wrong.

Gaston, his cook, had told the household steward what he needed, and Herbert Jolliet had dutifully recorded and ordered the items. Thinking that was all that needed to be done, George had given Herbert permission to ride out to meet his brother. Now, however, Gaston was in a state approaching a fit, for he claimed that he had asked for twenty dozen eggs and had instead received only eighteen.

George looked at the list again, but he could barely make out the words, for Herbert wrote in a singularly cramped hand. "So we'll eat fewer eggs," he muttered in exasperation as he shoved back the chair and stood, laying a hand on the small of his back and stretching like a cat after a nap.

He strolled to the window and looked out, scanning the road leading to Ravensloft Castle.

No sign of Sir Thomas and his party, at least on the main road. He had spent the whole of the past fortnight in anxious preparation for his marriage, and thought to see Sir Thomas and his daughter tomorrow, just before the wedding. Although George had invited them to arrive earlier, his future father-in-law had refused to spend more than one day away from his castle.

At least that had been the plan agreed upon before his departure from Dugall Castle. It would be just like Sir Thomas to mount a surprise attack by arriving early and by an obscure route. He might not even use the main gate, but the smaller one to the south, to test the guards' readiness.

George leaned against the cool stone frame and sighed pensively.

What the devil was he doing, marrying Aileas Dugall? To be sure, she was different and exciting, but what else did he know of her, except that she dressed outlandishly and acted in no way ladylike?

She was also incredibly capable of arousing his emotions as few people could, and surely that was not good.

If he had been wise, he would have taken more time to consider this betrothal. He would have lingered at Dugall Castle and learned more about Aileas. He would have waited before signing the marriage contract.

He would have been calm and not carried away by the idea of Aileas Dugall in his bed.

But he had done none of those things, he thought as he sighed heavily and pushed himself away from the wall. "Too late now," he murmured.

"My lord?"

He was startled to discover a maidservant standing in the doorway. It was Elma, a young woman about Aileas's age whom George had chosen to be a maidservant to his bride.

Elma was clever and quick, neat and polite. She had been a lady's maid before coming to live in Ravensloft and seemed eager to assume her new position.

"What is it?" he asked warily, fearing another domestic disaster.

"Nothing bad, my lord," Elma replied. The reason for Sir George's unaccustomed manner and sudden zeal to have everything perfect about his castle was certainly no secret, and his tension had been the talk of the servants and soldiers since his return—albeit with sympathetic understanding, for he was like many another bridegroom in that regard. "It's Sir Richard back from London, and Herbert Jolliet with him."

"God's wounds, I'm glad!" George cried with a mixture of relief and joy. He gestured helplessly at the parchment. "I need help."

Elma smiled genially.

"Go to the kitchen and bring us some wine in the hall. I'll meet them in the courtyard."

"Aye, my lord," Elma replied, dipping a curtsy.

George hurried past her, running lightly down the stairs. Now that both his estate steward and his household steward were here, he could ignore that part of the daily business and concern himself with more important matters, like impressing Sir Thomas. And Aileas.

A swift survey of his hall showed him that everything was as he had ordered it to be, so by the time Richard and Herbert and their entourage entered the gate, George had once more achieved his usual state of unruffled tranquillity.

Indeed, George looked so calm as he strolled to greet his stewards, one would believe he had nothing more pressing on his mind than how to say hello. "Greetings, Richard!" he called out merrily as the older man dismounted. "I trust all went well in London?"

"Excellently so, my lord," Sir Richard replied. "We shall have to pay a few more marks, but nothing you will miss greatly."

"No doubt I have you to thank for keeping the amount so small," George said. "I suppose your brother has told you the news."

George glanced at Herbert, who was dismounting awkwardly. That was not so surprising, for he rarely rode a horse or ventured far from the castle or village.

"Indeed, my lord!" Richard replied, smiling broadly as he bowed to George. "My best wishes."

George put an affronted look on his face. "You don't sound at all surprised, and here I had been hoping to astonish you."

Richard, who knew his master well, continued to smile.

"Indeed, I was sure Herbert had gone mad when he told me," he said.

"He was quite taken aback, my lord, as, I confess, we all were," Herbert replied gravely.

"No more so than myself, I daresay," George remarked as he led the way toward the hall, wondering, as he often did, how two men who were brothers could be outwardly so different. Richard was all jolly affability, where Herbert was usually as dour as a penitent with many crosses to bear.

Together they entered the large, well-appointed hall. It was nearly fifty yards long, with a high roof and the innovation of a large fireplace near the dais. Clean, brightly colored tapestries covered most of the walls. The rushes on the floor were freshly laid, and the smell of the herbs sprinkled on them pleasant. Three tall, narrow windows that faced into the courtyard provided illumination.

As it was not yet time for a meal, the unassembled trestle tables leaned against the walls, the benches in front of them. On the dais, the chairs for the highest-ranking guests were set, and there was a small table bearing wine goblets.

George threw himself in his chair and reached for a goblet. "You find it surprising that any woman would consent to marry me? You wound me, Richard!" He frowned mournfully and laid one hand over his heart as his estate steward sat nearby. Herbert also took a chair, albeit farther off.

"I'm surprised you found a woman to meet your exalted standards," Richard replied, likewise taking a goblet. "I was beginning to despair that such a creature existed."

"Ah!" George slipped down further in his chair and sipped his wine contentedly, happy to be in his steward's company again. "Well, she was conveniently to hand."

Richard shook his head. "My lord, are you never serious?"

"Not unless it is completely unavoidable."

"Well, she is a lovely woman."

A genuine frown crossed George's face for the briefest of moments. Aileas lovely? As he considered her features, he had to admit she wasn't conventionally beautiful. She was too sun-brown, and her features lacked the symmetry of true beauty.

But no other woman had such sparkle in her eyes or a countenance more fascinating, at least to him. "Yes, she is."

Richard's fingers toyed with the stem of his goblet and he cleared his throat. "A good portion of my surprise, my lord, comes from the fact that you made this arrangement without my assistance."

George suddenly felt like a child being scolded for a mistake and took a sip of wine to hide his annoyance. Yet he couldn't deny that his steward had a point. "It wasn't a complicated contract," he said by way of explanation. "I knew Sir Thomas would not part with any land."

"Not even a portion of his wood?"

"Not a yard."

"You did *ask,* my lord?" Richard cautiously inquired.

This time, it was George who cleared his throat. "No. Considering that Sir Thomas has six sons, I didn't think it necessary."

Richard sighed but said nothing.

"Her dowry is movable goods, worth five hundred marks," he said, trying not to sound defensive. "That was more than I expected," he finished honestly.

"What kind of movable goods?" Herbert asked, reminding George that the household steward was there.

"I assume the usual items—plate, linen, fabric, that sort of thing."

"You...you didn't ask?" Herbert's voice was pitched so high he squeaked.

Richard gave him a sharp look, while George waved his goblet dismissively. "It doesn't matter. He is my neighbor, and the alliance is a good one."

"Yes, you're absolutely right, my lord," Richard agreed quickly. "As long as you stay on his good side, you will be sure of an excellent ally, should you ever have need of one. I look forward to meeting Lady Aileas again. I'm sure she will not act the peasant maid on your wedding day!"

George could not begin to guess what Richard would think of Aileas when next they met, especially if she wore her usual attire.

Then he decided he was worried about nothing. Her father would ensure she was properly dressed when she arrived at the castle of her betrothed. "Tell me all the news of the court, Richard. Is Hubert de Burgh in or out of favor?"

The conversation turned to matters at the royal court, but just as Richard was delving into some very interesting news concerning the king's opinion of the French ambassador, Elma came hurrying into the hall. "My lord!" she cried breathlessly.

"What is it?"

"It is *them!*"

George banged down his goblet and half rose from his seat. "What them?"

"Sir Thomas and his party! They're at the gate!"

"God's teeth, I knew it!" George cried. "That old—"

Richard and Herbert set down their goblets while

George straightened and tugged his tunic into place before hurrying from the hall.

Whatever hopes George had harbored about Sir Thomas persuading his daughter to dress appropriately were dashed the moment he laid eyes on the party riding through the inner gate.

Aileas wore the same bizarre attire as she had during his recent visit. To make matters worse, she rode astride her horse and beside her father, not behind him, as a modest maiden might. Not only that, but she had a bow slung over her shoulder, a quiver on her back and a brace of pheasants tied to her saddle, as if she were a member of a hunting party rather than a wedding procession.

Behind her came a sizable group of men-at-arms and wagons bearing what had to be the dower goods.

Sir Thomas held up his hand and all the men in his train halted at once. He nodded at George, then scanned the walls like a conquering hero surveying his prize.

George forced the scowl he wanted to make into a smile. Indeed, Sir Thomas could look all he liked. He would find nothing amiss with Ravensloft, which had been built during his father's lifetime and therefore had all the latest innovations in construction. The towers were round, not square, to deflect rocks and arrows and any other missiles, and placed not only at the corners of the walls but at intervals between, too. The outer curtain wall was six-feet thick, the inner three.

The gate had not just heavy, iron-studded wooden doors but a portcullis, too, which could trap men between. A murder hole was above that space, to rain down rocks or boiling liquid if necessary. The hall itself was spacious, the apartments roomy, and even the barracks decidedly more comfortable than anything Sir Thomas provided.

And yet Sir Thomas's lip began to curl. "Are these walls whitewashed?" he demanded incredulously.

"With lime," George replied. "I bid you welcome to Ravensloft, Sir Thomas." He made a deep obeisance at the older man, then his daughter. "I bid you welcome, Lady Aileas."

Aileas threw her leg over her saddle and jumped down from her horse without waiting for assistance. She quickly removed her bow and quiver, slinging them over the raised front of her saddle. "A most impressive fortress, Sir George. It must have been costly."

"A fortress is not something one should be frugal with," he remarked lightly, "as I'm sure you'll agree, Sir Thomas. Lady Aileas, Sir Thomas, allow me to present my stewards, Sir Richard Jolliet, my estate steward, and his brother, Herbert, my household steward."

Both men bowed, while Aileas stood motionless and Sir Thomas dismounted with more dignity. "I thought coming one day early would give Aileas more time to get settled before the wedding."

George was certain that this early visitation had to do with a desire to test Ravensloft's readiness rather than Aileas's comfort. "Whatever the reason, naturally I am delighted," he said, once more bowing politely at his betrothed.

As he looked at her, Aileas was suddenly reminded of the embraces they had shared, and a fresh, anticipating excitement coursed through her body, along with considerable relief. Despite her misgivings, she was glad she had persuaded her father to journey here sooner than agreed. Fortunately, that had been easy. He always preferred to come upon both friends and enemies unexpectedly.

In the past several days, she had been thinking— and thinking—about the decision she had made to accept Sir George de Gramercie, and while she could not completely regret it, especially when she recalled Sir George's kisses in vivid, exciting detail, she couldn't help wondering if she had been too hasty. What *did* she know of him, after all? Very little, except that he was not Rufus.

Fortunately, there had been enough to do to keep her busy during the day. It was only at night, when she tried to sleep, that she would toss and turn and try to convince herself she had been right, and that she would be happy.

She had not spent much thought on what Sir George's household would be like until she set eyes on the soaring walls and towers of Ravensloft, gleaming white in the sun, looking as if they had been carved from one single, gigantic rock. She had not anticipated the size of the castle, the prosperity of the village outside it, the perfection of the situation with its view of the river and its valley, or the wealth that could command such impressive stonework and masonry.

As they had entered the outer gates, she had been as impressed by the troops they encountered as her father had, to judge by the approving expression on his face.

Inside the inner wall were a number of buildings of more obvious recent construction than her father's castle. The main ones were of stone and also whitewashed. Others were composed of wattle and daub, with the beams darkened over time. Several soldiers stood outside one of these buildings, watching with interest, while others came out to join them, leading Aileas to suspect she was looking at the garrison barracks. Across the courtyard was a similar building, but with large windows, and the windows contained glass. Probably that building was intended as guest quarters.

She spotted a stone building nearly hidden by the hall. Smoke billowed out of a chimney—the kitchen, no doubt.

Besides the soldiers, several servants, both male and female, bustled about the yard, pausing to give the new arrivals a curious glance. A few engaged in whispered conversations, and Aileas couldn't dismiss the notion that they were whispering about her.

Then Sir George himself had hurried out of a doorway across the wide courtyard. How different he looked, here in his own home, and attired in a far more casual manner than she had yet seen. He wore only a plain tunic, albeit of fine fabric, and his breeches and boots were likewise plain. The sleeves of the white shirt he wore were rolled partway up, exposing his lean, sinewy forearms and reminding her again of being held in his arms and not wanting him to let her go.

Immediately, however, she realized that there was something...different...in George's manner toward her. The expression in his eyes was not one of unmitigated pleasure.

While the jovial estate steward smiled, as did his brother, neither man made her feel comfortable or particularly welcome.

She tried to keep her discomfort from her face, instead blaming her pique on the whole notion of having retainers so intimately involved with one's financial well-being, which was foreign to her. Despite the size of her father's estate and the number of men in his household, he had always insisted upon being in control of his money, for he said no one would care about his money the way he did.

Nor could she deny that the disapproving look on Sir George's face was responsible for her sudden ill-humor, no matter how quickly his expression changed.

Sir Richard, whose appearance gave every indication that he enjoyed a well-stocked larder, walked toward her. "Allow me to apologize for my behavior when we met before," the estate steward said deferentially, bowing again. "Had I known who you were, I would have spoken with more respect."

"I'm sure you would have," Aileas replied coldly.

"Shall we all go to the hall and have some wine?" George asked, looking at Sir Thomas. "Or would you prefer to be shown to your quarters first?"

"It is early yet," her father said. "I haven't been here in years. Seem to be some improvements. I'd like to see them."

"Very well, Sir Thomas," Sir George agreed with a courteous bow. "But I daresay Lady Aileas wishes to change from her traveling garments."

"I would rather have some wine," she said honestly, for the ride had been slow and they had not stopped for anything but the briefest of rests since setting out at dawn. "Those pheasants should go to the kitchen."

"As you wish," Sir George said lightly. He beckoned to one of the idle servants watching them, and the fellow took his time obeying.

"Fitzgibbon!" Aileas shouted, and her father's serjeant-at-arms nudged his horse into view. She hurried toward the stocky middle-aged soldier, glad of an excuse to show Sir George how one's men should obey. "See that the horses are taken care of, and then this man—" she pointed at Herbert Jolliet "—will show you where to take our baggage."

Fitzgibbon immediately took charge of the rest of the men and Aileas turned back with a smile of smug satisfaction.

To see her father and Sir Richard looking up at the battlements, obviously in deep discussion, while Sir George was regarding her with a most peculiar expression as he sauntered toward her.

"What's the matter?" she demanded, crossing her arms over her chest.

"Your orders were audible to the entire castle," he observed.

She frowned with displeasure. "At least our men know how to follow orders and be quick about it."

She thought she saw a brief flash of annoyance in his eyes, but if she did, it was gone the instant he blinked. "I have asked my cousin, Lady Margot de Pontypoole, to come to help me prepare for your arrival. Unfortunately, you have arrived before she has."

"My father likes to travel at first light," Aileas informed him. "I'm sure everything will be satisfactory."

"I hope so, but I fear my home is lacking a woman's touch."

Aileas had to laugh at that. "What, pray tell, is a woman's touch?"

"A woman's touch is a hundred little things one doesn't notice until they are missing," he said softly, his melodious voice low and intimate—so intimate her knees felt strangely weak.

Or perhaps that was only the effect of her long ride this morning.

"I...I..." She cleared her throat and straightened her shoulders defiantly, determined not to sound like a blithering fool. "I don't know what you're talking about."

"I'm hoping Lady Margot will help you learn."

"Since I am a woman, surely I already possess the knack," she reminded him, bristling slightly at the implication that she needed to be taught anything.

His immediate response was to raise an eyebrow skeptically. Then he made that slow smile that always completely disarmed her. "She has been a widow for some years and is, unfortunately, childless, with little to occupy her time, poor woman," he said quietly. "I confess I thought this would be a good excuse to have her visit. Her own home gets very lonely, I think."

Aileas suddenly felt very mean and petty. It was kind of him to help his poor old relative this way— although the notion of having to listen to any talk that didn't concern weapons or horses struck her as exceptionally boring. However, she nodded her head in silent acceptance.

He looked at her with blatant approval, and she felt as if she'd never been truly appreciated before. "Let us go inside," Sir George declared, his voice not as loud as hers had been, to be sure, but it carried to the others nonetheless.

She let him lead her forward, all the while very aware that he was touching her. Then they entered his hall, and for a moment, Aileas was too stunned to notice much beyond that.

She had expected luxury and plenty, but she felt as if she were in the king's palace instead of a knight's hall. The size alone was unexpected, and as for the accoutrements...! The tapestries were as beautiful as anything she had ever seen, the colors delightful, the scenes wonderful. The huge hearth was fascinating as much for the decorations around it as the novelty. The furnishings all appeared to be new. Even the smell of the place, of herbs and freshly hewn wood, was delightful.

"Welcome to my home," Sir George said softly, his lips seemingly at her ear, his deep voice low and thrilling. "Soon to be your home, Aileas."

Chapter Seven

Sometime later, after Aileas and her father had been shown the fortifications of Ravensloft, Aileas followed a bright-eyed maidservant up the tower stairs to dress for the evening meal.

"I thought the other building contained the guest apartments," Aileas remarked, taking the shallow steps two at a time to keep up with the briskly trotting servant.

"Oh, the one across the way?" the maid asked. She was rather short and pretty, with tawny hair and snapping black eyes and a wide smile. "It does. But Sir George thought that you might as well use his bedchamber, to save moving your baggage after the wedding. He's already had what he needs taken out and left the rest."

"Oh." It made sense, of course, but Aileas had never slept in a man's private bedchamber before, and this information both excited and frightened her.

All her emotions seemed to be a mass of confusion lately. Today, she could blame such a state on fatigue and unfamiliar surroundings. She feared it would be some time yet before she could retire and think over the events that had recently passed, as well as ponder the man she was about to marry.

Ever since she had arrived, she had been too aware of his presence to be completely composed. Whenever he touched her or even brushed her sleeve, she became hot and flustered in a manner quite new to her. She could only hope nobody else noticed.

"Here you are, my lady," the maidservant said as she pushed open the door and stood back to let Aileas enter the airy upper chamber.

The room was easily the size of three bedchambers at her father's castle, she thought as she moved past the servant to the center of the chamber. Beautiful tapestries covered the stone walls, and white linen shutters were open to let in the fresh spring breeze. A thick carpet lay upon the stone floor.

Two windows looked out onto the inner courtyard; near one stood a delicately carved table of a size that would have been necessary if she had possessed more than one brush and comb, which she rarely used. A similarly delicate stool, which she suspected would collapse if she ever dared to sit on it, stood before it. Near the other window was a more sturdy table bearing a bronze basin and ewer wonderfully wrought. A tall candleholder held a dozen of the finest beeswax candles, and a brazier, piled with coal, was across the room, beside the bed.

Aileas swallowed hard and her gaze seemed pulled to the most impressive piece of furniture in the room. The large bed was made of age-darkened oak, with a feather bed even thicker than the one Sir George had brought to her father's castle. The coverings were as rich as those she had seen before, and as beautiful, in shiny shades of deep red and blue and green, shim-

mering like a lake in the sunshine. The tall posts had
been carved with the shapes of vines and leaves, and
heavy damask curtains, to keep out the night air, hung
about it.

"Is something the matter, my lady?"

How could she begin to explain the effect the sight
of such ostentatious luxury had upon her? Part of her
wanted to examine everything in exquisite detail, yet
another part, which spoke in her father's voice, reminded her such extravagance was a sinful waste.

Aileas regarded the maidservant lingering in the
doorway. "You may leave."

The young woman glanced about and there was an
awkwardness to her manner that Aileas didn't understand.

"If you please, my lady," she began, "Sir George
said I'm to be your maidservant from now on."

Aileas turned away to mask her confusion and uncertainty. She had never had a maidservant; her father
deemed such use of servants another waste.

"I assure you, my lady, I'll work hard. You'll see."

"I'm sure you would."

"Besides, my lady," the young woman said matter-
of-factly, "it's my lord's orders."

Aileas didn't know what to say. She didn't want or
need a maid, yet if Sir George had given an order, it
should be obeyed.

The maidservant waited expectantly.

"Since it is your lord's order," Aileas said at last,
"I will accept your service. What is your name?"

"Elma, my lady," the maid replied happily. "And
I'm glad you're agreeable, I must say," she went on,
coming farther into the room to stand near Aileas. "I
was trained as a lady's maid, you see, in another

household. But then that lady died, so I came home. Sir George was kind enough to give me a place in the hall, but that's not what I'm used to.''

"I see," Aileas replied, thinking the life here at Ravensloft was not what she was used to, either.

"Now, I'm to help you dress." Aileas's plain brown leather chest had been placed near the door and she couldn't help noticing that there were five other brightly painted chests beside it. "Those are Sir George's things," the maidservant said helpfully.

"So many?"

Elma laughed softly. "Sir George likes to dress fine, my lady. And why not? A good-looking man like that, eh? Not that he dallies with the maidservants, my lady. No, we're not for him, I assure you."

Aileas was relieved, even though it had never crossed her mind that Sir George, like many nobles, would think nothing of seducing his maidservants, until Elma pronounced George good-looking.

Elma bustled over to Aileas's chest and threw up the lid. "What gown would you like?"

Aileas cursed the flush she felt stealing over her features. "I suppose this is necessary?" she demanded. "I'm perfectly comfortable in these clothes."

Elma regarded her with a somewhat wary expression. "There's blood on your skirt," she noted, nodding at the spot where some of the pheasants' blood must have dripped onto her from the brace tied to her saddle.

"Oh, yes, I didn't see that. Well then, the green one," she said reluctantly. She despised that green velvet gown, with its awkward sleeves and tight waist. She would far rather wear what she had on, blood or no blood.

Elma pulled out the gown and shook it, surveying it critically. "I hate to say this, my lady, but whoever packed this didn't know what they were doing. It's all wrinkled." Then she looked closely at the cuffs. "It should have been cleaned, too."

"I packed the chest," Aileas replied.

The maid blushed. "Forgive me, my lady. I shouldn't have—"

"Then obviously I cannot wear the gown," Aileas interrupted, attempting to sound sorry for this unforeseen outcome. "I shall simply have to wear what I've got on."

"With the breeches, too, my lady?" Elma asked timidly.

"No, I can do without them."

"But your skirt will be too..." The maidservant hesitated, and Aileas quickly realized the problem. She had cut off her skirt at midcalf so that it was easier to walk without tripping and to mount her horse without the bulk of unnecessary fabric. Without her breeches, however, she would be exposing her bare legs.

"Well, Elma," she said, "since you are trained as a lady's maid, what is worse, bare skin or wrinkles and a food stain or two around the cuff?"

She was sure it would be the wrinkles and stains, but to her chagrin, the maid did not hesitate before replying, "Bare legs."

Aileas was very tempted to override the maid's opinion, until she reflected that Elma probably knew more about such things than she did. "Then it will have to be the gown," Aileas answered with a sigh of resignation.

Before she could don the hated garment, however, a shout came from the vicinity of the gate. It didn't sound urgent enough to be an alarm, but Aileas hurried to look out the window nonetheless.

Another group entered the courtyard, but there was no familiar redhead leading it.

What had she expected—Rufus coming to demand that she marry him instead? He had already made his choice, just as she had made hers, and she would be content.

What she did see was a slender woman wearing a gown the color of daffodils, which peeked out from beneath a plum-colored hooded cloak trimmed with ermine. She rode upon a palfrey at the front of a guard of five men, each attired in chain mail and overtunics of sapphire blue, their horses' accoutrements colored to match. The woman pushed back her hood, revealing both a silken yellow scarf, which matched her dress and was held in place by a circlet of silver, and, as Aileas could tell even from this height, a very beautiful face.

"That's Lady Margot," Elma noted from behind her.

"Who?" Aileas demanded, not hiding her surprise. Wasn't Lady Margot old and destitute? This woman was clearly neither.

"She's Sir George's cousin, and come for the wedding."

"Yes, yes, of course," Aileas said, trying to sound nonchalant. "I was expecting someone older, though."

"Well, she's about two years older than his lordship. She was married very young, poor creature, to a man who was her father's choice." Elma leaned closer and whispered, "They were not happy together.

Everyone said it was a mercy when her husband fell off his horse and died.''

"Including Sir George?" Aileas couldn't help asking.

"I don't know," Elma said with a shrug. "He wasn't here."

"She doesn't look very impoverished, either," Aileas remarked. "Her men are very finely dressed."

Elma giggled. "Impoverished? Who told you that?"

Aileas did not reply, telling herself she was not pleased with this servant's sudden familiarity.

"She was left quite a fortune in her own right," Elma said in a more deferential manner. "There are some who say her father took pity on her just before the wedding and made sure it would go that way." Elma leaned even closer. "And some say she had a hand in her husband's death, but I don't believe it. She's a sweet lady and Sir George adores her."

Aileas glanced sharply at Elma, who blushed and giggled. "As a cousin, of course. Here he comes now!"

Aileas watched as George hurried toward the new arrival. "George!" Lady Margot cried in a dulcet, extremely feminine voice. Her joyful tinkle of a laugh reached to the tower windows.

George answered with his own deep, rich laugh, something Aileas had never heard before, and she could see a warm, welcoming smile on his handsome face. "I thought you might miss my wedding. Naturally you would blame me for not giving you enough notice, and then I should never hear the end of it." He reached up to help Lady Margot dismount, clasping her about her narrow waist.

Lady Margot gave him a kiss of greeting on each cheek, rising on tiptoe to do so. Entirely proper, really, but Aileas's hands bunched into fists.

"You are looking very well, Margot. I do believe riding agrees with you."

"It does not," the lady replied firmly. "It's so uncomfortable."

Aileas's lip curled in a sneer, and she was sure she had the measure of the lady in that moment. Anyone who did not care for riding was an idiot.

The beautiful Lady Margot laughed again and took hold of George's arm. Their voices lowered so that Aileas couldn't hear them, and their heads nearly touched as George bent to listen. No doubt he didn't want to miss a word of everything Lady Margot was saying in those womanly, silvery tones while escorting her inside the hall.

Aileas forced her hands to straighten and wiped her sweating palms on her skirt. "Smooth out those wrinkles as best you can, Elma," she said firmly, turning to face the maid.

If any warrior had seen her face at this instant, he would have recognized her expression at once.

Aileas Dugall was ready to do battle.

George surveyed the hall, now prepared for the evening meal, and tried to feel pleased. The tables had been set up and spread with pristine white cloths. Delicious odors emanated from the kitchen corridor, where Gaston was sure to have concocted a superb feast.

George could easily guess Sir Thomas's reaction to the furnishings and the meal: he would condemn the apparently wanton extravagance and the money spent on such unessential items, even though it was all in honor of his daughter's marriage.

Naturally, Sir Thomas had said nothing about the money spent on the fortifications of Ravensloft Castle as George had conducted them about it before they had finally retired to prepare for the evening's feast, leaving George free to greet the few guests who had been able to come on such short notice and who had arrived after Sir Thomas's party. Fortunately, Margot was one of them. He was quite sure that with Margot's help, Aileas would lose some of her rougher ways.

George sauntered past the high table, where he would sit in the center, Aileas on his right, her father on his left.

Despite Margot's comfortable presence, ladies would be distinctly lacking, both at the high table and the hall in general. This didn't please George, for ladies assured a more civil tone to such proceedings. Without them, the celebration would surely have something of the soldiers' barracks about it, despite the fine linen and excellent cuisine.

No doubt Aileas would feel more at home under such circumstances, he reflected with a disgruntled frown as he leaned back against the hearth.

No decent woman would dress as she did, and ride astride at the head of a company of soldiers, as well as insist upon joining her father and her betrothed on a tour of the fortifications the day before her wedding. She had asked all sorts of questions, too. A properly demure noblewoman wouldn't have opened her mouth.

Not even when her remarks were pertinent, succinct and usually complimentary.

George's reverie was disturbed by the sound of

someone approaching, and he looked up to see Richard Jolliet ambling toward him, a pleased smile on his face as he ran a cursory gaze over George's clothing, which included a white linen shirt beneath a finely embroidered scarlet tunic, scarlet hose and black boots.

"I thought you'd still be dressing, my lord," the steward remarked. "That tunic's rather plain for you, isn't it?"

"I didn't want to dazzle the bride too much," George replied lightly, and with a smile. There was no need for anyone to know that he had any doubts about his marriage to Lady Aileas.

The men of the garrison began filing into the hall and taking their places, their conversation a steady hum. Too interested in the feast to come, they paid little heed to the familiar sight of Sir George and his steward talking together.

"Ah, of course!" Richard replied with a chuckle, a deep bass rumble that began in his chest and expanded to fill the room. "I should have known. But I'm sure she's already overwhelmed by your magnificence."

"She is not the kind of woman to be easily overwhelmed," George replied, a hint of his doubts entering his tone.

"Is she not?" he asked, and George couldn't tell if the steward intended that response to be serious or not. "Nevertheless, I understand the lady was favorably impressed by Ravensloft."

"I believe she was."

"I had it on good authority—Herbert overheard one of Sir Thomas's men say so."

"I'm glad to know it," George answered honestly, "for she certainly asked a lot of questions." Then, deciding he was sounding much too serious, he said jovially, "Spare me an inquiring mind, Richard! So tedious to have to think of the answers—or evasions, where necessary."

"Evasions were required?"

"I didn't think either Sir Thomas or his daughter would approve the sum I spent on the masonry, so when Aileas asked me about it, I fear the answer was somewhat less than completely accurate." He sighed with a dismay that was not a complete fabrication. "Fortunately, Sir Thomas required much less effort."

"He asked no questions?"

"Not as many as she did, I am relieved to say."

Richard shook his head, feigning sorrow, or so George thought. "Sir George," he warned, "this does not bode well. Honesty in a marriage is to be desired above all things."

"You sound very sure of that for a man who's never had a wife," George answered lightly.

Richard chortled again. "Indeed, you are right! However, my lord, it doesn't take a great deal of perception to see that she's one of the more forthright of her sex, and therefore, I doubt she'll countenance evasion from anyone. Even you."

George shrugged his shoulders. "It is my opinion that no man should ever be completely honest with his wife, about anything, if he wishes to ensure domestic tranquillity."

"And is the wife never to be completely honest with her husband, my lord?"

"Of course she should."

"That hardly seems fair."

"We are not talking about a court of law, Sir Richard," George said with an airily dismissive wave of his hand. "We're talking about marriage. Besides, why would she ever want to lie? There would be no point dissembling about the price of a new gown, or hair ribbons, or the linen."

Richard frowned, although his eyes continued to sparkle with merriment. "I fear you are very mistaken about the majority of the fairer sex, Sir George. I believe most of them lie all the time. They're taught to do it from the cradle, whether to maintain domestic tranquillity or from fear of punishment.

"Forgive my impertinence, my lord, but I think you should appreciate Lady Aileas's honesty. It must be terrible to be married to a woman you cannot trust, especially if she is to oversee your household and all the attendant expenses."

"You're absolutely right, Richard." George pushed away from the hearth and clapped a friendly hand on Richard's shoulder. "I'm sure any daughter of Sir Thomas Dugall would never dream of being dishonest, even if she does dress rather oddly."

"Sir George!" Both men turned to see Herbert Jolliet hurrying toward them, his face red and worried.

"What is it?" George demanded.

"It's the dowry, my lord. It's not what you expected and—"

George made a wry face. "I might have guessed Sir Thomas's idea of movable goods is not quite the same as mine," he said, envisioning rough, unspun wool and sheep-tallow candles instead of fine linen sheets and pure beeswax candles. "Is it worth five hundred marks?"

"Yes, but—"

"Then it will do."

Suddenly, the hall fell silent, so that when Sir Richard cleared his throat, it sounded like a clap of thunder on a quiet afternoon. He gazed over George's shoulder, his expression one of wariness—and surprise. "Here is the lady now, my lord."

George turned on his heel and saw Aileas standing at the bottom of the tower stairs. She wore that same green dress, and her hair, long and unbound, hung nearly to her waist, rippling in waves, thick and luxurious, the kind of hair a man could bury his hands in. Her fearless brown eyes shone in the light of the flambeaux, and she had a proud, defiant expression that belonged on the face of a queen. No timid maid this, but a woman of passion and fire and spirit.

The sudden silence in the hall made him aware that his men were likewise spellbound by this unexpected and unusual vision. George gave Richard and Herbert a quick glance, to realize that his stewards were surveying his wife-to-be not with admiration but with blatant disapproval.

A few men began to whisper, their tone snide, and a muffled snicker reached his ears. George fastened a keen eye on the men, who quickly fell silent again. Herbert bowed and hurried out of the hall as if George's look had been an order to go.

George turned back to face Aileas—and had to subdue the urge to groan aloud, for he saw the cause of those reactions. She was wearing that same green gown, which exposed more than it should, was tight where it should not be, and whose cuffs had not been cleaned.

Didn't she have something else to wear?

Then he met Aileas's gaze as she looked around the hall, and there was something in her eyes, beneath the pride and defiance, that made him believe she realized how ridiculous she looked. He would not have her feel humiliated in his hall for all the world. "Lady Aileas," he said in his most respectful tone and with his most sincere smile as he approached her. "You look lovely."

"Sir George," she acknowledged coldly, the pain of her embarrassment buried deep inside her. She saw the men's reactions and the mocking laughter lurking on the steward's face, try as he might to hide it. She knew she looked like a fool.

But Aileas had borne the brunt of mockery before. No woman with six older brothers would be spared such treatment, and so she was quite capable of hiding her regret at her wardrobe choice beneath a visage of austere dignity.

Nevertheless, she could not help but be pleased with the respect in Sir George's tone, although she could have done without the pity in his eyes, which pricked her pride. Therefore, when he took her arm to lead her into the hall, she would have him know she was not a fool or blind to the faults of this hideous garment. "I know exactly how I look," she whispered, even as she tried not to trip over the unfamiliarly long skirt.

He gave her a startled glance and was about to speak when Lady Margot swept into view at the other end of the hall, wearing the most lovely gown of ivory silk embellished with scarlet embroidery, her waist encased in a chain belt of what looked like gold, and her thin silken scarf barely concealing her bountiful raven hair. "Come," he said eagerly, taking Aileas's arm almost roughly, "I would have you meet my cousin."

"The poor old widow?" Aileas asked archly as he led her down the center of the hall.

He gave her a curious glance, but by this time, they

were before the lady. "Lady Aileas Dugall, allow me to present my cousin, Lady Margot de Pontypoole."

Lady Margot curtsied very prettily, and Aileas did her best.

"I am delighted to meet you," Lady Margot said, smiling at Aileas with apparent friendly sincerity.

"Sir George led me to believe that you would be considerably older," Aileas declared.

George's smile became somewhat pained. "I never—"

"He told you I was an old widow woman, did he?" said Lady Margot, looking at George, the expression in her eyes teasing. "Compared to you, my dear, I am old."

George smiled again, and Aileas felt that her remark had been neatly turned aside. "I have never seen you looking better, Margot," her betrothed said. "I am shocked that no man has offered to marry you."

"Who told you they have not?" she chided playfully, her voice as warm and sweet as honey. "Since you did not deign to pursue me, there was no one else worth taking."

"Ah, but my manners are too rough for your taste," George answered.

Lady Margot laughed prettily, while Aileas listened in stunned surprise. How could anyone consider Sir George's manners "rough"?

"Indeed they are," Lady Margot continued, "for you are forcing us to stand far too long."

"Forgive me!" he cried at once. He held out his arm for Lady Margot, who seemed very eager to take it. "Oh, but here is Herbert Jolliet," he said, gesturing toward the steward, who had returned to the hall. "I know he is looking forward to meeting you again. I fear I must force you to stand awhile yet, but you may sit, Lady Aileas.''

Sir George let go of her arm and sauntered away with Lady Margot, leaving his bride-to-be standing alone. She turned and marched toward the dais, until the estate steward moved to block her path.

''They are like brother and sister, my lady,'' Sir Richard noted, holding out his arm as if he would escort her the rest of the way to her seat, a matter of a few feet.

''Indeed?'' Aileas replied dispassionately, not taking his arm.

''Allow me to escort you to the table,'' the steward said, and Aileas felt she had no choice but to comply without being even more blatantly rude.

Aileas assumed the chair to the right of the largest one at the table—undoubtedly Sir George's—would be her father's, so she paused at the seat to the left of the center chair.

''I'm sorry, my lady,'' Sir Richard said, ''that seat is for Sir Thomas. You have the favored seat.'' His arm came around her, indicating where she was to sit.

''Oh,'' she murmured, surprised by this honor. She moved quickly to her place, noting with some satisfaction that Sir Richard was not to sit at the high table, for he moved to the table nearest. There was something about the man she did not like, although she would be hard-pressed to say exactly what.

Sir Thomas entered the hall, trailed by his men, and Aileas was pleased to see that Sir George abandoned Lady Margot with the same speed he had her. For all his apparent polish, it seemed Sir George de Gramercie could be rude, too.

Then she watched as he led her father toward the

demurely smiling Lady Margot, and more introductions were made. To her chagrin, her father nodded politely and seemed pleased to meet her, while his men were all grinning like besotted simpletons.

Including Sir George de Gramercie.

Chapter Eight

Aileas had never been so disgruntled in her entire life.

Wasn't she the bride here? Yet every man around her seemed besotted by Lady Margot de Pontypoole, including her father and the bridegroom. She might as well have been in another country for all the attention they paid her as the meal progressed.

Her gaze roved over the hall, taking in the fine tapestries that moved ever so slightly in the warm air, the faces that glowed like bronze statues in the golden light of the flambeaux and candles, the fresh white linen, the gleaming silver goblets and polished wooden trenchers, the large, nearly waked hounds that grazed beneath the tables. A host of lovely smells rose about her, too, from the spiced dishes that arrived in endless array to the rushes on the floor. Servants and pages scurried about, constantly bringing new dishes or filling goblets. Voices hummed and buzzed about her, with snatches of laughter reaching her. Somewhere nearby were minstrels, for she could discern the playing of instruments above the other noise.

If only she could leave the high table and sit with

the men of her father's household. They were having a merry time, eating and drinking and talking and laughing. Surely being there would be infinitely better than having to sit in exile beside Sir George. She couldn't even talk to her father without having her betrothed in the way.

How was she going to feel tomorrow, when her father had left for home? He did not intend to remain for the wedding feast. When she had proposed arriving at Ravensloft a day early, he had agreed with this condition. He truly did not like to be away from his castle for more than a day.

She stabbed at the roast duck before her with her dagger and shoved the tasty morsel into her mouth, washing it down with a gulp of wine. Once again, her cuff snagged on the trencher, and a smear of grease soiled it.

Frowning, Aileas went to wipe it clean with the fine linen napkin at her elbow, then decided it would not be worth the ruin to the napkin. What did it matter how her gown looked? Nobody cared.

After tomorrow, when she was married, she would dress as she pleased.

If she was married.

She ripped off a piece of the fine white bread and began to chew it meditatively as she once again scanned the hall. Her one consolation at the moment was that Sir Richard and his brother had retired already, before the seventh course. Why, she had no idea and didn't care. They made her nervous, those two, as if they knew in great detail everything she could *not* do.

And never had she felt more lacking than now. She had grown ever more aware that not only did she not dress like Lady Margot or act like Lady Margot, but neither did she eat like Lady Margot, or Sir George. They toyed with the food laid before them as if actually consuming food were the last thing they should consider, and certainly less important than polite and witty conversation.

She felt completely out of place, even though whenever she looked at George, he smiled at her with a hint of boyish mischievousness in his eyes that would have charmed her, if she could have thought of anything brilliantly clever to say.

A burst of trilling, feminine laughter drew her attention back to Sir George, her father and Lady Margot. "If you insist, Sir Thomas," Lady Margot was saying regretfully, "but I really am quite certain George's men can take care of your horses well enough."

"Be that as it may," her father said with only a hint of his normally stern tone, "I always make it a practice to see that the beasts are fed and watered and properly bedded down for the night."

This was true. He always did, at home or away, for he never completely trusted any except his sons, even in so small a thing.

Her father rose and glanced at her. "If you will excuse me, I'll return shortly," he said, then bowed and marched off the dais. He strode down the side of the hall, nodding at two of his men to accompany him. Those selected gave their companions rueful glances, but there was no question of remaining behind.

"My, he is a commanding presence, is he not?" Lady Margot said, gazing at Sir George and leaning over Sir Thomas's chair while emitting another charming laugh. "Quite overpowering."

George, acutely aware that Aileas had not said three words since the meal began, moved his head toward his betrothed and gave Margot a significant look. Fortunately, she caught on at once. ''A very fine man, too,'' she said sincerely.

Aileas crammed another piece of bread in her mouth.

His betrothed didn't seem to be listening, but George knew better. He could see the tension in her shoulders, the furrow in her brow and the way she avoided coming into contact with even so much as his elbow. The few times he had caught her eye, she had looked so stern and severe, he had had the unpleasant sensation that he was marrying a serjeant-at-arms, not the woman who had been so passionate and desirable. He had hoped that her father's presence might explain her attitude; unfortunately, that esteemed gentleman's departure had not noticeably lightened her mood.

Margot made a little frown. ''You know, George, I really must protest this marriage,'' she announced gravely.

''Why?'' George asked, seeing the teasing look in her eye and hoping that Aileas would realize she was only joking.

''I have it on the best authority that several young ladies of marriageable age were quite beside themselves when they heard word of your nuptials,'' Margot replied.

''Name one,'' he challenged.

''The Earl of Dunstable's daughter.''

''I have no idea who you're talking about.'' He turned toward Aileas, who was taking yet another enormous gulp of his finest French wine. At this rate, she wouldn't be able to get up when the meal was over. "Margot delights in tormenting me in this fashion."

"You seem to enjoy it," Aileas replied coldly. She turned a disapproving face to him, looking so like her father at that moment that George took refuge in a gulp of wine himself.

What was the matter with her? Margot was being charming and friendly, and Aileas was treating her with such obvious discourtesy it was embarrassing. He would not have Margot feel unwelcome in his home.

"Do you truly not remember Isobel de Barlough?" Lady Margot asked archly, apparently immune to Aileas's reaction, or rising above it. "She will be devastated to be forgotten."

"Isobel de Barlough? Is she the one who sniffles all the time?"

Margot laughed delicately. "She suffers much from colds." She leaned over Sir Thomas's chair again and spoke directly to Aileas, who finally looked at her. "Indeed, my dear, I can think of several young ladies who have probably wept into their pillows after they heard you had captured this valiant knight. Once, at a tournament, two women tried to pull out each other's hair over him."

Aileas shrugged and turned her attention to a boisterous group of her father's men who had burst into an extremely ribald song.

George decided it might be best to ignore Aileas as one would a sulky child. Her rudeness had distressed Margot, and now he feared his cousin might not want to remain at Ravensloft after the wedding, and that was absolutely necessary. "Who *was* that?" he mused aloud.

"Let me see..." Margot's shapely brows contracted

with concentration. "Wasn't it Lady Jane Pomphrey and her friend? Or, at least, they *were* friends. They haven't spoken to each other since."

Suddenly Aileas shoved back her chair and rose with surprising majesty for one who had imbibed five full goblets of wine.

"Are you ill?" George asked, rising, too.

"I need some air," Aileas replied. She gave Margot a cold, fierce look. "Fresh air."

With that, she began to walk away. She stumbled once, but quickly righted herself before George could even get out of his chair to assist her. Then she marched out of the hall as her father had before her.

George noted that the hall had fallen conspicuously quiet. "I had better go after her," he muttered as the door banged shut behind her. The assembly began to talk again, albeit in subdued and incredulous whispers.

"George, I'm so sorry!" Margot said softly. "I didn't mean to upset her."

"I know," he replied with a wan smile. "She is the most temperamental woman I have ever met."

"You should go after her."

"It certainly wouldn't do to find the bride passed out in the courtyard," he noted quietly as he rose.

Margot leaned forward and grabbed his sleeve. "Tell her she has no reason to be jealous of me."

This time, it was George's turn to stare. "Is that why...?" He felt like a fool for not seeing it himself. He had been too intent on impressing Sir Thomas with talk of his friends at court and the plans to add yet more to his castle. He hadn't paid much attention to Aileas at all.

Again, Margot nodded. "Absolutely."

He bowed gallantly. "I shall do as you command, my lady, and after my hot-tempered bride go I."

"Hush!" Elma hissed to her companions as they stood in the shadowed recess between the stables and storehouse. "Somebody's coming."

They watched Sir Thomas stride past, and Herbert heaved a sigh of relief. "I'll be glad when he's gone home."

"But his daughter stays behind," Richard reminded them.

"Are you sure? She doesn't look very happy about it," Herbert noted. "And if Sir George finds out about the dowry..."

"What about it?" Richard demanded.

"It's not household goods at all."

Elma and Richard stared at him. "Well, what is it?" Richard asked impatiently.

"It's weapons—swords, bows and arrows, lances."

"God's wounds!" Elma said softly. "What kind of mistress are we going to have?"

"Maybe that saucy girl will get angry enough to leave. Maybe he'll marry Margot de Pontypoole instead."

"Lady Aileas won't leave," Elma said, shaking her head. "She wants him."

"How can you be so sure?" Herbert demanded in a whining whisper.

Elma shrugged. "I just am. I've been watching her. She's jealous about Lady Margot, too."

"That's what I thought," Richard confirmed. "This could work very well for us, if she is unsure of her place here. We just have to do what we've planned all along—get her trust and keep it, especially you, Elma."

Elma nodded.

"What if Sir George's new wife wants to examine the books of account?" Herbert demanded. "She'd be perfectly within her rights to do it. I can't say no."

"What if she does?" Richard retorted. "She won't find anything amiss, unless you've been careless." His eyes narrowed ominously. "You haven't, have you?"

"Of course not!"

"Then we shouldn't have anything to fear. She's only a woman, after all. The important thing is to keep a cool head and watch which way the wind blows. If the marriage is troubled, so much the better for us and our plans."

"I agree," Elma said. "Now, I had best get back before I'm missed. Something tells me the lady may wish to retire early tonight."

"And you will be a sympathetic, friendly servant," Richard added.

"Of course," Elma said with a throaty laugh as she slipped out of the shadows and back to the hall.

The two men waited a few moments, then went their separate ways.

George wasn't quite sure where to look for Aileas, once he had ascertained that she had not passed out in the courtyard. It took him several minutes to discover her pacing beside the chapel, looking more like a soldier on guard duty than a woman on the eve before her wedding as the silvery light of the moon shone down on her. "Aileas?" he called out softly. "Are you all right?"

She halted abruptly, then faced him, her chest heaving as if she had just run miles, her bodice gaping with each breath. "What do you want?" she demanded.

"I was worried about you. I thought you might be ill. That wine—"

She straightened even more, and if her expression could have killed, he would have been stone-cold on the cobblestones. "Do you think I am drunk?"

"Well, no."

"Good. It would take more than that thin red stuff to make me drunk."

He should have guessed Aileas could drink any other woman under the bench, too. "Forgive me," he said with a courteous little bow.

"Now you have done your duty and you may return to your charming companion."

"Who is very concerned that you are jealous of her when you should not be," he said gently. He came closer. "I fear you misunderstand my relationship with my cousin."

Her response was a harsh bark of a laugh. "I fear I understand all too well, my lord."

Her answer and its implication made his hands curl into fists as he fought to control himself. "No, you don't," he said, enunciating each word.

"Tell me, Sir George, why...why you are not marrying *her*?" Her question began defiantly, but he caught the tremulous repetition that told him what he wanted to know.

"If I wanted to marry Margot, I could have done so before this," he reminded her. "I want *you*."

"Why?" The word was flung at him accusingly.

Instead of answering with words, he reached out and pulled her into his embrace, looking intently into the dark pools of her eyes before giving in to the irrepressible desire to kiss her.

For a moment, he thought she might pull away—but she didn't. She responded in kind, with that untamed urgency he had felt from her before, an urgency that seemed to reach into him and release something he had long tried to suppress.

Fiercely, he drove his tongue into the wet warmth of her mouth, the contact thrilling in a way totally new to him. Her strong arms tightened about him, and she pressed herself along his body, a low moan escaping her lips.

He broke their kiss to trail his mouth along the fine curve of her jaw and down her slender neck toward her gaping bodice. "I want you, Aileas," he murmured. "God's wounds, I want you."

Only half-aware of what he was doing as he claimed her mouth again, he pushed her back against the chapel wall.

Then, with a boldness that shocked him, she reached inside his tunic and shirt to rub her fingers lightly over his nipples. "Oh God, Aileas," he moaned, bending to kiss the flesh of her exposed breasts, wanting to give her something of the pleasure she was rousing in him.

"You there! Have you no respect—"

Aileas gasped and George spun around to behold Sir Thomas Dugall bearing down on them. The outraged nobleman hesitated for a moment, his expression growing even more angry, then he barked, "Stay here," to the two men with him, as if they were his hunting hounds. He strode toward his daughter and her betrothed.

Between the passionate excitement she had been experiencing and the shock of seeing her father, Aileas could scarcely draw breath. She had seen her father angry before, of course, but he had never looked so wrathful as he did at this moment.

What had happened here? Why was it every time Sir George kissed her, she seemed to lose all control?

"Daughter, what is the meaning of this?"

"Sir, I—" George began.

"How dare you accost my daughter as if she were a common whore!" he growled. Then her father raised his gloved hand and smote Sir George full on the face, sending him staggering.

Sir George recovered swiftly, straightening, his back to them. Aileas feared he would retaliate in kind, in which case her father would surely draw his sword and kill him. She quickly stepped between them. "Father! He didn't!"

"Forgive me for any overzealousness, Sir Thomas," Sir George said lightly behind her. "I must plead the impatience of a bridegroom as my excuse for any liberties I have taken."

Aileas turned to stare at him and found him leaning back against the chapel wall as if nothing much were amiss at all.

How could he be so cool in the face of her father's anger? She was trembling, terrified for him—and he was smiling!

"I think you are not the man for my daughter after all," Sir Thomas declared.

"Oh, I think my actions, as inexcusable as they are, would indicate otherwise, don't you?" He crossed his arms, his expression enigmatic. "Need I remind you, Sir Thomas, the marriage agreement has been signed. You have given me your word."

"You are an impertinent rogue!"

"I am Sir George de Gramercie, Sir Thomas, and I am betrothed to your daughter."

Her father's eyes narrowed as he abruptly turned on his heel to face Aileas. "Do you want him still?"

Aileas regarded her father steadily, knowing that once again, she had a choice to make. "Yes," she replied softly.

"Well then, marry him," her father snapped. "But if he ever lays a hand on you or causes you pain in any way, you are to come home to me at once. No blame shall attach to you."

She nodded slowly.

"Get to bed!"

Aileas didn't linger but obeyed at once, while Sir Thomas turned his glaring gray eyes on Sir George. "If you ever hurt my daughter, I will kill you. Do you understand?"

"Perfectly, as I am not stupid, nor hard of hearing," Sir George said.

Then the impudent fellow shoved himself away from the chapel wall and sauntered off without another word.

"Are you all right, my lady?" Elma asked timidly as she regarded her mistress, who stalked into the bed-chamber like a man who had lost his finest hawk.

"Perfectly," Lady Aileas replied.

"You look a little flushed."

"I'm tired."

That was a barefaced lie, Elma thought. She tried again. "Would you like me to fetch you some wine?"

"I think I have had quite enough. Please, leave me."

"But you'll need help—"

"I can undress myself. Good *night*."

Elma knew there was nothing else to say, so she reluctantly left this most puzzling of women.

When she was gone, Aileas let out a long, weary, trembling sigh and collapsed onto the bed.

What in the name of the saints was happening?

Did Sir George want to marry her or not?

Did she want to marry him?

Did it matter what either of them wanted tonight, when the marriage contract was already signed?

Sighing again, she rose and went to the window. Could she climb out of this window and leave this place? Then she wouldn't have to worry that she was about to do something she would regret for the rest of her life.

If she tried to climb out of here, she would surely fall and break her neck.

Which would be one end to her dilemma, she thought with a sad and rueful smile.

She leaned her elbows on the stone ledge and regarded the surrounding countryside. It all seemed so peaceful after the noise of the hall, where the men were still celebrating. Lady Margot, she had noted as she had hurried through the hall to the stairs, had apparently retired.

In the village, light could be seen shining palely from a window or open door. Somewhere an owl hooted.

Below, she caught the murmur of voices and saw two men talking together. One she immediately recognized as Sir George, the other Sir Richard. She watched as Sir George bade the other good-night, then strolled away with his easy, athletic gait toward the barracks.

Why did he want her? She could not believe he would want her for herself alone. She was too different from the type of woman he no doubt preferred, the beautiful, demure, witty ones, like Lady Margot.

Just to form an alliance with her father? That could be—yet he would get no land, and her dowry, while not small, was not sizable, either. Surely a man of his attributes could have his choice of many richer, more educated, beautiful women.

Why her?

If she knew the answer to that, then she might feel comfortable here, instead of feeling that she didn't belong. She knew that she was different. She had spent too much time in the company of her brothers and her father's soldiers to be like other women.

Sir George made her feel like a woman, especially when he took her in his arms and kissed her. Surely that boded well for her marriage.

Then she recalled the times her brothers and their friends had spoken of their lovers.

She moved away from the window and began to smile a different smile. A pleased smile. A triumphant smile.

Maybe she didn't know how to eat with the proper etiquette. Maybe she didn't dress like Lady Margot de Pontypoole. Maybe she was abysmally ignorant of many things most women of her station knew how to do.

But there were some things she did know, precisely because she had spent so much time in the company of men. Surely her husband would overlook those other faults in view of her exceptional knowledge.

Chapter Nine

At noon the next day, with the sun shining brightly in a cloudless sky, George made sure to put a very pleased and contented smile on his face as he arrived at the chapel. He would not have anyone think he was less than delighted by the step he was about to take.

Another step on the journey had begun that horrible moment when he realized that his father was truly dead and he was now the lord of Ravensloft, with all the attendant privileges—and duties.

The wedding ceremony would take place inside the chapel, attended by those guests of higher rank. Outside, men-at-arms and other retainers would assemble in the courtyard until after the ceremony's conclusion, whereupon they would follow the wedding party into the hall for the feast. Several of his men and those of Sir Thomas were already milling about. A few saluted, others bowed or tugged their forelock, but all grinned, no doubt anticipating the celebrations and feast.

George wished that he, too, had only to anticipate carefree revelry. Certainly he had been a guest at enough weddings to share in their current mood. Now

that he was the groom, however, he felt completely
different.

He could not help wondering if he had chosen his
bride unwisely. Perhaps he would have done better to
pick a younger, more amenable woman, one less defiant and proud, who would easily bend herself to her
husband's ways. One who knew how to dress properly
and eat properly and speak when spoken to.

One who would probably squeal in horror at the
sight of a man's naked body and have to be cajoled
into the nuptial bed. Who would then lie stiffly terrified as he took her, no matter how gentle he was.

Who would not meet him with exciting, feverish
passion.

Yet who would not also enrage him, as he had not
been enraged in years.

George entered the dim, incense-scented stone
building. A few candles on the bare altar and the sunlight pouring in through tall, narrow windows of
stained glass illuminated the inner room, casting a
muted light of yellow, red and blue that seemed somehow more holy than natural sunlight.

He rubbed his temples, as if by doing so he could
think with better clarity. Perhaps it would help if he
said a prayer.

"Fatigued, George?"

Startled, he realized Margot was standing near the
statue of the Virgin Mary.

Margot looked lovely, as Margot always did. She
wore a simple, but elegant, gown of pale green silk
with a darker overtunic of emerald samite. Her scarf
was likewise green, of a shimmering fabric that moved
when she breathed. Her face, framed by that delicate
scarf, was pale, and he did not think he was the only

one fatigued. The journey here must have been tiring for her, for she did not like to travel. She always gave that as an excuse when he had asked her to visit before.

He gave his cousin a warm, brotherly smile. "A little. Too much fine food last night, I fear."

"Did you speak to her?"

"Yes," he said, coming to join her near the statue.

Margot's gaze grew more intense. "Did you reassure her?"

"I tried to," he said, fearing this was not quite the truth.

Margot nodded, apparently satisfied. "Good."

"Margot?"

"Yes?"

"I have a great favor to ask of you."

She smiled. "Oh?"

"I would like you to stay here for awhile, to help Aileas."

"To help her do what?" she asked, obviously puzzled.

"You saw her last night," he said, the words coming in a rush, for he had not given full voice to his opinion concerning his bride before. "She eats like the roughest man in my retinue. She has no proper clothes—usually she wears the most incredible combination of breeches, tunics and skirts you can imagine. She has no notion of decorum or etiquette. I want you to help her learn to be a lady."

"She is a lady," Margot pointed out, turning away from him and brushing her fingertips over the wooden kneeling rail before the sacred statue, "for she is a lord's daughter."

"Don't dissemble now, Margot!" he pleaded softly. "I mean a proper lady. A respectable lady."

"So I am to be a teacher, like a nun in a convent?" she asked, her face still averted.

"Margot, please, I need your help. There is no one else I can ask. Won't you do this for me?" he pleaded fervently, reaching out to take her cool hand in his.

She turned toward him then, and he couldn't perceive what she was thinking, whether she would agree or tell him that she had to go back and manage her own household. "Why do you not do it yourself?" she asked softly, regarding him steadily.

He dropped her hand and shrugged. "I cannot. I have not the patience."

"But you were always the peacemaker," she reminded him.

"That is an easy thing to be when one doesn't have any particular affection for the people quarreling," he observed.

She came close to him, so that he could detect the attar of roses she always wore, despite the constant presence of incense. "Then you have a 'particular affection' for Aileas Dugall?" she asked softly, looking at him with a sympathetic expression.

"I believe so," he confessed.

"I am glad to hear it, since you are to marry her." She walked past him toward the altar.

"Margot?"

"Since *you* ask this of me, George, I will stay."

"Thank you, cousin," he said, with happiness and considerable relief. With Margot to show her the proper way to do things, Aileas's faults could surely be corrected.

Margot looked at him over her shoulder. "My pleasure, cousin."

Father Adolphus, a short, rotund priest dressed in fine vestments, came bustling out of a door at the side of the chapel, followed by his clerk. He started when he saw Lady Margot, and then Sir George. "My lady, my lord, you are rather early."

George heard the chapel door open and glanced back to see Richard and Herbert Jolliet enter. "A little, perhaps. I suppose I am as impatient as any bridegroom."

"And I came to say a prayer to the Holy Virgin to bless my cousin and his new wife," Lady Margot said with a lovely smile.

The priest beamed. "A very kind sentiment, my lady."

Margot went to stand beside the stewards as other wedding guests began to file into the small building. Soon, the only people missing were the bride and her father.

When an excited murmur ran through the gathering, George knew that Sir Thomas and Aileas were at the door.

He turned to look at them—and his jaw nearly dropped at the sight.

It seemed Aileas did own one dress that fit, after all, a lovely gown of eggshell-colored brocade. The square neckline could not have been more appropriately placed, and it, like the long, flowing sleeves, was trimmed with gold embroidery. Her long hair had been adorned with a garland of spring blossoms. A supple girdle of embossed leather hung about her narrow hips and seemed to emphasize their womanly sway as her father, attired in severe black, led her forward.

God's holy heaven, she looked like a woodland nymph or some kind of spirit of nature come to earth as a beautiful bride. George smiled, suddenly sure he was making no mistake taking Aileas Dugall for his bride.

Aileas clung to her father's arm, unusually bashful as all the people in the chapel turned to look at her. Indeed, she was tempted to turn and run, until she saw George staring at her, his eyes wide with wonder.

Then he smiled, and all her uncertainty vanished.

"My lords and my lady," the priest intoned when she came to stand beside him. "We are come together here to ask God's blessing upon the union of Sir George de Gramercie and Lady Aileas Dugall as they are joined together in holy wedlock...."

The hall was filled with the cacophony of happy revelers. The soldiers were half-drunk before the second course had appeared, but fortunately, their rambunctious behavior took the form of jokes and laughter. The maidservants, giggling and dexterously avoiding unwelcome advances, weaved their way around the tables. Dogs scuffled in the rushes or gnawed contently on bones, aware only that an unusual amount of meat was falling to the floor. Smiling pages served the noble guests. The musicians in the gallery, sure that they would be well paid, played with a will.

Pleased with his bride, mellow with fine wine, secretly delighted that his stern and severe father-in-law had chosen not to stay for the wedding feast and less secretly looking forward to his wedding night, George was in a mood to be generous and delighted with everyone. "I would dearly love to be able to feast all the knights of my acquaintance," he remarked in an expansive tone as he surveyed the happy company. He turned to Aileas with a sly and mischievous smile. "And to show you off, my lady."

Aileas's face flushed like the blushing bride she was. "I gather your acquaintance numbers in the hundreds, my lord. Surely the cost would be prohibitive!"

"Who cares about the cost?" he replied, waving his goblet dismissively. "I would have all men envy me!"

"But surely we could not afford it," she demurred.

"Let us ask Richard, shall we?"

"Right now?"

He gave her a quizzical look, until he felt her squeeze his thigh in an astonishingly bold gesture. "No, I suppose not. I fear I would not have the concentration to attend."

"Nor I, my lord," his bride said gravely.

"Perhaps later, when you go through the household accounts with Herbert, you will see that I can afford to have more than one or two feasts in a year."

Aileas moved her hand away. "Household accounts? With Herbert?"

"Oh, I know, this is not the time to discuss such business. Come!" He grabbed her hand and pulled her to her feet. "Clear the floor!" he bellowed. "My bride and I wish to dance!"

"George, I—" Aileas began desperately as servants rushed to do his bidding. She didn't know how to dance. She could ride as well as any man, shoot an arrow better than most, use a sword if need be, and a mace if she must, but she had never been taught to dance.

Ignoring her, George tugged her around the table

and to the center of the floor, where the tables had been taken down with the dispatch one might expect if they were suddenly attacked. At the moment, Aileas thought that would be preferable.

"Musicians!" he called. "A *carole.* Something lively, for truly, my feet feel winged tonight!" Holding her hand aloft, George slowly walked in a circle. "It is true, gentlemen, that there is, unfortunately, a dearth of ladies. Still, join us and dance, for I must and shall have dancing on my wedding day!"

"George, please!" Aileas protested, her grip tightening, but the leader of the musicians had already lifted the bow of his *fithele.*

Perhaps no one will join us and I will be spared, Aileas thought desperately.

Sir Richard quickly got to his feet and made a deep bow toward Lady Margot, who rose at once. As several other revelers came forward, Aileas wished the musicians would all suddenly drop down in a faint. Or maybe she could. "Sir George," she said weakly, "I don't think—"

Before she could finish, however, the music for the *carole* began.

Aileas never did know how she managed to keep on her feet for the entire dance. She felt as if she were being pulled this way, then that, then made to whirl around like some kind of demented madwoman. It was a wonder she *didn't* faint, or get thrown aside like meat for the dogs, or trip and fall headlong into a table. When the dance finally ended, she had to hold on to George by the shoulders to keep steady.

Panting, she looked up at him. He was regarding her with an expression she couldn't quite read. "You've never done that before, have you?" he asked quietly as Sir Richard led an infuriatingly serene Lady Margot back to her place. The other dancers staggered over to the remaining tables and downed their wine or joined in companionable laughter.

"No," she confessed. "That was what I was trying to tell you."

"Do you know an *estampie?*"

She let go of him. "No."

"A round dance?"

"No."

"Well, no matter," he said indulgently.

As if she were an ignorant child.

But she wasn't. She simply didn't know how to dance.

She began to bristle, until he took hold of her hand, and all her annoyance fled at the touch of his lean, strong fingers. "Perhaps you would care to retire?"

Her heart, already beating rapidly from the exercise of the dance, seemed to pound against her ribs. "As you wish, my lord," she replied quietly.

Her body throbbing, her heart racing, she managed to make her obeisance to her new husband. As calmly and regally as possible, she walked to the tower stairs with all the dignity she could command.

But the moment she was out of sight of the company, Aileas gave a throaty chuckle, hoisted her skirt and took the stairs two at a time, knowing she was about to experience what her brothers and Rufus and all the other men in her father's castle talked about almost constantly. What had dominated her thoughts this past fortnight, despite her best efforts, when she wasn't worried about fitting into the life of Ravensloft Castle.

Living in the countryside as she did, she had learned

early the nature of breeding. Later, though, as she
spent time in the company of her brothers and the
soldiers, she had come to realize that there was much
more to it than mere procreation, at least when it came
to people. She had seen the secretive smiles, nudges
and winks the men shared, as if they were all enjoying
some truly marvelous jest. Once, she had asked what
they were talking about, but they had grown suddenly
and frustratingly silent and then commanded her to
leave, as if she had committed a great sin.

Therefore, she had learned to shrink back in the
shadows when the talk turned to women, so that she
was quite forgotten.

Not that they described their activities in great detail. No. Just enough to let her guess the rest, including
the notion that there seemed to be an astonishing number of variations and positions, and that the basic act
was just that—basic. Like anything basic, be it a
weapon or a piece of furniture, it could be improved
upon with creativity.

The one great given was that whatever they had
been doing with women, each one of them had enjoyed it immensely and was equally certain that the
women had, too. And certain women were held in high
esteem—even awe—based upon their abilities in bed.

Now, as she recalled those overheard conversations,
a host of wild imaginings coursed through her brain,
each one featuring her charming, handsome husband.
She was very determined to be as enthusiastic and cre-
ative as any woman she had ever heard about.

She reached the bedchamber and shoved open the
door. Inside, Elma, who had obviously been awaiting
her, gasped and jumped up from the stool upon which

she had been sitting. "My lady!" she cried. "I thought you would be some time yet."

"Alas, I do not dance!" Aileas replied, twirling around as if to give the lie to her statement.

Elma gave her an odd look. "Shall I help you with your gown?"

"Yes. And fold it carefully, although Lord knows when I'll ever have need of it again." With some effort, she managed to stay still while Elma unlaced her and helped her from the gown, so that she stood clad only in her thin white shift.

"It's very warm in this room, isn't it?" she demanded, going to the window and opening the linen shutter as Elma carefully folded the gown. "There is too much coal in the brazier."

"Forgive me, my lady."

"Of course I forgive you, Elma. It's too late in the season for a brazier, anyway."

"I suppose Sir George didn't want you getting cold, my lady."

"Or himself. Look at all the coverings on the bed—" Aileas glanced at the bed, blushed and hesitated. "Well, no matter. We'll pack most of them up tomorrow."

"As you wish, my lady."

"And all these candles! So much light is not necessary, Elma." Aileas quickly went to the candle stand nearest the bed and blew out each of the fine beeswax candles.

"Shall I help you with your hair?"

"No, thank you. I'm sure I can manage the rest by myself, Elma. Why don't you join the other servants in the kitchen? I'm certain Sir George has arranged fine food and drink for all of you, too."

Elma nodded and went to the door with reluctant steps. "Good night, my lady."

"Good night, Elma."

When she was gone and the door closed, Aileas regarded the bed for a long moment before being overcome by an irresistible temptation, which she acted upon at once.

She ran and jumped, falling back into the softness of the feather bed and giggling. "Such a sinful luxury," she said aloud, running her hands over the satiny coverlet.

"I see nothing particularly sinful about luxury, as long as one also does one's duty by the poor."

With a gasp, Aileas sat up and stared at her husband, who was leaning against the closed door with a goblet held lightly in his hand, as if he had somehow been magically transported there from the hall below. "I...I didn't hear you enter!"

"I can be as quiet as a cat when I wish to be, my lady," he said, and to her, it was as if he could purr like a cat, too. He took a final sip from the silver goblet before setting it down on the nearest table. Then he sauntered toward the bed, removing his belt as he did so. "I'm afraid I was rather rude to our guests. By rights, I should still be below, acting the perfect host."

Aileas could think of no response beyond attempting to swallow, for her mouth was suddenly very dry. He slowly ran his gaze over her while he set his belt on a chair, and she instantly realized her shift was rather far up her legs. A modest maiden would have tugged it down at once.

She didn't, for she felt powerless to do anything except watch him as he began to undo the lacing at the throat of his tunic, his blue eyes continuing to regard her steadily, as inscrutable as a cat's.

"Do you like my castle?" he asked.

She nodded.

"And this room? Does it meet with your approval?" he inquired before pulling his tunic over his head and tossing it aside, leaving him in a fine white shirt that hung to the middle of his powerful thighs, which were encased in tight breeches.

The tunic landed on the floor with a muffled thump, and the sight of an expensive garment being treated in such a cavalier manner finally gave Aileas the impetus to move. She scrambled off the bed and picked it up, folding it over her arm, aware of its soft texture, and that it smelled of him.

"Forgive me, my lady," he said softly, with a little smile. "I wasn't thinking."

Neither was she, exactly, she realized as she set it down on the closest of his chests. When she turned back, his shirt was neatly folded and laid on a table.

He stood before her, half-naked, his chest gleaming in the glow from the brazier, his hair brushing his broad shoulders.

He was marvelous, magnificent, with a look of purely primitive desire on his face. No longer was he the coolly charming, eloquent Sir George de Gramercie. He was a man yearning for a woman. For *her*.

No matter how many women he might have had, she would make him feel as he never had before. She would show him that even if she could not dance, and if she had no knowledge of the proper way to eat a dish, there were other things she did know that would make those seem unimportant.

She remembered everything she had heard and

wanted to do it all, at once. With him. For him. She went toward him swiftly, not as a timid virgin, hesitant and modest, but as a woman equal in her urgent need. A desire that was as strong, as overwhelming and as primitive as anything she had ever felt in her life overwhelmed her.

As if he sensed her wishes, they came together in mutual heat and passion. She pressed herself against him, kissing him with all the fiery hunger he inspired.

And tonight, it was she who invaded his mouth with her eager tongue. Her hands that caressed and stroked and touched. For a moment, he was motionless—but only a moment, until he responded with equal fervor. With a growl, he grabbed her buttocks and ground against her, letting her feel his arousal.

She knew of so many things to do. So many ways to give him pleasure. And that was what she wanted more than anything now, to give him pleasure.

A low moan escaped his lips as her tongue flicked across one nipple, then the other. Then harder, using tongue and lips, while her hands continued to stroke and caress his back, his chest, his thighs. Teasing him. Cajoling him. Inflaming him.

Pushing his breeches lower.

She gripped him lightly, gently rubbing. Then she knelt.

He gasped when she took him into her mouth. "What are you—" His words dissolved into a groan as she continued, feeling the tension in him increasing. He began to move inside her, thrusting and panting.

Then he stopped and moved away, his eyes dark with desire as he swiftly yanked off his breeches and pulled her to her feet.

Once again, he took her mouth, possessively, ur-

gently, stripping the shift from her body before he
picked her up and laid her, panting, on the bed. His
body covered hers and he pressed another heated kiss
to her lips.

She was not remembering any overheard whispers
now; she was acting for herself as she opened her legs
for him, arching to meet him. He eased himself into
her, and she bit her lip against the slight pain so that
she would not cry out and interrupt this moment.

For it was but a brief discomfort, soon forgotten.
With a sure rhythm he moved inside her, tension
building in her, too. Her body seemed strained with a
sweet, unearthly tautness, increased by the play of his
hands and mouth upon her.

She wrapped her legs about him, urging him with
half-muttered words and entreaties, hardly knowing
what she was saying, crying out when tension finally
broke like the clap of thunder heralding a storm. Then
he, too, gave a strangled, guttural cry and fell against
her, his breath hot on her breasts.

Each satisfied and spent, they slept a pure, deep
sleep, entwined together, the luxurious covers a crumpled tangle beneath them.

George awoke with a long, slow, blissfully contented sigh. It was morning, of that he was sure, for
his eyelids could not shield out the light completely.

And yet he was in no hurry to get up. He let his
mind drift lazily, remembering his wedding night.

A slow smile spread over his face as he recalled
with what haste and incredible desire he had made
love to his bride. God's wounds, he had never experienced making love with such passion and fervor and
excitement and...shock.

He had expected to take some time. To go slowly
and gently. Instead, she had ambushed him right from
the start, his control slipping away from the moment
he entered the bedroom and saw her naked legs on the
silken coverlet, her shift shoved up invitingly. It had
taken a great effort then to sound calm and act composed.

Indeed, his composure had lasted only a little time,
for each move she made sent new waves of passionate
desire coursing through his veins, whether bending to
retrieve his clothing so that her breasts, visible through
her thin shift, were silhouetted in the dim glow from
the brazier, or stroking his tunic. It was as if he had
never truly wanted a woman before.

When she had come to him, meeting him boldly, he
had been delighted. When she knelt, and then…well,
of all the things he might have hoped his bride would
do on their wedding night, he had never dared hope
for that. At once he had been overwhelmed and completely without control.

Without control.

He stiffened instinctively. His father's face appeared
before him with that wondering, disappointed look.

George opened his eyes and stared at the roof of his
bed. This was different, he told himself. Last night he
had felt love, not anger. Passion, not rage.

He reached out to touch Aileas, to draw her to him,
intending to make love with her again, only this time
slowly and leisurely, to give her pleasure.

Aileas wasn't there. The bed was empty, save for
himself. He sat up and surveyed the room. Her gown
was not in sight, and his breeches were now folded
and laid upon his largest clothing chest, along with his
shirt and tunic.

He might have known that Sir Thomas's daughter would not act like most brides after their wedding night, and that a daughter of Sir Thomas's would not allow herself the luxury of resting past dawn, even on this morning. The fact that she could rise and leave without disturbing him was something to be glad of, too, and not to wonder at.

Whistling jauntily as he dressed, he congratulated himself on his considerate and wonderful bride.

Chapter Ten

George left the bedchamber and trotted down the stairs.

Aileas wasn't in the hall, directing the servants, as he had expected. Indeed, the hall still bore every sign one could expect of last night's feasting. Several of his men slumbered, apparently right where they had been sitting until overcome by exhaustion, leaning back against the wall or spread out on the benches.

Looking rather the worse for celebrating, a few servants made desultory attempts to clean up the remains of food that even the sated dogs had left. When they saw George, their movements quickened. Upon questioning, each was very clear that they acted on their own marvelous initiative; the new mistress of Ravensloft had left the hall without a word or order to anyone.

Hungry and puzzled, George continued to the kitchen, which looked even worse than the hall. If the servants had gone berserk and rioted, the place would have been only slightly more unsightly. The pots were unscrubbed; the tables were covered with leftover pastries and scraps; the fires were out; and the only inhabitant was a loudly snoring Gaston, lying on the ground and clutching what appeared to be an empty wineskin to his plump chest.

George grabbed the heel of a loaf of bread and wondered where the devil Aileas could have gone and what she could possibly be doing.

Outside, a quick glance at the sun proved that it was already well beyond the time for mass, so he doubted Aileas would be in the chapel.

His gaze lit upon the stables and he grinned with satisfaction. She had probably gone to see that horse of hers.

He started across the courtyard, noting that only one man, whose helmet was sitting lopsided on his head, stood on duty at the gate. The fellow straightened so abruptly when he saw George that he let go of his spear. When trying to retrieve it, his helmet fell to the ground and rolled away. The guard lunged for it and nearly tripped over his weapon.

"Not so much ale next time!" George called out cheerfully. "I'm glad to see you are in your place, at least."

The man grinned with sheepish camaraderie and saluted.

Inwardly, however, his master was not nearly so pleased as he looked. Anybody could ride in, he thought grimly, if they had a mind to. It was a good thing Sir Thomas had already gone home, or he would have bent George's ear, pointing out the lax behavior of his men.

George glanced about, wondering if Aileas had noticed.

The moment he thought it, he was sure she probably had.

Then it occurred to him that if anybody could ride in unchallenged, they could ride out, too.

His steps quickened. Surely Aileas wouldn't have been so stupid as to go riding alone. His land was safe enough, but no lone woman should risk such a venture.

He pushed open the stable door, his eyes quickly adjusting to the dim light as he entered. Bits of chaff swirled in the sunbeam and a horse whinnied. Another stamped, and he realized that was Aileas's beast, who was still in its stall, thank the Lord.

"Tom?" George called out, looking for the head groom. Or any groom. Even a stable boy would do.

A low moan, a sneeze, a giggle and a cascade of loose straw from the open hatch of the loft overhead heralded the appearance of the head groom. Tom was of middle years, with a long, thin face and long, thin nose, so that he looked rather like a horse himself. "Me lord?" he asked stupidly, as if he'd never seen George before.

A woman's bare foot appeared and started to play with the groom's ear. "Stop that!" Tom muttered, shoving it away so that it disappeared from George's sight.

"Have you hired a new stable hand?" George asked gravely.

The foot reappeared, moving slowly up Tom's beefy arm. His grip tightened on the hatch, his face bloomed scarlet and his voice became a little strained. "No, me lord."

"It that Elma?"

A younger woman, whom George recognized as one of the laundresses, showed her face, which was not the most attractive George had ever seen. Her shoulders were bare, the rest of her not visible. "I'm Tilda, my lord."

She batted her eyelids, but her brown lashes were so sparse the effect was quite lost.

"Hello, Tilda. Don't you have table linens to wash today?"

Her face fell. "Yes, my lord," she muttered.

"Have either of you seen Lady Aileas lately?"

They shook their heads.

"It seems that the bridegroom has misplaced his bride," he said ruefully, turning on his heel to leave. "Now, to work, both of you."

Once outside, George stood for a moment in the courtyard, wondering where to look next, when a burst of hearty laughter came from the men's barracks. He thought he detected a familiar feminine note among the boisterous sound.

He strode over to the wattle and daub building, then shoved open the door and stood on the threshold, his arms akimbo as he regarded the men gathered there around Aileas. She sat on a stool in the midst of them, with one ankle resting on her knee, holding court like a queen—or something rather different.

"And so he said, 'Then next time, watch where you aim!'" Aileas concluded, eliciting another roar of laughter from the men.

What in the name of the saints was she doing? She was a lord's wife now and had no business hanging about with his foot soldiers like a camp follower, no matter what her father might have countenanced. "Then there was the time Sir Ralph's squire lost a boot," she began.

"I think you have amused the soldiers quite enough," he remarked coolly.

Aileas's foot hit the floor with a thump as she twisted to look at her husband standing in the doorway, his hands on his hips. Surprisingly, there was something about his lips that altered his grin from one of jovial good humor to something indicating very slight disapproval.

Happy and quite comfortable in the spartan barracks among the soldiers, Aileas glanced around, wondering what was amiss, and noticed that the soldiers all looked completely stunned, as if George's presence were not just a surprise but something extremely unusual.

Despite their peculiar reaction—for surely a lord who commanded his men well often arrived unannounced in their quarters to inspect their weapons or armor—and the fact that his grin was not quite a grin, her mind was quickly overtaken by the memory of being in George's arms and then watching him this morning as the first streaks of dawn tinted the clouds a rosy pink.

She had delighted in how young he looked as he slumbered, with a stray lock of blond hair falling across his smooth brow, his darker eyelashes like fans against his skin and his mouth temptingly half-opened. She had wanted to kiss him very much. She had not, reflecting that he might need to rest after all his efforts.

And such efforts.

So, quickly and quietly, she had washed, including the few smears of blood on her thighs. She gently and cautiously raised the covering from George, who slumbered on, and with a stifled giggle, she had cleaned him, too. And bestowed a light little kiss.

Then she had dressed in her usual clothes, delighted to feel the comfort of her breeches and shortened skirt, although the rough fabric of her shirt made her wince. It seemed too much attention had rendered some parts of her rather sensitive.

"You woke up," she said cheerfully, standing. "I feared you would sleep the entire day away."

"Someone else should be on the gate," he replied, sauntering into the room and running a measuring gaze over his soldiers.

"Derek is there, and Baldwin," she replied, for she had ascertained first thing that the proper men were at the gate. Indeed, that was what had brought her to the barracks in the first place.

"I saw only one."

"Baldwin must have been inside the gatehouse. I sent him there myself. Otherwise, anybody could have ridden in unannounced."

"My thoughts exactly."

"By the time you got out of bed and saw to the guards, we could have been overtaken," she observed. "It's a good thing I am a light sleeper."

"The soldiers are not your responsibility," he reminded her. "The hall is."

Aileas flushed. "You were—"

"Herbert can see to the household this morning," he said, in no mood to hear any excuses, even from her. "However, he takes his orders from you now."

"It seems your household can run by itself, my lord, without anyone to issue orders," she retorted.

George suddenly took her by the arm and said, "I believe we should continue our discussion elsewhere, my dear."

His grip was strong and his expression, although he smiled, inexorable. Rather than let it appear as if he were pulling her away, Aileas turned and stalked from the barracks, leaving the men glancing nervously at one another. The moment she was outside and saw that nobody was nearby, she faced him angrily. "You made me look foolish in front of them!"

George leaned his weight casually on one long leg and regarded her with what looked suspiciously like bemused condescension. "Perhaps, then, you shouldn't have gone there."

"But I wanted to see about the guards. There was only one there, and he's half-drunk yet."

"I see. So then you felt compelled to stay and entertain them rather than return to the hall and direct the servants?"

"I..." Her gaze faltered and she felt as if the wind had been taken from her sails. She shrugged her shoulders sullenly, wondering if he could possibly understand. She gave him a sidelong glance. "I was enjoying myself, that's all," she muttered.

George suddenly smiled, all hint of displeasure gone. "I should have expected Sir Thomas Dugall's daughter to think first of guards and watchmen before the usual tasks of a chatelaine," he said, his tone more amiable. "I will have Richard ensure that the guards are always on duty."

"Richard? *You* should do it."

"Aileas," he chided gently, "your father may have commanded his castle and his family with an iron hand, but he is the exception, not the rule. Richard is more than capable of seeing to such things."

Aileas was about to protest, but she was afraid of risking that look of censure in his eyes and decided to keep silent. There were other expressions she would rather see upon his handsome face. With that in mind, she embraced him and gave him a playful nip on his earlobe, although she had to subdue a cringe at her abrupt movement. She was rather sore elsewhere, too.

Yet whatever pain she had to endure was immaterial, for she had surely shown her husband that, in some things, she was a very worthy bride.

And, indeed, the reality had far surpassed anything she had ever overheard.

He gently, but deliberately, pushed her away, then took her hand and placed it formally on his arm. "You shouldn't do things like that in public," he said softly. "It's not proper."

She grabbed hold of his arm and pulled him into a narrow recess in the stone wall between the barracks and armory, then pressed against him in a provocative embrace. "We are in the courtyard of our home and I see no reason why anyone should doubt that we are happy in each other's company," she said huskily.

"Aileas," he warned, albeit without a convincing tone as he tried to maintain some semblance of self-control.

She looked about in a furtive manner, her brown eyes twinkling mischievously. "Oh, dear me! Look! A kitchen boy drawing water at the well has seen that I like being close to my husband! What a scandal!"

George bit back a curse at her blithe response, fighting the impulse to take her at that very moment, despite the location. "You are embarrassing me, Aileas. You are not a soldier in some barracks," he reminded her. "You are a lord's wife and—"

"And you are a lord," she whispered, her fingers toying with his tunic, then slipping inside to brush his naked skin. "A marvelous lord. The lord of lovers. And such a lover." Her voice grew huskier, her breath warm against the hollow of his neck. "I thought I would die when you took me, or that I was already in heaven."

"Aileas!" he moaned, not wanting her to stop, telling himself she must. "Please!"

To his relief and chagrin, she finally obeyed.

He took a deep breath and willed himself to be dignified. "Aileas, a lady doesn't talk that way or entice her husband as if she were a whore in an alley."

She looked up at him sharply. "What?"

"God's wounds, I didn't mean to use such language," he said, embarrassed by his coarse comparison. "Forgive me."

He felt her relax, her body grow soft against his, and again had to fight his impulse to make love with her there in the courtyard.

Aileas spoke, her head against his chest. "I accept your apology, although I'm quite sure you use such language when you are with your friends. Or even more colorful terms."

"I do not!"

She drew back with a decidedly skeptical look. "Truly? When you are with your companions, you do not talk about your women? Or what you will do the next time you go to a brothel?"

He winced at the last word. "No, I do not."

She raised her eyebrows and grinned, and there was mockery in her eyes. "Then you are indeed a rare man."

"Aileas," he began, fighting to keep his tone even and casual, "there is a time and a place for such conversations among men, perhaps, but never—"

"Among women?" She regarded him studiously. "Not even alone, with one's wife?"

"No."

She frowned a little but mercifully remained silent.

Having won his point, he grew calmer, inwardly as well as outwardly. "I daresay women also discuss certain personal subjects when they are alone," he remarked, "but never...that."

She grinned suddenly and stroked him in a most intimate place. "I will try not to embarrass you anymore. I will not touch you in front of the soldiers or servants," she whispered slyly. "Or kiss you before the stewards. Or caress you where the tenants might see."

"Aileas!" he moaned, losing the battle to maintain his outward calm.

She withdrew her hand, and he was suddenly as frustrated with the cessation of her caress as he had been by the initiation. "As long as you do not intend to stop doing what we are talking about," she said, "I suppose I can be silent upon the subject in company."

She broke away and gestured toward the stable. "Come! Let's go for a ride. I simply cannot stand to be cooped up inside another moment and I want to be alone with you— Oh!" She put her hand over her mouth, although her eyes danced with merriment. "I'm not supposed to say such things, am I?"

"Aileas!" George warned, his anger less than it might have been, subverted by the excitement engendered by her words.

She laughed gaily and dashed away.

"A short ride," he called after her. "Then you must address the servants about their duties and talk to Herbert concerning household matters."

By then, Aileas had reached the stable door, where she turned and stuck her tongue out at him before she disappeared inside.

* * *

"Sir George, forgive me if I am disturbing you…"

George awoke with a start and a snort. "What?" he demanded. He rubbed his bleary eyes and saw Herbert Jolliet standing before him in his solar.

He must have fallen asleep here after a short, but swift, gallop over the fields in Aileas's wake. Fortunately, she had taken pity on either him or his horse, or perhaps herself, for she had slowed as soon as they entered the wood.

How lovely she had looked, astride her horse like some kind of Amazon, her face glowing, her eyes bright. They had talked of her brothers, all six of them, from the oldest, who was twenty years her senior, to the youngest, only one year older than she and nicknamed Snout, because he had a tendency to snoop. No secret was safe around him, and in self-defense, she explained, she had learned to keep very close counsel.

She was so delightfully frank and open, a wonderful contrast to women who simpered and smiled too much. Even with Margot, he often sensed that she was talking only to tell him what she assumed he wanted to hear, not what she really thought.

Then they had stopped and sat beneath a large oak tree and… He smiled at the memory of their heated passion and covered his secretive smile by rubbing his chin. They had stopped short of making love, however, because the ground was too rocky.

He regarded his grave steward. Upon returning to Ravensloft, he had suggested to Aileas that she would find Herbert with either the pantler or the bottler, and that he was probably anxious to discuss the state of the food stores with her. She had nodded and walked off toward the larder; he had retired to his solar—and promptly nodded off.

"What is it?" George asked, wide-awake now and quite certain that some kind of domestic catastrophe was responsible for this uncharacteristic behavior. Herbert wasn't the kind of man to wake his lord, even during the day, unless there was an emergency that required his immediate guidance.

"My lord, James was just telling me that the wine merchant from Venice is going to be here soon. Unfortunately, James has heard that his prices have increased again, due to some very unfortunate weather in Italy this past year."

"You're speaking of Guido Valleduce?" George asked, relieved that his steward's concern was of no great import, yet puzzled as to why Herbert had come to him at all over this.

"Exactly, my lord."

"Then pay the extra. His wine is always excellent."

"As you wish, my lord," Herbert replied with a small bow. "Also, Lady Margot sends her regrets that she will be unable to join you in the hall this evening. She says she is too tired from the feasting and begs to be excused."

George nodded, still confused as to why Herbert was here. "Of course. Make sure Elma or one of the other servants takes her something to eat. She likes bread and cheese and a little mulled wine for a light supper, if memory serves."

"As you wish, my lord." Herbert cleared his throat deferentially, as he always did when broaching an awkward subject. "I also thought to speak with you about the household accounts."

"You should have talked to my wife about that,"

George replied, trying to keep his frustration from his voice. "That is her province now."

Herbert's already gloomy frown grew deeper.

"Unfortunately, my lord..."

"What?" he demanded impatiently.

"She doesn't seem to want to speak to me. Every time I've seen her since you returned, she's sent me away."

George's first impulse was to frown, but he forced himself to smile. "Perhaps she's too tired to want to deal with such things. And I'm sure you didn't want to insist." Herbert neither confirmed nor denied George's comments, so he continued. "I can understand your reluctance. Rest assured, Herbert, I will make sure she understands her duty as my wife and she will go through the accounts with you tomorrow. Where is she now?"

"I believe you will find her in the armory, my lord."

"The armory?"

"Yes. She said she wanted to ensure that her dower goods had arrived in good order. My lord, I—"

But Sir George was already on his feet. "My father-in-law must have sent me a sword for a wedding present," he murmured as he walked past his steward. "Thank you, Herbert."

Herbert listened to his lord's retreating tread before going to a cabinet and removing one of the parchments there containing a list of the castle weapons.

A sardonic expression darkened his face. *Wait until you see the dower goods,* he thought glumly. Sir George was in for a surprise.

What kind of creature was this new lady of Ravensloft? Herbert wondered, with her outlandish clothes and masculine manner? That she was pretty and spirited was obvious, and of course some men liked that kind of woman, so it wasn't necessarily surprising that Sir George had chosen her.

But was she intelligent? Would she watch over the accounts with those sharp brown eyes, or did her preference run to sport and entertainment? For her sake, he hoped it did.

At the same instant George opened the door of the armory, an arrow thudded into a knothole in the door frame three inches from his left eye.

George stared, and Aileas, reacting to the startled look on her husband's face, burst out laughing.

"I hardly think murdering the groom is an appropriate way to begin married life," George observed as he came inside the stone building. Windowless, it was dimly lit by a flambeau and the light from the open door, which slowly swung shut.

Lances and unstrung bows lay against the wall, and swords, sword belts and quivers of goose-quill arrows hung nearby. A few straw targets stood in a corner, and a bag of goose feathers on one of the wooden shelves had split, spilling its contents, so that several feathers lay upon the dirt floor.

His wife stood opposite the door, a longbow of yew in her hands and a smiling, but guilty, expression on her face. "I wasn't aiming for you," she said, "or I would have hit you."

"I'm glad to hear it. But what are you doing here?" he asked, coming farther inside. "Do you always make it a practice to inspect people's weapons?"

"Some people's," she said with an unmistakable leer.

"I thought you had ascertained all you wanted to know last night," he said.

"Oh, no, my lord," she said with mock seriousness. "That will take months or years yet."

He noticed several additional wooden crates and barrels and wondered what they were. He would have to ask Richard. Later. "This hardly seems the place for such intensive examinations," he noted, sauntering closer, remembering that morning in the courtyard. And the afternoon under the oak. And last night in the bedchamber.

"I was trying this out." She pulled on the bowstring as she held it up for him to examine. "It's made of the finest, most supple yew, with the very best leather for the string."

"I've never seen better," he agreed, putting his hands lightly on her slender waist.

She embraced him quickly with her right hand, while her left held the bow. "Nor will you," she said proudly. "My father has six Welshmen in his castle to make bows, and he's given a hundred of the best for my dowry," she explained as she pulled away and began to unwrap a leather strap bound around her left wrist and forearm.

Then she took three steps back and made a sweeping gesture at the crates and boxes, smiling happily. "I came to make certain all my dowry is here." She pointed at the wooden crates and barrels in turn. "Bows and arrows for your archers." She nodded at another corner, where something long and wrapped in leather leaned against a wall. "Ten very fine lances for you." She nodded at another small pile of large wooden chests that he hadn't seen. "Fifty swords and the same number of helmets and suits of chain mail."

She went to a quiver and selected an arrow. "And a thousand goose-quill arrows."

"Your dowry is composed of weapons?" he asked incredulously.

"What would we do with more linen? Or plate? Or tapestries? You have more than enough already. Indeed, I think we have enough to last for several years. Besides, my father would not give you such useless things."

"I thought your father had given me a sword when Herbert said I would find you here."

A slight frown creased her brow at the mention of the household steward. "He told me you kept sending him away," George remarked.

She should have guessed a man like that would squeak on her. Next time, she would take care to avoid being seen at all, for she had absolutely no desire to talk over boring household business.

Nor could she rid herself of the baseless and surely foolish notion that he was an evil man and so was his brother. "I didn't see any great need for immediacy in discussing the accounts," she said, giving George a sidelong glance and what she hoped was an enticing smile to take his mind away from matters of business. "After all, it is only the day after our wedding. Besides, I think it would be preferable to converse with a statue, something that man seems determined to emulate."

To her relief, he smiled. "Well, he isn't the happiest of mortals, I grant you, but he's very good at his work. Tomorrow, you must let him explain things to you. It is your duty now."

"I know full well what my duty is," she grumbled.

George raised an interrogative eyebrow. "You just don't want to do it?"

That was so close to the mark, she blushed. If he said she lacked the knowledge to do it, he would have hit the bull's-eye. She had never learned about household duties and responsibilities; she had never wanted to, and apparently it had never occurred to her father that she should be taught such things.

"George," she said in a cajoling tone, taking hold of his arm. She felt warmed by the contact and pressed even closer. "George, let's not talk about such things today."

Aileas's smile was glorious, and instantly George was convinced she was absolutely right—he had been too hasty about asking her to get involved in household matters so soon after their wedding. "Well, tomorrow will do well enough, I'm sure."

Then he gathered her into his arms and kissed her, meaning to be tender and gentle.

Until she responded with hot, fierce passion. He kissed her again, and her response was every bit as passionate as last night.

They were not in public now. They were alone.

His exhaustion vanished as desire and need overtook him and his kiss deepened. Pushing her gently until her back hit the wall, his mouth still possessing hers, he tore at the lacing of her bodice with one hand while the other lifted her skirt. She moaned softly, responding to the urgency of his passion.

His lips trailed along her cheek and down her neck while his hands caressed and cupped her breasts before moving lower. His mouth, too, continued its downward path and his hands their passionate quest until—

"God's wounds!"

"What?" she gasped, opening her eyes to see frustration on his face.

"I *hate* these breeches you wear!"

"So do I right now!" she replied, smothering her laughter by leaning into his broad shoulder.

"How the devil am I to—"

"The same way I do with you, I daresay," she said seductively. "Undo them."

His expression softened, although the fires of desire still burned in his eyes. "I would rather cut them to ribbons."

"Then do that," she murmured.

Chapter Eleven

"I never thought I would find an armory inspirational," George said with a deep sigh. "Unfortunately, I fear my back may never recover."

Aileas was easily the most amazing lover he had ever known. She seemed to know instinctively how to move, and when. She knew that the sensation of her legs around his waist was incredibly exciting for him, and she had already discovered, with astonishing speed, the exact points on his body where a light touch or scratch would send the blood surging through him. The soft sounds she made were never too loud or too quiet to be distracting, but perfect. As she was perfect.

"*Your* back?" Aileas muttered as she lowered her legs from around his waist. "It is mine that is against the wall."

George chuckled softly. "You've left me feeling a husk."

"After all that sleep?"

George was in too serene a humor to discuss that particular point again. He planted a light kiss on her forehead. "Let's to the hall for some sustenance before I faint."

She reached down and held up what was left of her breeches. "I fear these are beyond repair."

"What a pity," George said with absolutely no sincerity as he grinned like the very embodiment of devilment. "Throw them into a corner. They can be used as a rag."

"What a waste!"

"Herbert will be glad to hear that you favor economy. He's always telling me I spend too much."

His wife eyed him sharply, and he wished he'd kept silent on such a point. To be sure, Herbert did occasionally recommend prudence; however, George was wealthy enough not to worry about a single article of clothing. "Rarely," he said firmly.

"I am glad to hear that," Aileas said, tossing the clothing aside, albeit with a regretful frown.

George took her hand. "Come, before everyone wonders where we are. Herbert will think we've fallen into the well."

They left the armory and strolled toward the hall.

"I must say I'm surprised you have such a dour man in your employ," Aileas remarked pensively.

"Are you? Perhaps the contrast between his manner and mine makes me look all the better."

"Would you really have a man as a steward for such a reason?" she demanded, halting and staring at him. "Or are you teasing me?"

"What, I, my lady?" he replied with a shocked tone and mockery in his blue eyes as he laid a hand to his heart. "Never!" .

She laughed and punched his arm. The laugh was loud and the punch so hard he winced. He hoped none of his garrison saw that reaction, he thought as he looked around. His gaze rested on the castle apartments where noble guests resided while they visited Ravensloft. "Margot will not be joining us in the hall for the evening meal," he remarked. "She danced too much last night."

"Or had too much wine."

"Margot never imbibes overmuch," he replied. "She loves to dance, and often does so beyond her strength." George gave his wife a rather pointed look. "However much she enjoys dancing, her manners are beyond reproach."

Aileas didn't say anything, but he felt her hand tense on his arm.

"Of course, she is not nearly as fascinating as my wife," he said softly, and her hand relaxed.

By now they had reached the hall, which was no longer empty. Indeed, Aileas realized, it was nearly as full of people as it had been for the feast the night before. She was also pleased to note that the festive debris had been cleared away, the tables washed and set up anew, and the servants seemed to be going about their tasks competently, despite not having their mistress standing guard over them.

It could be, she thought with some relief, that she need not interfere very much in the day-to-day running of the household.

Just as George didn't seem to have much to do with the day-to-day running of his castle.

"I fear we are a little late," Aileas whispered as George led her to their places at the high table, for Father Adolphus was already in his place.

"Shall I tell them why?" he offered, his face grave but his eyes full of laughter. Until he noticed her bare legs below her shortened skirt.

She grinned ruefully and hurried to take her seat as the priest began grace.

When Father Adolphus was finished and everyone had started to eat, George said, "This seems to be a day for tardiness. I am surprised Richard isn't here. He will be soon, no doubt. And Herbert, too. I know you will want to meet with him at once, to pick a daily time to discuss household matters."

Aileas gulped her ale to hide her dismay, then wiped her lips with the back of her hand. "*Daily* discussions?"

"Can you not use a napkin?" George asked in a whispered aside.

"I do not see one," she countered.

His brow furrowed, her husband scanned the table. "Your first command as chatelaine," he said, "can be to make certain there are napkins at the high table for every meal."

"*Every* meal?"

"Yes."

"But surely it isn't necessary to use such linens daily. They will need more washing and will wear out sooner."

He turned to her and elevated one of his eyebrows ever so slightly, so that she immediately felt extremely silly and parsimonious. "Very well, my lord," she said. "Napkins at every meal."

"A small thing, I know," he said, "but etiquette makes life so much more civilized and pleasant."

"And my lack of concern for such matters makes me uncivilized and unpleasant?" she charged.

"Aileas, that isn't what I meant at all!"

Pleased by his rapid denunciation of the implication, she smiled and moved her hand toward his lap. "Last night I think we were both uncivilized, but it was very pleasant indeed."

He started when she touched him. "Aileas! We are in company."

Stung by the rebuke in his tone, she clasped her hands together in her lap and, truth be told, began to sulk. She had only thought to please him. Would he really rather talk about napkins than enjoy a little…teasing? If so, he was unlike any other man she had ever encountered. Why, to hear Rufus and the others talk, they would rather play such games than eat or drink or even fight.

"Ah, here is Herbert now!" George declared.

Aileas followed his gaze and spotted the household steward making his way along the wall like some kind of spider, and she shivered at the notion. A quick glance at George gave evidence that he did not share her sense of distaste for the man—and why should he, if he had known him ten years or more?

"Greetings, my lord," Herbert Jolliet said in a voice as mournful as his countenance. "I trust I find you and your lady wife well."

"Indeed—never better!"

"Even if somebody forgot the napkins," Aileas muttered.

George turned to her sharply, a smile on his lips and what appeared to be a warning in his eyes.

"Good evening, Herbert," she said.

"If it pleases you, my lord, I thought we could begin tomorrow morning by, um, talking about the dower goods."

"Ah. Since the dower goods are all in the armory, I think we may leave that for Richard."

"I...I see you have discovered what they are, my lord."

A discouraged expression appeared on his sallow features.

"You look as if you do not approve," Aileas said sternly.

"Aileas," George said, hoping to diffuse the building tension.

"It is not for a steward to pass judgment on my dower goods."

"I'm sure Herbert was doing nothing of the kind."

"Certainly not, my lord," the steward added immediately. "Forgive me, my lady, for giving you that impression."

"Very well," Aileas said, not believing that his apology was sincere.

Her skepticism was obvious to George from her still-offended tone and her pouting lips. Gracious God, she was as sensitive as a man with a toothache.

Nevertheless, the way she pouted, with her full bottom lip pushed ever so slightly forward, only served to make him want to kiss her again. And as for sensitive—that need not always be a problem, as her incredibly sensitive reactions to his touch had demonstrated. Besides, she wasn't used to Herbert's manner, which he supposed was not the most agreeable in England.

"At any rate, there is no need to concern yourself with the dower goods, Herbert," he said placatingly. "Tomorrow, perhaps you could show my wife the linen?"

"The linen, my lord?" Herbert echoed, a worried frown creasing his permanently wrinkled brow. "Much of it will be in the process of laundering."

"Then go over the foodstuffs Gaston thinks we need for the next fortnight."

"Whatever you wish, my lord. I shall be happy to wait upon you, my lady, whenever it will be most convenient," Herbert offered.

"Well then, I leave you two to work it out," George announced. "In the morning, I am going to speak to the reeve about the mill rate."

"You fear something is amiss, my lord?" the steward asked.

"Not at all," George replied. "I only thought I should speak with him about it. He wanted to raise it a week ago."

Herbert nodded and made his obeisance, then turned and left his lord and his sharp-eyed bride to go in search of his older brother.

Richard Jolliet glared at Herbert in the dim light cast by the glowing coals in the hearth of the main room of his house, a large edifice just outside the main gate of Ravensloft. "She wouldn't speak with you? At all?"

"She spoke to me," Herbert answered in a low whine, "to send me away."

"How did you offend her?"

"I didn't!"

"You must have done *something*," Richard growled.

"Nothing," his brother declared.

"Then it must be that face of yours that repelled her."

"We cannot all be as pleasing as you," Herbert sneered.

"You should try. It goes a long way to avert suspicion."

Since Herbert couldn't deny the truth of that, he fell into a sulky silence.

"So you know little about her, then?" Richard asked.

"Only that she is a most peculiar woman."

"To judge by her dress alone, eh?" Richard confirmed with a laugh. "Yet she seems to suit his lazy lordship well enough."

Herbert nodded, falling, as always, under the spell of his brother's boisterous nature, something he both envied and loathed. "She was up before dawn but said nothing to the servants. She spent the morning in the barracks—"

"The what?"

"The barracks. The men seem to adore her now, too."

"No doubt."

"You are disgusting."

"What did Sir George make of this outrageous behavior?"

"As far as I can tell, nothing at all."

"He *is* a fool." Richard picked at his teeth with his fingernail. "What else did she do? Did Elma spend any time with her?"

"She didn't get the chance. They went riding, then he slept in his solar."

"Where was she while he was snoring?"

"Apparently in the armory. With the dowry—the weapons."

Richard cursed softly. "There's no money at all?"

"Not that I've heard of."

Richard grunted. "The parsimonious Sir Thomas.

The daughter will not be so free with money as Sir George, if she is like her sire.''

''I agree,'' Herbert replied. ''She had the servants take away several candles and most of the coal for the brazier in their bedchamber, as well as half the bed-clothes.''

''Indeed?'' Richard said, raising his bushy eye-brows. ''What about the accounts? Do you think she'll be able to figure them out?''

''I don't know,'' Herbert replied honestly. ''I was as careful as I could be, but she doesn't strike me as a stupid woman.''

Richard laughed scornfully. ''You who are so wise when it comes to women!''

Herbert flushed hotly. ''I can manage Lady Aileas.''

''You'd better. Now, how many weapons?''

''I don't know. Sir George said he would speak to you about it. He also intends to talk to Rafe about the mill rate.''

''Why?'' Richard demanded, sitting forward. ''Does he doubt the need to raise it?''

''He didn't tell me.''

Richard slumped back, disgusted. ''And you didn't ask.''

''Some of us are not so forward as others. Some of us know our places. Some of us—''

''Are cowards, content to have others do our talking and thinking for us,'' Richard concluded sarcastically. ''And that includes Rafe, who might have considered that a man who had to pay for a wedding feast might be very concerned about his money.''

''You said there was plenty enough that he wouldn't notice.''

Richard scowled. ''Of course there's plenty. But the

additional expenses for a feast might make an intelligent man worry about any decrease in income—even a lax fool like Sir George.'' His expression grew less angry. "Still, there is no cause for concern just yet, I think, as long as everyone keeps their head. A newly married lord is liable to be too busy with nuptial matters to trouble about the business of his estate.

"So let us toast Sir George and his bride—and may they be too filled with lust for each other to examine the accounts closely!''

The two men raised their goblets and drank deeply.

George took his time going up the stairs toward the bedchamber. Aileas had retired soon after the fruit and cheese appeared; he had lingered, gaming with some of his men, for he was determined to regain some semblance of calm normality before he encountered his wife again. Her behavior toward Herbert had been confusing and rather upsetting.

Unfortunately, he was finding it extremely difficult to concentrate on anything other than having Aileas in his arms when he was with her.

George opened the door to the bedchamber—and nearly fell over, for Aileas was already in bed, and quite obviously naked, the coverlet around her waist. She made no move to cover herself, but regarded him with the merest hint of a smile on her face.

How was he to deal with such a woman?

He closed the door and tried to think, then cleared his throat and commanded himself to control his passion. It was important that Aileas understand what he expected of her at once. "I was not pleased by your conduct toward Herbert Jolliet today,'' he began in a reasonable tone.

Her brow furrowed slightly. "I explained that I was tired," she replied calmly. "You agreed the accounts could wait."

God's wounds, he wished she would cover herself, for the sight of her was making it very difficult for him to concentrate, let alone reprimand her. "That you would not be demurely polite, I rather expected, but I did not think you would be discourteous outright."

Her lips turned down in another pout, and the sight, coupled with her state of undress, was incredibly arousing—so arousing, he walked toward the window and looked out at the dark, moonless sky, for he was determined to settle the matter of her impolite conduct at once. "I expected better of you, Aileas."

"I apologize for being rude to Herbert," she said.

He came toward the bed and sat beside her, leaning toward her and taking a lock of her hair and rubbing it between his fingers.

She wasn't looking at him. Her brow slightly creased, she was looking at her intertwined fingers laid in her lap, those same incredible fingers that had worked such magic last night. "I want you to be happy here, Aileas," he said softly.

She looked at him boldly. "I don't trust either one of your stewards."

"What?" The candid nature of her words, as well as their import, shocked him.

She flushed, but her expression remained defiant. "Perhaps I shouldn't have said that, but it is what I think."

"You've only just met them," he observed with a scoffing laugh. "I concur that Herbert doesn't immediately give a good impression, but he was my father's steward, too, and never gave a single cause for any mistrust.''

"I know that I have no reason to distrust them,'' she continued defensively, ''and so I have said to myself, yet I cannot help feeling uneasy about them.''

"I assure you, Aileas, they are completely trustworthy. When you know them better, you will agree with me.''

"I hope so,'' she answered truthfully, telling herself that George must be right and her own misgivings foolish. After all, her father had said nothing against the stewards, and he was an excellent judge of men. If he had thought them dishonest or untrustworthy, he would have warned her. Convinced that she was worried for nothing, and far more interested in George than either of them, she smiled and said, ''Forgive my hasty words.'' She brushed her fingers lightly over his. ''I would rather know you better, husband.''

"Soon, Aileas, you will know me as no one else ever has.''

He stood and quickly tossed his tunic aside and pulled his shirt over his head. He went to blow out the candle and realized many were missing. ''Where are the candles?''

"I had Elma take some away. So many were too wasteful.''

"Oh.'' He put aside any annoyance her words caused and hurried to remove his boots and breeches, then chuckled softly as he slid beneath the coverlet. ''Then I shall simply have to feel my way.''

"Let me guide you—''

He took hold of her wandering hand and rolled on top of her, taking his weight on his elbows. ''Not tonight, Aileas. Tonight *I* am in command.''

Aileas drew in her breath sharply. "But I—"

"No!" he ordered, staring down at her with intense seriousness. "Tonight, I will lead the way."

Aileas stiffened for an instant—but only an instant, for George's featherlight caresses and increasingly passionate kisses soon created tension of that other, wondrous kind before she could dwell on his unexpected words.

Then she forgot them, too caught up in the burning desire that coursed through her heated flesh to think of anything at all.

But later, as George slumbered beside her, Aileas did remember his words, and the way he had loved her—with astonishing skill, but also in a slow, measured, practiced way, as if she were someone else, until near the end. Then he had once again become the impassioned lover she had known on her wedding night.

He had wanted to be in command, he said. He would lead the way.

Because she hadn't done things right? Because she had been too hasty or too clumsy? Because she was ignorant of how to please him in their marriage bed?

Had she failed at that, too?

She couldn't dance. She couldn't sing. She couldn't sew. Her manners were appalling. And now, she knew, she couldn't even make love properly.

What would George say when he found out she couldn't read or write, either? That *that* was the true reason she didn't want to talk to the household steward?

She could guess what he would think, even if he proved too polite to say it. Soon enough, he would begin to lose patience with her. He would grow annoyed, then angry. Eventually he might even hate her. He would be certain he had married the worst wife in all of England. He would be sorry he had ever laid eyes on her. He might even send her back to her father in disgrace.

How could she bear that? How could she bear to be away from him, now that she knew how kind and delightful a man like George could be?

A man like George? Surely there was no one else like him.

Aileas felt the hot tears sting her eyes and ground her fists into them as if she could push the tears back from whence they came.

She wouldn't cry, she told herself. Tears were for fools. Tears were a weakness she wouldn't indulge.

Tears were for women.

Aileas's hands slowly uncurled until her whole face was covered, as if she would hide herself and her shame from prying eyes.

Tomorrow, she would be strong again. No one would know the pain she felt. No one would discover that she was a complete disgrace to her sex. She would hide the fact that she couldn't read or write as best she could, for as long as she could. She was Sir Thomas Dugall's daughter, and she had her pride.

But her tears seeped out between her fingers and her shoulders shook with silent sobs.

Chapter Twelve

"George, it's time to get up," Aileas commanded loudly. "You should not stay in bed all morning."

He opened his tired eyes to find her face inches from his. He reached out and pulled her to him for a long, slow kiss. She was as rigid and unyielding as a plank, as she had been in the beginning last night. It had taken a little more time to arouse her than on their wedding night, but surely that was nothing to be concerned about. Once kindled, her passion had been as fiery and exciting as any man could wish.

It could be that their many activities during the day had tired her before they got to bed.

"George!" she protested, pulling away with an annoyed expression. "It is time to get up."

"But the sun has barely risen."

"How can you tell from there?" she demanded, shoving wide the bed curtains so that light streamed in, making him close his eyes against the sudden brightness. "It is surely well past prime. The mass might even be over."

"The windows face east," he said by way of explanation for what appeared to be the lateness of the hour. "I heard no bells."

"You slept through them."

"But you did not. How creditable," he said with approval. "But is it any wonder I am tired? I am not Hercules, my love. Or Eros."

"No, you are not," she agreed in a tone that he didn't quite like.

He rose on one elbow and saw her put an ancient leather belt over an equally ancient, male tunic, frayed at the bottom, and cinch it tight. He bit back a curse, for she was already attired in her usual combination of breeches, short skirt, men's tunic and belt. He had hoped to suggest she don something more appropriate for a lord's wife before she got dressed.

"I told you, it's late," she said. "You should get up."

He would get those clothes off any way he could, he decided, and later, he would find a diplomatic way to get her into a proper gown. "Come back to bed with me, Aileas," he cajoled, giving her his most seductive, persuasive smile.

For a moment, he thought she was about to comply, but then she primly said, "We should go to mass. It's our duty."

"I know what my duty is," he answered, trying not to sound as frustrated as he felt. Clearly, she was in no humor to indulge him. Indeed, she seemed as peevish as a mare with an irritation under her saddle this morning.

So he got out of bed. The moment his bare feet touched the cold stone floor, he shivered and wrapped his arms around himself. "God's wounds, light the brazier!"

"Oh, it's not that cold!" Aileas chided. "You just have to get dressed."

He remained silent as he went to the chamber pot. When he was finished, he turned around to find her sitting on the bed, holding out his oldest, most worn breeches, apparently intending that he put them on. "I meant to get rid of those," he muttered, heading for one of his clothing chests.

"There is nothing wrong with these," she charged.

"Those?" he said. "I haven't given them away because I didn't think they were even fit for one of the village beggars."

"They've only been mended twice!" Aileas protested.

He threw back the lid of the chest and pulled out a clean white shirt. "And how many times do you have to be told that I have plenty of money?"

"We won't if you continue to be so wasteful," she countered.

"I will not dress like a pauper."

"Then I'll wear them."

He slowly turned to face her, still completely naked. "No, you won't."

She frowned darkly. "I—"

"You will not," he ordered before putting on the shirt, whose hem fell to his thighs. "As a matter of fact, you shouldn't be wearing breeches at all, as you should know."

"I've always dressed this way."

He went back to rooting in his chest. "While you lived under your father's roof, it was his place to comment on your choice of clothing. Now you are under mine, and those clothes are not acceptable."

"I don't own a gown suitable for wear during the day."

"Wear that green one. Elma can alter it so that it fits you better," he said as he pulled out a long tunic of red wool.

"It's too fine."

He clenched his jaw as he tugged on the tunic. "No, it isn't," he muttered.

"I shall consider your request," she replied haughtily.

He spun around on his heel and glared at her, to find her still holding the torn breeches expectantly. "Aileas, I can afford to throw those things out the window and I can afford to buy you as many dresses as you would like."

"You wouldn't do anything so ridiculous, and I don't like dresses," she said sullenly.

He marched toward her and snatched the offending garment from her hand. "I did not ask you whether you *liked* wearing dresses. You *must* wear them." Then he took the breeches and threw them out the window.

She jumped up from the bed and glared at him. "That was a silly thing to do!"

"This is my castle and I shall do what I like!"

Her eyes narrowed and her lips thinned as she crossed her arms over her chest. "You sound like a child—or one of my brothers."

"I am not a child or your brother," he said very slowly and deliberately. "I am your husband, and I do not take kindly to being addressed in that tone. As for how you spoke to your brothers, I can assume that it was not as a noble lady should."

"If by that you mean I did not dissemble and mince

and simper and say they were always right, you are absolutely correct," she retorted, flushing hotly. "Nor would I speak that way to you, as if I didn't have a brain in my head! Is that the kind of woman you really prefer—someone like Lady Margot?"

"I told you before, if I wanted Margot, I would have asked for her," he said as he struggled to keep his temper. He strode toward his chest and pulled out his finest pair of breeches. In truth, they were too costly for everyday wear, but he yanked them on nonetheless.

"Perhaps you should have. I'm sure she would have said yes. Now I am going to the chapel."

"Not in those clothes, you're not," he said, wheeling to face his recalcitrant bride.

"Do you think you can stop me?" she demanded before coming straight toward him. As she made her way to the door, she shoved past him, deliberately pushing him with her shoulder.

He raised his hand, then halted, motionless save for his heaving chest, as she slammed the door behind her.

George took a deep breath and let it out slowly, fighting to regain control. He walked to the ewer and splashed cold water over his face, leaning over the basin as if he were about to be sick and gripping the side of the table until his knuckles were white with the effort.

God's wounds, he had almost hit her.

He took another deep, shuddering breath. He must and would master his feelings, he commanded himself. He must and would dominate his rage.

He had to conquer his emotions or else he knew, as surely as he stood in this room, that the result would be disaster, for him and for her.

He closed his eyes, and once again, he saw the poor, dead creature in his arms.

The memory returned with as much force as if it were yesterday, although he had been a boy of ten at the time. That horrible day played through his mind in excruciating detail, reminding him of the consequences of his uncontrolled emotions.

Then, as always, the same tremendous sense of shame and loss filled George until it seemed his whole body burned with it.

With a weary sigh, he opened his eyes and strode to the window, looking out unseeing at the blue sky dotted with clouds.

For years, to protect those around him, he had forced away strong emotions, becoming the man everyone thought they knew: the charming, the elegant, the jovial Sir George de Gramercie. A man apparently without temper. A man who kept the peace between others. A man tolerant and perhaps a little lazy, who did not upbraid his servants.

Until he had met Aileas Dugall and married her, and discovered that those volatile emotions were still there, buried deep, to be sure, but more than capable of exploding. It was as if Aileas had lifted the lid of his own Pandora's box, so that the evils he had dominated so long by sheer force of will had finally escaped.

How naive he had been, to believe that he could govern himself completely, even when he had felt that first flush of anger at her impertinence and experienced the slight stab of jealousy when he saw Aileas with Rufus.

He spotted Aileas marching across the courtyard toward the chapel. Well, he would not go to mass this morning, let her say what she would.

What about *her* duties as his wife and chatelaine of Ravensloft?

And why was she so different last night and this morning? What had changed to make her so irritable? What had he done? Or was the fault with her alone?

George laid his cheek against the cool stone.

The peculiar nature of their first meeting as adults should have been a warning to him to turn around and return to Ravensloft immediately. He should have realized that Aileas Dugall, with her wild hair and insolent manner, was the antithesis of the wife he should seek.

Instead, his curiosity about the Aileas he had known in his childhood had led him onward. As for the reason he had married her…he could only describe it now as a perverse fascination aided by an overwhelming physical desire such as he had never felt before.

A desire she seemed to share. She made love like no woman he had ever known, exciting him as no other ever had, with a passionate abandon and skill—

And skill.

She did things one might expect of the most experienced courtesan, not a maiden bride.

Where had she learned…?

He went to the bed and yanked back the coverlet to stare at the bottom sheet. The unstained sheet, bearing no sign of a broken maidenhead.

With a savage growl, he tore the linen from the bed as if it were leprous.

Moments later, Elma knocked softly, and opened the door of the bedchamber when bidden to do so to behold a smiling Sir George standing in front of the window.

"I've come—" she began, curtsying on the threshold.

"To tidy the bedchamber," he said. He glanced ruefully at the bed, and Elma saw the pile of linen on the floor beside it. "You have your work cut out for you, I'm afraid."

Elma nodded as she entered, while he strolled past her toward the door. He paused to look back at her. "You will find a pair of breeches lying in the courtyard," he remarked as nonchalantly as if he stored his clothing in that location. "Burn them. Then you will take all of Lady Aileas's clothing except her shifts and her gowns, and you will burn them, too. And then the linen from this bed."

"I...I beg your pardon, my lord?"

"I want it all burned." He gave her a conspiratorial grin. "I have reason to fear that fleas were something of a nuisance in Dugall Castle. Therefore, I would also like you to find some fleabane and spread it on the floor, and the feather bed will need a good beating."

"Ah!" Elma nodded her understanding. "Of course, my lord."

"Thank you, Elma," his lordship said as he shut the door softly.

George rose as Lady Margot joined him at the high table for the noon meal. He had spent the morning at the mill, arriving back in time to eat. "Ah, here you are, and looking as lovely as ever!" he said pleasantly.

"Where is Lady Aileas?" Margot asked, slipping gracefully onto her chair beside George. "I trust she is well?"

He had no idea where Aileas was, except that she was not here. Perhaps she was once again in the barracks, he thought, instantly regretting conjuring up that image. "She is seeing to that horse of hers," he lied smoothly.

"You look tired."

"I am as exhausted as a bridegroom should be," he answered flippantly.

"That bodes well for your happiness," Margot said with a sweet smile.

"Did you entertain doubts?"

His cousin didn't meet his gaze, instead daintily reached for some bread. "She is not quite the bride I had expected you would choose, I must confess," Margot said softly.

"Nor I," he replied, trying to sound merry. He tore a piece of his loaf into tiny pieces and tossed the bits to a nearby hound, who sniffed at it in a desultory manner before ambling away. "She has the manners and speech of a villein, and dresses like some kind of jester."

"Why *did* you marry her?"

George leaned toward Margot and whispered secretively, "I must have been bewitched."

"I've known you too long for you to play these little games with me, George de Gramercie," Margot said. "I assure you, I am quite serious. Why did you marry her?"

"My father wanted it, her father wanted it, and I saw no reason not to."

Margot twisted to regard him steadily, a frown marring her expression. "Will you never be serious with me, George?"

Surprised by the intensity of her tone and look,

George felt himself blush. "Very well," he said gravely. "I had no wish for a boring wife and Aileas never ceases to amaze me."

"If you don't wish to answer me honestly, very well," Margot said, turning away, "and I will go back home."

"I was being truthful," George admitted quietly.

Margot's eyes searched his face. "I believe *this* time you are sincere. Will she make you happy, though?"

He opened his mouth to confirm her estimation, but his natural honesty prevented him from speaking. Instead, he took a drink of the ale before him.

When he set his goblet down, he spoke in his usual jovial tone. There was no need for Margot to suspect that there was anything seriously amiss with his marriage. "It is only that she doesn't know how to dance or dress properly, but I'm sure she'll learn those things from you."

"She looked well enough dressed to me."

"Now who is not being serious?" George demanded lightly.

"Granted, the skirt was a little short, but that is easily fixed."

"She wears *men's* clothing."

"Because it is what she is used to. I daresay she hasn't ever had the services of a good dressmaker, and you must believe me, George, when I say that there is nothing so uncomfortable as an ill-fitting gown."

"Except ill-fitting armor," he observed.

Margot laughed melodiously. "I'm sure you are right. Still, Aileas might feel differently about gowns when they fit properly. May we have some new ones made?"

"Of course you may. In fact, I insist upon it—and it is now something of a necessity. I had her other clothes burned."

Margot stared at him, appalled. "You did what?"

"I told Elma to burn her other clothes today. She wouldn't stop wearing them otherwise," George said defensively. "I'm not talking about dresses, you understand," he continued. "The breeches and her brothers' old tunics, not her shifts or the two gowns she does own. Those other things were probably full of fleas, anyway."

"Oh."

"Yes. As well as completely improper for the wife of a lord."

"What did she say when you did that?"

"I don't know if she's found out about it yet."

Margot slowly shook her head. "I'm surprised you resorted to such measures, George. That doesn't sound like you."

No, it didn't—as he well knew. "Aileas wouldn't listen to my point of view, so I had no choice."

"You got angry at her, didn't you?"

"My dear Margot," George protested, "I do not get angry."

"No, you don't," she admitted. "But she does, I'm sure."

He made a face of distaste. "I confess I am not looking forward to her reaction."

"Tell me, George, did she act the demure maiden at her father's castle?"

"No, she didn't," George admitted. "But I thought—"

"That you could improve her? Or would *train* be a more accurate word?"

A strange expression crossed his face before he smiled sardonically. "You make it sound as if we were speaking of a horse or a hawk," he remarked. "I will confess that I thought I could do something about her wardrobe, and with your help, amend her more barbarous mannerisms."

"Instead you find she resists such efforts."

"Stubbornly," he confirmed.

Margot smiled wryly. "You, on the other hand, are never stubborn."

He eyed her warily but said nothing.

"Need I point out that burning somebody's clothing, however much you hate it, bespeaks a certain stubborn insistence on having one's own way?"

"I couldn't think of an alternative."

"You were not angry?"

"I don't get angry," he reminded her.

"Or frustrated?"

"Perhaps a little."

"I see. Perhaps she won't be upset if the dressmaker is here," Margot speculated.

"That is an excellent notion, Margot," George said, some relief in his voice.

"Is there a good one in the village?"

"I would say there must be at least one. I have noticed several well-dressed women in the market."

"That I can believe. Then we shall have to have a dressmaker come here this very afternoon."

"Very well. I shall send Elma to fetch the one she thinks best."

Margot gave her cousin a sidelong glance. "George?"

"Yes?"

"Did you really only ask me here to be her teacher in matters of dress and deportment?"

"Yes."

"Not to show your wife what you rejected for her?"

This time it was George's turn to stare. "I never rejected you, Margot!"

She patted his hand and smiled sympathetically. "No, you never thought of me that way at all. I know. I never thought of you that way, either," she lied as smoothly as George had before. "I simply wanted you to see that she may interpret my presence in a manner far different from what you intend."

"There is no excuse for her discourtesy, to you or anyone else."

"I didn't mind. I could understand. And truly, George, I would rather she launch her barbs in a direct assault than a sneak attack or an ambush."

"She is nothing if not direct."

"And you admire her for it."

"Yes. Yes, I suppose I do."

"Of course you do. Just as you care for her more than you're willing to acknowledge."

George eyed his cousin skeptically. "Have you been consulting with that astrologer again, that you can read into my heart?"

"Not at all," Margot replied. "I know you, that's all, and I shall do my best to teach her."

Margot meant what she said, and she did know George well—well enough to know that he had never loved her, except as a sister. She could also tell that he cared very much for his unusual wife, no matter how flippantly he spoke.

It was written in the depths of his eyes, although only a woman in love with him herself might see it.

* * *

"What are you doing?" Herbert asked Elma as she stood in the outer ward beside a smoldering pile of cloth, a long stick in her hand.

"Burning most of Lady Aileas's clothes," the maid replied, giving him a sidelong glance. "Sir George commanded it."

"Whatever for?"

"Fleas, he says. But I think he wants her to wear better clothes and this is his method of enforcing his edict. After I am finished here, I am to fetch a dressmaker."

Sir Richard appeared around the corner tower. Seeing his brother and Elma talking, and noting the curling smoke, he quickened his pace and joined them. "What is this?"

Elma explained to both of the brothers what had happened that morning when she had gone to Sir George's bedchamber.

"That doesn't sound like our George," Richard noted sardonically. "Was he angry?"

"No," Elma replied, shaking her head. "He was as cool as a brook in the spring, as always."

"I take it Lady Aileas was nowhere in sight?"

"No, she had gone to the chapel for mass. I saw her go myself." Elma took her stick and stirred the nearly completely destroyed clothing.

"Did he go to mass?"

"I don't know," Elma answered bluntly. "I had work to do." She looked at Herbert. "Did he?"

Herbert shook his head. "No. He went to the village. He said he was going to speak to the reeve, and I suppose he went to do that."

"Rafe?" Elma asked sharply. "What about?"

"The mill rate," Richard said, his tone placating. "I'm sure it's nothing to get worked up about."

"The miller is getting anxious," Herbert said with a nervous glance over his shoulder as if he feared someone spying upon them from the battlements. "He worries that we'll all be caught and exposed."

"Why? Has he heard anything?" Richard demanded.

"Nothing specific," Herbert acknowledged, albeit reluctantly. "I think it was a mistake to enlist him. We could have managed without him."

"Yes, we could have," Richard agreed. Then he dropped his voice to a harsh growl. "But at half the profits. Without the miller with us, we couldn't have switched the weights as often. Besides, he might have discovered them anyway, and gone running to Sir George." He glanced at Elma. "Not everyone would see the opportunities."

"You should both be glad I found out what you two were up to. You need someone who hears the servants' chatter," Elma observed. "And Herbert might be right. I'm not sure the miller can be counted on to keep quiet. I can see him going to Sir George and claiming it was all our doing to save his own skin."

"Then we'll just have to make sure he doesn't talk, won't we?" Richard retorted.

"What do you mean?" Herbert asked.

"You know very well."

"I will have nothing to do with murder!"

"Would you rather run the risk of having our schemes exposed?" Elma demanded.

"Of course not!"

"Of course not," Richard mimicked. "For then you

would never be able to afford Lisette, and she would
have to find another man.''

"She loves me!" Herbert declared, but there was
doubt in his eyes, and Elma turned away to hide her
scornful smile.

"She loves your money, Herbert,'' Richard said
harshly. "Without that, she will leave you.''

"Still, I shall not do murder,'' Herbert replied, although with a conspicuous lessening of resolution.

"My dear brother, have I actually asked you to murder anyone?'' Richard asked scornfully. "I only want
him warned, for the time being. He is a coward, so a
good beating should be sufficient. Or even a good
threat.''

Herbert slowly nodded.

"I know just the men for the job, too. I shall tell
you where to find them.''

"Me?'' Herbert croaked.

"You,'' Richard snarled. "Unless you want to have
to beat the fool yourself. Now, don't you have things
to do—accounts to go through with our new chatelaine, for instance?''

Herbert gave them both a resigned nod and walked
away. When he had disappeared around the corner,
Elma glared at the older man. "I knew you shouldn't
have included him. He is going to ruin everything.''

"Now, my dear,'' Richard said in soft, appeasing
tones, "he will do what we tell him to, so there's
nothing to fear.''

"He's a sentimental fool.''

"You know I shall keep my eye on him.''

"You'd better!''

Richard flushed and turned his attention to the fire.

"What do you make of this? Do you think there is trouble between the lord and the lady?"

"It's too early to tell. It could be that he does fear fleas."

"It would be to our advantage if they didn't get along. Divide and conquer, eh?" he offered.

"She is not the confiding sort," Elma noted. "She will keep her own counsel and probably never trust a servant with her fears or worries."

"Then we shall work upon Sir George. Yes, that might even be better," he mused. "Herbert and I can plant some seeds of doubt about the bride's worthiness, and a lonely, unhappily married lord might like a sympathetic maidservant to talk to. Or even to spend his nights with."

Elma regarded him contemptuously. "I slept with you, Richard, because you paid well for the privilege. Sir George, though, is an honorable man who does not believe in sporting with his servants, as you well know."

Richard's face reddened. "And because he would not sport with you and pay for the privilege, you don't mind stealing from him."

Elma's expression was as cold and hard as one of the stones in the wall behind her. "We all have our reasons. Now go, plant whatever seeds you will, as long as no one suspects us of any wrongdoing."

Chapter Thirteen

Aileas surreptitiously wiped her sweaty palms on her skirt while she glanced up at Herbert Jolliet, who leaned over the parchment-covered desk as she sat in the solar.

With his glum face and pale color, it was almost as if she had Death hanging over her right shoulder. His brother, whose smiles didn't help but instead made her feel as if he considered her something of a child, stood on her left.

She had no idea why Sir Richard was here. He had nothing to do with estate business. It was bad enough having Herbert hovering over her, trying to explain what each list meant and each notation thereon.

She felt woefully ignorant and desperately wished they could finish this. Indeed, she wished she had hidden in the hayloft, as she had during the noon meal, or the armory, or sneaked out of the castle altogether, not foolishly decided that she could endure such a meeting once in a while. Her head ached from staring at the indecipherable writing and the effort of pretending that she understood.

She looked back down at the parchment in front of

her, but could make no better sense of the flowing lines of script than when she had first sat here. The numbers she knew, but she could not quite comprehend the additions and subtractions, and every word was a mystery.

"So you see, my lady, that the measure of flour will need to be increased," Herbert finished.

Sir Richard fidgeted beside her and then placed his finger beside a line of writing.

"Oh, yes, of course," she murmured, squinting where Richard pointed. The increase sounded necessary and reasonable.

"I think that is all we need to discuss today," Herbert said in his customary monotone.

She sighed with relief as the household steward picked up the parchment and began to roll it up. "Will this business always take so long?" she demanded, rubbing her painful temples and feeling the blood throbbing beneath her fingertips.

"No, it shouldn't," he replied. "I thought we should be very thorough, this first time."

"Now that you understand how things stand, my lady," Sir Richard said, "it will simply be a matter of attending to any necessary changes or alterations."

"Are you ill, my lady?" Herbert asked, regarding her quizzically. "Is there something you did not understand?"

"No. Of course I understood. It has…it has been a long afternoon, that's all." She gave them a wry smile. "Surely you men don't expect Sir George's bride to be well rested?"

Herbert blushed like a maiden, and even Sir Richard looked a little taken aback, but then he chuckled. "Yes, of course, my lady."

Elma appeared in the doorway and eyed them all before curtsying. "If you please, my lady, and if you are finished with the stewards, the dressmaker is here."

"Dressmaker? I don't want a dressmaker."

The stewards and the maid exchanged glances in a significant way that infuriated Aileas. "Who asked for a dressmaker to come?" she demanded.

"It was Sir George's order, my lady," the maid said respectfully.

Then Lady Margot arrived at the door of the solar. "Here you are," she cried gaily, her smile lighting her lovely face. "Shall we retire to your bedchamber for the fitting?"

So, George wanted her to emulate Lady Margot, Aileas thought as she regarded the woman. Lady Margot of the delicate, graceful gestures and movements. She of the soft speech and dewy eye. George wanted his wife, whom he obviously found so lacking, to become like this prettily attired, pliant creature.

"I don't want a fitting!" Aileas said, rising slowly and crossing her arms defiantly. She had the sudden feeling she was the victim of a conspiracy.

"Sir Richard, Herbert, would you excuse us, please?" Lady Margot asked calmly. The men nodded and left at once. "Elma, show the dressmaker to my lady's bedchamber."

Elma curtsied again and departed with alacrity, while Lady Margot glided into the room. "I'm sorry if this request disturbs you, Aileas," she said kindly. "But it is your husband's order that you be fitted for new gowns, as many as you would like."

Aileas scowled darkly, and Margot suppressed a sigh. Although Margot had no true knowledge of what had happened between her cousin and his wife, it did not take a seer to understand that there was trouble between the newlyweds.

She reminded herself not to be swift to cast blame. After all, it was quite different being a wife to a man instead of a cousin, and she was not blind to George's few faults. He had a singular inability to talk about serious matters, and one rarely knew exactly what he thought about anything. That he had a serious side she didn't doubt, even if she had never seen it. She had always rather envied his future wife, for surely he would reveal his innermost thoughts to her, and Margot was quite certain that would be fascinating.

She had never imagined he would choose such a headstrong, unusual woman for his bride. Nor had she ever dreamed he would want *her* to act as peacemaker, for he had always assumed that role in any family dispute when she was a child. To be sure, he had been somewhat older, but he seemed to have a patient, imperturbable temper even then.

"I told my husband," Aileas growled slowly and deliberately, "that I don't want any new gowns."

Margot began rolling up the loose parchments so that she wasn't looking at Aileas. "I'm afraid you don't have much choice, my dear," she said quietly, "unless you would care to go naked."

"What are you saying?"

"George ordered your old clothes burned."

Aileas's hands slapped down hard on the table and she glared at Margot. *"Burned?"*

Margot met her gaze steadfastly. "Burned."

"Why?"

"Whatever reason he gave Elma when he ordered her to do it, I think you know the true explanation."

Aileas straightened abruptly. "So he will try to make his ignorant brute of a wife into a lady, with your help," she said scornfully. "How kind of him!"

It was all Margot could do not to shout at Aileas that she was acting like a spoiled child. Didn't she see how much George cared for her?

Then, she happened to get a brief glimpse into Aileas's eyes.

George was not the only one in pain, it seemed, and she should remember that it took two to make a quarrel. "Would you rather he denounce you?" she asked softly. "Or annul the marriage and send you home?"

"He wouldn't dare!"

Margot doubted that he would, but she remained silent—and tried not to hope.

"I won't allow him to blame me if he is unhappy in his choice. I am what I was when he chose me— the fault lies with him if he now has regrets."

Margot took a deep breath and went forward. "Aileas, I think I should make something very clear right now. George thinks of me as a sister, not a lover."

"So he said."

"You should believe it."

"You are so ugly and ill-tempered, then?" Aileas asked mockingly.

Margot remembered that she was here to help. "No. If George had ever wanted me, he could have asked for me long ago, before I married. He never did."

"Perhaps because he was not ready to marry."

"I have been widowed for more than five years, Aileas. He could have asked for me at any time."

"And you would have taken him," she retorted. "You are a great comfort to me, my lady!"

"No," she lied. "I would not." Then she spoke the truth, burying deep her pain. "He has never, ever looked at me the way he looked at you when I first arrived."

"And how was that?" Aileas demanded defiantly. "With shock, because I do not dress the way he expects? With condescending pity? With assurance that he can improve this flawed female?"

"Can you not see for yourself how much he cares for you?" Margot demanded, trying very hard to keep her tone level. "If you are ignorant, Aileas, that is the ignorance that I truly pity you for."

"I don't want your pity!"

"No, but you shall have it nonetheless." Margot forced away any thought of herself. This was the woman George had chosen. "If you are so blind that you cannot see how he wants you, then I shall pity you. If you are so stubborn that you would not change for such a man's love, then I shall pity you more. If you throw away what he offers you, then you are the most pitiable creature on this earth!"

"I do not have to be upbraided," Aileas began, marching past Margot, who grabbed her arm with surprising and unexpected strength.

"Yes, you do! Aileas, don't be a fool! I want to help you, not take your place!"

Aileas regarded her steadily for a long moment, her expression inscrutable. "Very well, if you are so determined," she said at last, "and because my lord orders it, I will learn. But know you this, my lady—in some things I will *not* be taught."

With her back straight as a newly made lance and her chin jutting slightly forward, Aileas threw herself into a chair. "What do we do first, my lady," she sneered haughtily, "after my wardrobe is made acceptable? Dancing lessons?"

"George was not specific."

Aileas sniffed disdainfully. "That does not surprise me. He doesn't like to give specific orders, does he?"

Bringing this couple together was not going to be easy, Margot thought with dismay. Nevertheless, she knew that *something* must be done, because they were breaking each other's hearts. "George has probably angered you several times already," she noted dispassionately. "He can be very high-handed."

Aileas had not expected George's cousin to criticize him at all. "Nor is he the perfect lord," she said. "He leaves too much to his stewards, trustworthy though he thinks them. He doesn't oversee his men well enough, either. To be sure, his manners cannot be faulted and he dresses as well as any man I have ever seen, but those things are not important. Not really."

"What do you consider important?"

"Respect," Aileas replied without hesitation.

"You do not think George commands the respect of his men?"

Aileas thought of George in her father's hall and his own. "I suppose he does," she admitted.

"George simply doesn't understand the comfort of your old clothes," Lady Margot said sympathetically. "He has never had to do dance while too tightly laced."

"Or ride astride without breeches," Aileas suggested.

Lady Margot laughed. "No, I'm sure he hasn't. Unfortunately, George is not the most imaginative of men, I fear."

Aileas recalled some of the intimacies she had enjoyed with her husband and thought that wasn't quite accurate; nevertheless, she wasn't about to relate any specifics to Lady Margot.

"Like most men, he simply doesn't see a woman's point of view. Very few of them even try."

"They should," Aileas muttered.

"Oh, I absolutely agree," Margot hastened to reply. "But I believe that would require a miracle. We women, on the other hand, are constantly forced to consider theirs."

"I don't," Aileas said sulkily.

"That, if I may say so, is the problem."

Aileas glared at her husband's cousin. "Why should I consider a man's point of view if he will not consider mine?"

Margot's alabaster brow furrowed delicately. "Why should you be any different from the majority of women?"

Aileas barked a harsh laugh. "I am different from other women. Surely you have noticed. That is why George wants you to stay. To force me to change."

"Oh, I don't think—"

"*I* do! And you can tell my husband for me that I will *not* change, unless it suits *me!*" She rose from her chair, determined to leave at once.

"And you do not think it will suit you?" Lady Margot asked very, very softly.

Aileas stared at her, this woman who was everything she was not.

If she wanted to change... She did not. Yet if she didn't, she would lose any hope of making George love her as she—

She drew in her breath sharply, the truth of her realization striking her like a blow. Was that what she felt for him? Love?

If it was, she loved him not as she loved Rufus, as a friend and confidant, and an extension of the life and home she had known.

Perhaps the emotion she was experiencing was what a wife should feel for her husband, as lover, confidant and companion, a partner in a new life and a new home, one they made together.

If she did not change, she would lose him and that feeling. That love. Indeed, it would be like surrendering without even a battle.

"Let us go to meet the dressmaker," Aileas declared in ringing tones, as if the words were a call to arms, before striding from the room.

Margot sighed as she followed her cousin's wife, although whether with relief or resignation, it would have been hard to say.

Richard grabbed Herbert's arm and pulled him into the empty buttery. "This is too marvelous," he whispered with a subdued chortle. "We are lucky men!"

"Why?" Herbert demanded peevishly. "I thought she was never going to understand. What did you mean by complimenting her comprehension? I was certain she was completely confused half the time."

"Absolutely! She was! And didn't you notice how she had to have every item pointed out to her?"

"Yes. What of it?"

"And that she sat there with puzzled brow over the most simple of things?"

"What does that signify?" Herbert asked. "I want to get some food, not answer riddles."

"You fool," his brother replied, not totally in jest,

"she cannot read! I doubt whether she can add or subtract, either."

"Of course she can. She's a lord's daughter."

"She's *Sir Thomas's* daughter. I can believe he wouldn't consider it worth the time or expense to have his only daughter taught to read."

"But all noblewomen should have some learning," Herbert protested, for he truly believed that his brother had to be wrong.

"And I tell you, she can't. Didn't you see where I pointed when we were discussing the flour, there at the end? My finger was at the notation for wine."

"I wondered what you were doing."

"She didn't say anything. Don't you think she would have?"

Herbert slowly let out his breath. "She would! You may be right."

"Of course I am. That would explain why she didn't want to have anything to do with you right from the start. I tell you, she's the most ignorant noblewoman we've ever met!"

"Do you suppose Sir George knows?"

"No, or he would have said something about it, made some little joke. Or helped her. She is too proud, I suppose, to tell her husband."

"That could well be," Herbert agreed, more conspicuously excited. "Why, she will believe whatever we tell her about the list of supplies."

His brother rubbed his hands together gleefully. "A lazy, lustful husband, an ignorant wife who cannot keep accounts—this is nearly too good to be true."

The moment George saw Margot coming into the hall before the evening meal, he knew something was wrong. "Well?" he asked when she sat at the high table. "What happened? And where is Aileas?"

"She complains her head is aching, so she will not come to eat."

No doubt she would not be welcoming in their bed tonight, which was probably just as well. "Did she send the dressmaker away?"

"Not before the appropriate measurements were taken and the fabric selected."

George let out his breath slowly. "I was afraid she'd shove the poor creature down the stairs."

"She wasn't happy about it," Margot admitted. "I have never seen a grown woman fidget so much."

Their conversation paused while Father Adolphus pronounced grace and the first course arrived. During the second, third and fourth, they spoke of old acquaintances, although George found it difficult to concentrate.

"That disgruntled expression would do credit to your wife," Margot observed quietly. "She can scowl as no woman I have ever met. She was very angry and frustrated with you, you know."

"I know," George remarked, inwardly calm but secretly filled with anxiety. He would have very much liked to have been a witness to the conversation between Margot and Aileas, yet he was too proud to seem overly curious, just as he was too proud to confront Aileas about her "special" knowledge. He pushed away that thought as he took a bite of pheasant cooked in sauce.

"That's a good sign, George."

He couldn't quite mask his surprise. "It is?"

"Any strong feeling is cause for hope. If she were

indifferent to you, then I would be truly alarmed. Does she enjoy making love with you?''

"Margot!"

"George, if you want my help, I cannot be stumbling around in the dark. I've never known a woman quite like your wife, and I don't want to make things worse between you."

"And that gives you the right to pry into the most intimate details of our life?"

"If you would rather not have my help, you have only to say so."

George regarded his cousin's placid face, subduing the urge to tell her what he feared about his wife's honor, or lack of it. "As far as I can tell, she enjoys our intimacy immensely."

Margot smiled happily. "Excellent! Oh, that is wonderful!"

"I cannot disagree," he replied, while secretly wondering how often Aileas had enjoyed such... activities...and if there had been many men. Or only one with bright red hair.

"Nevertheless, George," Margot warned, "you cannot build a happy life based only upon what happens in the nuptial bed. There is the rest of the day to consider, too."

"I tried to get her to stay in bed during the day, but she has the foolish notion that no good lord or lady remains in bed past daybreak."

"No wonder she is angry with you, if this is the cavalier way you talk of the troubles between you."

"What would you have me do?" George countered.

"Treat her with patience."

"I *have!*" George protested with a smile.

"Not enough, I think. You can't expect her to

change overnight—assuming, of course, that you do *want* her to change, for clearly, she is willing to try."

"What are you suggesting? That I want a wife who eats like the least mannered of my soldiers? Who dresses like some sort of cross between a squire and a serving wench? Who would rather shoot arrows than dance?"

Margot eyed him shrewdly. "I must ask you this, George. If she does change to suit you, will you love her as much?"

George regarded her steadily, his expression frustratingly impenetrable. "You believe that I love her?"

"Yes, I do."

"Her current manner of behavior is simply too embarrassing to be endured," he said after a moment.

Margot wondered if she truly saw the danger in what he was attempting, and if she should try to warn him that some marriages would break from the strain of unmet expectations. She knew that from bitter experience, for she had not borne her husband the son he craved. He had cursed her for her barrenness every day after their first year together, including the day he died. "I will try to teach her, George. But you must forbear and leave it to me."

"I shall be the very paragon of a patient husband," George promised. "That will not be so very hard a task."

Margot was not nearly so sure.

Chapter Fourteen

Aileas sat on the stone floor of her bedchamber, her back against the wall, her legs tucked beneath her, thinking. Here at Ravensloft, she had no tree to climb, so she had cautiously and secretively returned to the bedchamber after Elma had finished tidying it.

She was also hiding, for it was time to go through the accounts with Herbert again.

She didn't want to be near anyone, not even Elma, tempting as it was to confide in someone. Her father had always made it clear that servants were the last people to trust with your state of mind, and although Elma seemed keen to listen, Aileas could not bring herself to break her father's rule, even here.

There was Lady Margot, but Aileas would not voice her fears and doubts to that lady, no matter how kind-hearted she seemed. Indeed, she found it difficult to be with her husband's perfect cousin, for she felt as if all her faults were magnified in Lady Margot's presence.

So she would be alone with her thoughts, and today, only for today, she would abandon her duty and avoid the strain of being with Herbert.

When she was in the solar with him, she was always trying to determine if her growing suspicions were correct. Every day he showed her the record of purchases of food, drink and other items for the household, with the most recent added to the bottom of the list. Several times now, she could swear that things that had been listed the day before were altered or missing, or that the notation had been changed somehow, one word replaced with another, the figures slightly different.

Yet because she couldn't read, she could not be sure if the mistake was hers. So many words looked similar!

And she had to admit to herself that it could be that she hoped to find something amiss so that she wouldn't have to endure Herbert's presence.

She found it difficult to even tolerate the Jolliets. While Herbert was the very model of a patient man as he explained things to her, she always felt he was secretly criticizing her and thinking her stupid. Richard, with his jovial bonhomie, disturbed her even more, although she would be hard-pressed to say exactly why.

She could not help feeling, and strongly, that both men were not to be trusted. Unfortunately, there had been nothing blatantly obvious to her eyes, and to voice her suspicions now would mean admitting that she had never been taught to read properly. Her ignorance would be common knowledge, along with her less-than-flawless deportment and inability to dance.

Nor could she assuage her dread that her husband was a spendthrift, although the dour Herbert had assured her that there was no need for concern. After voicing her apprehension the second time, and seeing

Herbert react with disapproving condescension, she decided she would keep silent and try to believe him.

She sighed wearily and laid her head on her knees. Her father had taught her to be an excellent soldier, not an excellent wife. Here at Ravensloft, she was never quite sure what to do or how to do it. Lady Margot tried to teach her, but every alleged duty of a chatelaine, such as counting all the linen, had been boring beyond measure.

The only times Aileas felt free and once again her old self were the occasions she went riding, although even then, all was not completely blissful. First, she had to endure an armed escort. Once, she had tried to outride the men George sent with her, to no avail, and Elma soon gave her to know that George had chosen his very best riders to be her guard.

She missed the comfort of her breeches. She found her new long skirts cumbersome and awkward and despised them.

Added to this was the uneasiness of trying to eat a meal without feeling George's censure. She felt he was watching her every move, which destroyed her appetite, although his cook always concocted delicious—and costly—meals. He sometimes told her what he thought she was doing wrong, or reminded her to chew with her mouth closed. Lady Margot, her alleged teacher, was much more subtle.

So much so, and so kindly into the bargain, that Aileas felt it would be easy to like her. Aileas had never had a female friend, and sometimes, she thought Margot might be the first.

If only she weren't so beautiful and exemplary.

If only George didn't seem to find her company preferable to his wife's.

Again, that nagging dread came to trouble her, try as she might to subdue it, that George had invited Lady Margot here not because he thought his wife needed a teacher, but because Margot was a beautiful, elegant woman who obviously liked him a great deal. Perhaps even loved him.

Had *she* not done enough, been enough? Had he found it necessary to go to another woman's bed? Was the other woman Lady Margot? Was he apparently loving to his wife only so that she wouldn't suspect him of duplicity?

Oh, horrible, horrible thought! She wanted to banish that notion, but it lodged in her heart, along with the incontrovertible knowledge that she desired him more than she would ever have thought possible. The moment he touched her, all that mattered was the love she felt for him and her passionate need for him.

Did he know this? Was he using this knowledge to blind her to the true state of things at Ravensloft?

She wouldn't believe it, Aileas told herself firmly. She wouldn't believe that he would be unfaithful to her so soon.

Her gaze rested on the bed. Here, more than anywhere, she felt adrift and lost since the night he had said he would be in command. Now she was always afraid she was going to do something wrong, say something wrong, prove that she was ignorant here, too, despite her best efforts.

She had tried to act as she thought a well-bred wife should, letting George lead the way here, as he wanted.

But she couldn't. Not when his touch was so exciting and his caresses so arousing. She simply couldn't lie there like a log. She had to touch and caress and stroke and move.

Yet every day he seemed to be drawing away from her more and more. Instead of learning more about her husband, she was learning nothing.

Why did he now seem so guarded in her presence, except when they made love? To be sure, he was inevitably polite and charming and smiled just as much, but something was very different. It was as if he were slowly and inexorably building a wall between them. Sometimes, even when they were alone together, she sensed that he was trying to pretend she didn't exist.

Would he ever again love her as he had on their wedding night, with a fierce, wild passion that overwhelmed her utterly?

What was she to do? she asked herself for the hundredth time. She felt as if she were bound with sturdy ropes, and every day the ropes were pulled tighter, as if they would eventually strangle her.

She untucked her legs and rose slowly, then walked over to one of his clothes chests and stared at the worked leather on the top, brushing it lightly with her fingertips.

She had tried to please him. She had struggled to change, for his sake. She had endured the dresses and the dancing. She had tried to comprehend the accounts and spent tedious hours listening to the steward. She had kept to the castle far more than she would have liked. She had tried everything she had ever heard her brothers and his friends describe that gave them pleasure with a woman, to make George feel the same delight and desire as she did for him.

For nothing. She had lost the battle and probably

the war. So what was she to do now? Lie down and die?

Admit her defeat? Go home like a whipped dog?

Never. *Never!* Her father had always maintained it was better to die honorably than be defeated.

So she would triumph—on her own terms, not his. No longer would she allow herself to feel constrained and anxious. Never again would she feel flawed and hopeless.

With a determined expression, Aileas opened George's chest and yanked out the first pair of breeches she found. They were big, but she was used to wearing her brothers' castoffs; all she needed was a belt. She went to her own clothes chest and tore one of the laces out of a new gown of blue wool. With a few swift movements, she hiked up her skirt, put on the breeches and tied her makeshift belt. Then she let the skirt fall to the floor.

The breeches were barely visible, and she permitted herself one small, sorrowful sigh. If her heart had been broken, she would hide that, too.

Then she marched from the bedchamber, going directly to the armory, where she took the fine yew bow and a quiver of arrows, slinging the bow over her shoulder and the quiver on her back.

She was going hunting.

The bell in the village church had tolled matins sometime before when George finally slipped into his bedchamber that night. He had spent the time after an enjoyable evening meal of quail—shot by his wife, or so Gaston had informed him—playing chess with Richard Jolliet.

Aileas had remained silent during the meal, but that

was usual these days. Nothing he said seemed to amuse her, and while her manners had improved, this sullen silence was growing nearly unendurable.

Despite what Margot still apparently believed, he was not so certain that Aileas's fierce emotions were a good sign. He could more readily believe that she disliked him and had married him only because the real object of her affection, Rufus Hamerton, had not asked for her.

He could also, unfortunately, believe that the fellow had been her lover, or one of them, and that Aileas Dugall was no virgin bride.

Even Richard Jolliet was implying—oh, so carefully, lest he upset his lord and friend—that Aileas seemed to spend an inordinate amount of time in the company of the garrison. He delicately indicated that the men seemed to enjoy her attention as much as she did theirs, and that perhaps the chatelaine of Ravensloft was a little too affable where the soldiers were concerned.

George had heard the rumors that were starting to be told about his wife, with her penchant for riding about the countryside with men who were not her husband.

Her behavior when she was with him would do nothing to dispel such rumors. Aileas pointedly ignored him, thereby making it obvious to all in the hall that the relationship between their lord and his bride was a troubled one.

But not all the time. Not at night. No matter what thoughts troubled him during the day, when he was alone with her in the bedchamber, nothing else seemed to matter but loving her. One touch of her skin, and he needed her. One kiss, and everything except desire melted away.

He was always overwhelmed by his feelings for her, losing himself completely in passionate surrender.

Now he stood just inside the bedchamber door, listening to Aileas's deep, even breathing, which told him she was asleep. He moved farther into the moonlit room. The brazier had not been lit, and there was no scent of a recently doused candle to tell him she had been awake and awaiting him.

He didn't know which he would have preferred, to find her waiting, annoyed at the lateness of his retiring, or to realize that she apparently didn't care how late he stayed below. Her bow rested against the wall near the window, the quiver on the floor beside it.

With a disgruntled frown, he cautiously approached the bed.

Clad in her shift, Aileas lay on her side facing him, her features relaxed with sleep and with one slender arm outside the covers, her long-fingered hand lying upon the satin coverlet. Her thick, wildly curling hair surrounded her face and spilled over the pillow, and her dusky lashes fanned her sun-browned cheeks.

How peaceful she looked! Like a sleeping Diana, goddess of the hunt.

He reached out and gently brushed a lock of hair from her face. Her lips parted slightly and she sighed softly before turning onto her back.

George felt his manhood stir. He pushed away the visions that tormented him, of a red-haired man lying with his wife. Touching her. Kissing her. Loving her.

He concentrated solely on his wife. Almost without conscious thought, his hand began to undo the lacing at the neck of his tunic as he looked down upon her.

She was lovely and exciting and special. He would join her in their bed and kiss her soft lips. They would share again the pleasure. The passion.

His clothing fell to the floor in a heap and he climbed into the warm bed beside her, quickly enveloped in the moist heat. He reached out and took her hand, pressing his lips on her palm. Then, with light, gentle motions, his lips began to move up her naked arm.

She smelled of the fresh air, so different from the heavy perfume that clung to other women's skin. Although he could feel the muscles and sinews beneath, her flesh was as soft and inviting as that of any woman he had known.

With his other hand, he began to caress her body, enjoying the different textures he encountered. He pushed her shift higher and moved closer as his hands continued their leisurely exploration. Always he had been too engulfed with excitement and need to take time to peruse her body.

She stirred again and sighed. "George?"

"Yes, my love."

"George," she whispered, leaning toward him and encircling him with her arms.

George wanted to be patient, to take his time so that he could arouse her slowly. Despite their troubles, he wanted to give her some measure of the delight she gave to him. He tried to hold back and maintain control, telling himself it was necessary if he was to pleasure her completely.

But the moment their lips met in a kiss, his resolution was destroyed. As always, her immediate, passionate response inflamed him further, beyond anything he had experienced before. She was fire and heat and light to him, her body the vessel of his pleasure. He could not have left her side if a battle were raging outside the door or his soul depended upon it.

All too quickly, the crescendo came and passed, and as George lay back, spent and panting, Aileas pushed her shift below her waist. "Where have you been?" she demanded.

"Paradise," he replied, his eyes closed and the sweat cooling on his naked chest.

"No, that is not what I meant. Where have you been? Why did you not come to bed before?"

"I was in the hall."

"With whom?"

He heard the suspicion in her tone. "With Richard Jolliet, if you must know."

"No one else?"

He did not appreciate her interrogation. He had done nothing wrong since they had been married. She had no cause for complaint, as he probably did. "It is not your place to question me," he said, opening his eyes and raising himself on his elbow to look at her, and the suspicion in her brown eyes angered him. "I can do what I wish, with whomever I wish. I am the lord and master here."

"I am your wife."

"I am well aware of that," he snapped, lying back down.

"Are you?" she charged before abruptly moving away from him. Aileas shivered from a sudden chill and cursed herself for being a weak-willed fool. She should never have welcomed him so quickly into bed, not when he had been so long before joining her. "Where have you been, my husband?"

"I do not have to answer that," he said with the

barest hint of anger in his voice as he got out of the bed and began to pull on his breeches. "But it is as I have said, Aileas. I was in the hall with Richard Jolliet. Then I sat before the fire, deep in thought—something I'm sure you cannot appreciate.

"I see I should have stayed below," he continued brusquely, "where I could at least comfort myself with the thought that my absence might be forcing you to contemplate the error of your ways."

"*My* ways?" she gasped, glaring at him. "What is so terrible about my ways? At least I do not waste hours with idle sport! Nor do I leave my duties to someone else! If you think I have shortcomings as a lord's wife, perhaps you should examine your own!"

He reached down for his tunic. "I do not idle my time away."

"Oh, forgive me for thinking that playing chess is important work. Or that sending your estate steward to speak with the miller when you learn he has been nearly beaten to death is fulfilling your obligations as lord, instead of investigating the matter for yourself!"

"It was a jealous lover's retribution and nothing more," George said, waving his hand dismissively after tugging the tunic over his head. "I suspected as much."

"But you didn't go yourself."

"I did when the mill rate was in question."

"Oh, yes, you did—and that is the only act of supervision I can recall in all the time I have been here!"

"Because I do not talk of such matters," he muttered as he put on his belt. "Your father might have enjoyed bragging about his labors. Some of us do not."

''My father knows what a lord's duties are, and he does them—and more.''

George suddenly whirled around and glared at her, his face flushed and hot anger burning in his eyes. ''Except for supervising his own daughter! Tell me, *wife,* am I better than Rufus?'' he demanded harshly.

''What?'' She stared in shock as he slowly approached the bed, like a cat stalking its prey.

''Am I a better lover than Sir Rufus Hamerton?'' he growled, so different from the Sir George de Gramercie she had known, it was as if a demon had replaced him.

''I don't know,'' she answered honestly, pulling up the sheet as if it were a shield that could protect her from that look. Then the full import of his question struck her and she gasped in shock. ''I have never made love with him!''

''Then who?'' he charged, wrath written deep on his face. She scrambled back until she could retreat no farther. ''Who taught you so well how to pleasure a man? Who was the lucky recipient of your virginity?''

''No one! You!'' she cried.

His hands balled into fists. ''Don't lie to me, Aileas,'' he said, his voice low and quaking with rage. ''Whatever you do, don't lie to me.''

''I am *not* lying!'' she protested. ''I have never loved any man but you.''

For an instant, his gaze seemed to flicker and he drew back, his whole body as tense as the bowstring before the arrow is released.

Then he straightened, the lover as well as the demon gone, replaced by the cool, inscrutable Sir George de Gramercie—yet it was a different Sir George, a new Sir George, as cold and hard as granite.

In that instant, a part of her wanted to die. She had failed, completely and utterly. How could any man who loved her look at her so?

But she had not betrayed him. She had not loved another. She had come to him pure and honorable; she would not let him say otherwise.

"By what right do you insult me?" she asked sternly, climbing from the bed and wrapping the sheet about her in one swift motion. "What evidence have you to back up this accusation?"

"There was no blood on the sheets."

So calm and so deadly cold.

"It was on me!" she replied forcefully. "And you. I washed it away."

"Very convenient."

"And do you not love your cousin, who has come to visit so *conveniently?*"

His eyes narrowed. "I love my cousin as I should, and nothing more."

"Is it not diverting to be accused unjustly, my lord who lives for diversions of many kinds?" she mocked.

"How many kinds of diversions do you enjoy, Aileas?" he asked. "You seem very accomplished— for a virgin bride."

Kicking at the sheet, she strode toward him, raised her hand, her palm open wide as if she were going to slap him full across the face.

He grabbed her hand, his grip as strong as oak, and she braced for his blow. Her father and her brothers would have struck her had they been so red-faced with rage—but he let go of her and walked abruptly to the door. Going out, he slammed it so hard it sounded like a clap of thunder.

She hurried after him, flinging open the door. She

took a step, determined to follow him and make him see the truth—until pride stopped her.

What would people think if she pursued him, clad in her shift, barefoot, in the dead of night?

That she was a woman who could not even keep her husband's affection for the space of a month and who was so desperate she had to chase after him?

She took another determined step. How dare he accuse her of dishonor!

She had been a virgin when she came to him, as he should have known. And as for those accomplishments—she had listened and learned, nothing more.

He did not know that. He suspected...

She leaned against the cold stone of the wall and closed her eyes. She should have seen this. He thought she came by her knowledge from practice!

His suspicions must have been driving a wedge between them. Perhaps that was why he had grown so distant! She would have to explain to him.

Suddenly, it didn't matter who would see her, or what reason they would ascribe for her absence from her bedchamber. She would find George and tell him how she had learned about love.

And then, please God, they could begin again.

George slumped down in the shadow of the well, hidden from the moonlight and out of sight of the guards patrolling the wall walk.

His heart wanted desperately to believe her protestations of innocence, but his mind urged caution. He would not be the first cuckold to be fooled by a convincing woman. His whole body flushed with the heat of anger and shame as he wrapped his arms around his legs and drew in deep, shuddering breaths, each one racking his body while what little self-control he had regained splintered and disappeared.

He could have killed her. She had enraged him so much, he might have killed her, had he held a sword or even a stick.

That had been his weapon that other day long ago when he had been so filled with frustration and anger that he had hit and hit and hit, insensible to anything but the action of striking.

Until the dog lay nearly dead at his feet, whimpering pathetically, his brown eyes as reproachful as a wounded child's. Horrified, George had cried out and dropped the stick before kneeling to take up the small body in his arms. He could feel it yet, the warm, limp weight.

And then his father had come, staring at George with that horrible, incredulous look....

That was what had happened the last time he had tried to teach, when he was a boy of ten.

He remembered the little creature so well, even now. One of a litter of his father's favorite bitch, the puppy had been especially appealing, the spriteliest of the bunch and adorable with its unexpected black ears, although the rest of it was brown.

More, there was a quality to its play that made George, young as he was, guess that it could be the best of the litter. The finest hunter. The most loyal.

So he decided to teach the pup a trick. Some little task, he thought, to show his father what a good dog he was, and how intelligent his son for recognizing it. George had envisioned what his charming, affectionate father would say: "An excellent animal—but I must not have the dog. Since you have trained it, it shall be yours forever."

Oh, what a selfish little brute he had been! And how transparent his desires, for he had wanted that puppy for his own almost from its birth.

For hours, it seemed, he had tried to teach that puppy to retrieve a pig's bladder filled with air. The puppy had been too young, however, and soon grew tired of the game. Nevertheless, George was determined to teach it this trick, despite its lack of attention.

Then the dog had nipped him, breaking the skin, and suddenly George had been filled with a rage so hot and overwhelming that he was lost to all control. He had grabbed a stick.

There was no conscious thought to what he did next, no deliberate attempt to punish or compel. It was all wrath and frustration and repetition.

Until the little animal lay dying.

His father had put his arm around his shoulders and asked what had happened. Very soft was his voice, and tender, and there was no denying the shameful act.

He had done murder, or so it seemed to him. With choking sobs, George had confessed, trying to explain the unexplainable.

His father listened patiently. Then, gently taking the dead pup from him, he had told George that while his remorse was plain to see, it would not help the puppy. There was no undoing such a thing. That was why no good and honorable man gave way to his temper. He controlled it, subdued it, commanded it. He was its master.

Then he had wiped away George's tears and told him that this was a hard way to learn such a lesson.

Yet despite his father's tenderness and sympathy and patience, there had been a look in his eyes...a look that told George something had changed between them, and he had understood that he had lost something forever.

Years later, he knew exactly what he had lost: his father's respect. Not completely, but enough that things never seemed quite right between them again.

So from that time, George de Gramercie had learned to hide his anger and frustration—indeed, any strong emotion.

Until he fell passionately in love with Aileas Dugall.

She could rouse his feelings as no one ever had, with her forthright manner and incredible, unfettered passion.

She stripped away every carefully constructed barrier between the world and his emotions.

Now, here, hiding in his own castle, he finally faced the one emotion he had denied until this very moment.

Fear.

He was afraid of his passion, his anger, his love and his jealousy. Afraid of what they could make him do, and what he could lose if he gave them free reign.

Aileas conjured up all those emotions and he could not be sure he would ever be able to subdue them completely. He would be their prisoner, not their ruler.

What was he going to do? he thought helplessly.

If he stayed here, in such turmoil that he could barely think straight, who could guess when he might finally lose his tenuous self-control?

But to leave her, to flee like a coward...

He had no choice. He would have to go, until he was once more his own master and had found the strength to govern his feelings. He had outlying estates that he could visit on pretext of attending to several small matters of business.

Determined to do just that, he rose from behind the well.

To see Aileas, clad in a thin cloak, her feet bare, creeping into his soldiers' quarters.

Chapter Fifteen

Aileas sneezed violently as she waited in the hall after mass the next morning. She felt ill, and not just physically, for she had been unable to find George after he had left her in anger last night.

She had spent what seemed an age cautiously searching the castle, wearing only her shift and thin cloak, and with her feet bare so that she would be as silent as possible. Unfortunately, that had been as stupid a decision as trying to find him had proved, for she was now most definitely ill.

Her eyes were burning, her nose running, her throat sore, and she had a cough, to boot. Every bone in her body ached, and she knew that she didn't dare to eat anything without risking what her brothers would call throwing her bread.

She wanted to go to bed and stay there, alone, in the peace and quiet. Only one thing could have brought her to the hall, and that was the absolute necessity of explaining to George that he had leapt to a disastrous conclusion.

Somehow, she would convince him that she had been a virgin on her wedding night. As for her feelings for Rufus... They were so different now. When she recalled how she almost begged him to marry her, it was with acute embarrassment, much as any adult could recall a shameful incident from their childhood.

She still thought of Rufus with affection, but she had never, ever felt the passionate desire for him that she did for George.

Somehow, she would try to recapture those happy, joyous moments she and her husband had shared at the wedding and the day after, when they had ridden together and talked as friends and confidants! Why, she had told him things about her feelings for her brothers that she had never shared with anyone. There *had* to be a way to make him believe her.

Someone entered the hall, and Aileas glanced up hopefully, only to see Lady Margot make her graceful progress to the high table.

Aileas glanced down at her own gown self-consciously, aware that her cerise gown of stiff *cendal* would never look as becoming on her as Lady Margot's lovely dress of a similar hue and fabric, which seemed as if it were somehow melded to her body. Aileas felt as if her body were carefully avoiding all contact with the fine gown. Similarly, Lady Margot's silky scarf and wimple only drew attention to her loveliness; Aileas disdained headdresses of any type and wore them only under duress. They chafed her neck and face; they slipped and got in her eyes. In short, she would have felt ill at ease even if she had been in the best of health.

"My dear, you are not well!" Margot cried as she hurried around the table and laid a cool hand on Aileas's forehead. "You should be in bed! I will send for the apothecary."

Aileas sneezed again, barely resisting the urge to wipe her nose with her silken scarf. "I shall retire after I eat," she said hoarsely. "I...I have to speak with George about something."

"Surely that can wait," Margot said, truly concerned. Aileas was warm, but not feverish yet. Still, her condition could worsen quickly, and the hall was the last place she should be.

"No, it cannot," Aileas said firmly, leaving Margot little choice but to take her seat.

Then George arrived, Father Adolphus and Sir Richard in tow. Her cousin sauntered toward the high table, not looking at his obviously ill wife. When he took his seat, he finally glanced at Aileas, then stared at her with an odd expression. "You're sick," he said, his tone one of casual surprise.

Aileas was about to speak, but she had to delay while Father Adolphus blessed the food. "I must speak with you," she said the moment the priest had concluded.

"Whatever you have to say to me can wait until I return," her husband replied. "I have decided to visit my outlying estates."

Margot realized Aileas was as surprised by this as she.

"I believe I have been somewhat lax with my supervision," George said with a hint of self-mockery as he looked at his wife. "I would not have anyone say I am remiss in my duties."

A puzzled look appeared momentarily on Richard's face, while Margot subdued a sigh of understanding. Aileas must have said something of that nature to George.

"Remiss, my lord?" the steward repeated.

"Yes. You do not think I have been negligent?"

"Certainly not, my lord," the estate steward immediately replied. George slid a snide glance at his wife, and Margot almost winced.

Perhaps it would be wise to hint to Aileas that no man liked his methods of governing criticized. Not even George.

"But I do think a personal visit would not be a mistake, my lord," Sir Richard added.

"We shall ride as soon as we can both be ready, before the noon today."

"Very good, my lord," Sir Richard answered. "I shall see to it at once." The steward rose, leaving his food unfinished, darted a look at Aileas—surely concerned for her health, Margot thought—and left the hall.

There was a long moment of silence as George resumed eating and Aileas sat unspeaking, her attention apparently taken up by a contemplation of the table linen.

When Margot could no longer stand it, she asked with a brittle brightness, "How long will you be gone?"

"I don't know."

Aileas rose unsteadily. "My lord, I would speak with you before you go."

"I will not have the time. My duties, as you know, keep me occupied."

"George!" Margot chided, keeping her tone as low as she could so that the others in the hall would not hear. "She is ill! Go with her to your bedchamber."

"You would make a better nurse, Margot, although I'm sure my wife's ailment is nothing but a cold brought on by improper attire and dashing about the castle in the middle of the night," he replied, biting off the last word.

Aileas went as pale as a bleached sheet. Thinking she was about to faint, Margot quickly moved to support her.

With an expression of alarm that lasted only an instant, George half rose. Then, seeing Margot with her arm about Aileas, he sat back down. "Please escort my wife to the bedchamber," he said to Margot, his manner so brusque and cold she could scarcely believe it was her cousin speaking. "Send for the apothecary to tend to Lady Aileas," he ordered Elma.

Margot opened her mouth to respond, then thought better of it. The first thing she had to do was get Aileas to her bed.

Surely they had not been married long enough for serious, unsolvable difficulties to have arisen, she thought as she helped Aileas toward the stairs. She hoped it wouldn't be terribly difficult to mend the breach.

It crossed her mind that it probably wouldn't be impossible to get this recent marriage annulled, either.

Herbert watched in dismay as his brother angrily tossed some clothing into a large leather pouch. They were in the bedchamber of Richard's house, a large, timbered structure that boasted a hall and kitchen, with buttery and pantry below, and two bedchambers above. Richard's bedchamber, the largest of the two, was as well furnished as Sir George's, with an opulence lacking in the public rooms below. Here, the only other person allowed besides his brother was his well-paid, and mute, body servant. Richard didn't want anyone speaking of the expensive luxuries, lest his master wonder how he could afford it.

Herbert thought of his own meagre lodgings in the other room. If Sir George saw that room, he might wonder why his household steward was so poor, for Herbert kept it a carefully guarded secret that he had a mistress who lived in a town ten miles away, in a very fine house luxuriously appointed.

"I thought you said he would never go," Herbert reminded the irate Richard. "That you could ensure he would stay away from the other estates. What if he asks to see their books of account?"

"I didn't think he would be bothered, idiot!" Richard growled. He banged down the lid of his clothes chest and cast a black look at his brother. "Why should I, when he has never gone before?

"It's *her* fault," he muttered, sitting on the chest. "That wife of his. That shrew! That harpy!"

Herbert entwined his long, thin fingers nervously. "Do you suppose he suspects we've been—"

"No, of course not!"

"Perhaps she's seen something in the accounts—"

"How could she, when she can't read?"

"Then why blame—"

"Because she's driven him out, you idiot!" Richard slapped his hands on the chest and rose abruptly. "Why else does he look like he hasn't had a decent night's rest in days?" he demanded, beginning to pace. "Why else would he suddenly take it into his head to go? I'd lay you good odds she denies him!"

"I thought you said we didn't have anything to fear from her?"

"From her directly, no, we don't—but I can't think of everything!" his brother cried. "How was I to

236 A Warrior's Bride

know she would prove such a terrible wife that he
would prefer to do business rather than stay home? I
hope she dies!''

"Richard!''

"Well, I do—she's sick already.''

"Sick?''

"Yes. She could barely stand when she left the table. It would have been wonderful if she'd fallen and
broken her head!''

"What's the matter with her?''

"I don't know. She looks to have no more than a
chill to me. They've sent for the apothecary.''

"I hope it isn't anything serious,'' Herbert said sincerely.

"I hope it isn't anything serious,'' Richard repeated
in a sweetly cloying tone. He grabbed a pair of boots,
then threw them across the room, where they struck
the wall and fell to the floor, leaving a black mark on
the whitewashed walls. "You sound as if you're in
love with her yourself,'' he said scornfully. "Lisette
will be pleased to hear that, I'm sure!''

"I am not! But what if Lady Aileas does die?''
Herbert charged. "He'll marry again—and perhaps to
a woman who *can* read.''

Richard crossed his arms and eyed his brother
shrewdly. "What's this? Don't tell me you're beginning to think for yourself?''

Herbert remained silent as he retrieved the boots
and set them beside the bed.

"You'll be in charge here while I'm gone,'' Richard
observed. "Don't do anything without my approval.''

"I am always careful.''

"Don't do *anything* without my approval—or else

those delightful fellows who showed the miller where his interests lie might have to pay you a visit, too.''

Herbert felt his blood run cold at the implied threat, yet he told himself his brother would never hurt him. Call him names, tell him he was stupid and fool-ish—but he wouldn't hurt him!

"Keep the lady confused, and don't make any de-cisions until I get back. Do you understand?"

Herbert nodded.

"Good. Now I had best get to the castle." Richard grabbed up his bag and strode from the room.

Herbert watched him go, then sighed wearily as he slowly left the house.

Everything had seemed so easy and free of risk when they had started. A few coins here, an inflated sum there. Enough to buy finer food and wine, enough to buy gifts for women. He had never guessed how far Richard was willing to go to get more money. He might have, if he had stopped to consider how trusting Sir George and his father were, and how greedy Rich-ard was.

Herbert continued through the village market, deaf to the noise of the merchants and their customers bar-gaining for the wares, blind to the vegetables, chick-ens, pig's heads, baskets and other goods displayed. He vaguely wondered if he should buy something new for Lisette at the stall of one of the fabric merchants. Or at the goldsmith's, where there was always some-thing to please her.

It was undeniable that he had needed more money than his wage as a household steward or the income from their family manor could provide to keep Lisette. That had been obvious from the first. So, when Rich-ard came to him with his initial plans, he had agreed.

When his brother had proposed other schemes, ones
with more risk yet sure to yield better profit for them,
he had agreed, too—although at the time, he had told
himself that he would soon tire of Lisette, and then he
would find another mistress, one with less expensive
tastes and habits.

He had not realized he might fall in love with the
petite, dark-haired woman from Paris. He had not
reckoned on how her attentions could make him feel
the equal of any man, even Richard. Or that he would
find her banter charming, taking him away from the
cares of his responsibilities. Unfortunately, he had, and
now the thought of losing Lisette was so unbearably
painful, he would risk almost anything to keep her.
Indeed, he was already risking his life, for if they were
caught, they would surely hang.

Suddenly, he heard a hiss and then his name. Startled and confused, Herbert peered down a narrow lane
between two fishmongers and saw Elma beckoning to
him. After looking around to make sure no one saw
him, he joined her in the alley.

"What are you doing here?" he asked in a whisper.
"Should you not be in attendance on Lady Aileas?
Richard told me she is ill."

"I have been for the apothecary. I sent him to the
castle, then told him I had an errand to run for the
lady."

"Perhaps you should return at once. They might
have need of you."

"She is not very sick," the maidservant replied
scornfully. "A touch of ague, nothing more. Tell me,
what does Richard think of his lordship's sudden interest in outlying estates?"

"He is not pleased."

"But we have nothing to fear, do we? Sir George won't find anything?"

"Richard assures me he won't."

"You don't sound convinced."

Herbert could only shrug. "I'm beginning to think we should leave here, before our dealings are discovered. Things were easier when it was only Sir George's father, and when it was only a few coins here and there. But we've done too much. We're bound to be found out."

Elma eyed him suspiciously. "You wouldn't be thinking of abandoning us, would you?"

"No, of course not," he lied.

"Good." She smiled. "I'm sure you wouldn't want to leave Lisette behind."

"I would never leave her."

"And she would never leave you, unless you were poor or in prison. Or dead, of course."

"You're lying," he declared bravely.

"We are all liars," she told him, "and cheats and frauds."

"She loves me!" Herbert cried fervently, wanting to believe it, but knowing that was a lie, too.

"Believe what you will," Elma said coldly as she pushed past him. "But don't ever think you can just pick up and run."

Elma proved to be right. Aileas was not seriously ill. Nevertheless, the apothecary, a middle-aged man with a bald pate and scraggly beard named Paracus, whose black robe seemed to bear evidence of every potion he had ever concocted, advised that she stay in bed. He also ordered her to drink a noxious brew he claimed would make her better in a few days.

One taste and the brew went out the window. Then Aileas carefully refilled the bottle with water. The bottle continued to smell of the substance, so that no one suspected what she had done, and the water was tainted by the brew's bitter taste, but it was infinitely better than drinking the potion.

Even without it, Aileas felt better within a few days, although she did feel more tired than usual. She blamed that on the dull, anxious days, which seemed excruciatingly long because George was not there. She had never had a chance to talk to him before he had gone. Nor had she any notion when he would come back.

She wasn't used to having people flutter about her like irritating, twittering moths when she was unwell, either. In her father's household, sick people were generally left to recover on their own, apart from having a servant bring them food and drink. Her father thought too much attention might encourage malingering, even among his own children.

Attentive Margot had offered to see to the daily business of the household while Aileas recovered. She was probably doing a better job of it than she could ever hope to, Aileas thought despondently.

To make matters worse, she heard nothing from her husband, even though Margot informed her that his farthest estate was just half a day's ride away. He might have sent a messenger asking how she fared.

Finally, on the fifth day, Aileas could stay in bed no longer, especially when Elma informed her that Lady Margot had taken to her own bed, for it was her woman's time.

That information gave Aileas a moment's pause. If there was one thing she lacked in her father's household, it was someone with whom she could discuss such matters.

Nevertheless, since her nursemaid would not be able to watch over her, Aileas thought with a sardonic smile, she could get up and out of the bedchamber, where everything reminded her of George and the nights they had shared.

Indeed, even attending to the household accounts would be preferable to staying here. That reason also proved the best excuse to convince Elma that she could not remain abed. Soon enough, Aileas was dressed and on the threshold of the solar, watching Herbert bending over his lists.

"My lady!" Herbert cried, shoving back his chair and rising quickly. "Should you not still be resting? The apothecary said—"

"I know what he said," she replied somewhat peevishly. "I simply couldn't endure staying in bed another moment. I thought I would go mad."

"Please, sit, my lady," the black-garbed steward said anxiously as he drew another chair toward the table. "I was just looking at the figures for some eels we had the other day. I'm beginning to think they are too costly to have weekly."

Aileas maneuvered her heavy skirt as she sat on the edge of the seat. Perhaps she should have listened to Elma and chosen something lighter than this gown of amber brocade, but it was the one she found easiest to move in, despite the weight of the skirt. It fit perfectly in the bodice, and she could move her arms freely, for its sleeves were tight, with no cumbersome, dangling cuffs.

She ran her finger around the edge of the wimple. She was not yet used to the constriction of the detested

headdress. She had put it on only because she feared
Elma would bar the door with her body rather than
see her mistress leave the room without it, claiming
that unless Aileas had something on her head, she
would catch a chill again, for the rainy day was as
gloomy as her mood.

Herbert pushed a list of foodstuffs toward her.
"Yes, I see," she said, scanning the page. She tried
not to think about the last time she had been here,
before George had gone away more than a week ago.
Unfortunately, everything she thought of these days
was now divided into two parts: before George left,
and after.

"Is something the matter, my lady?" Herbert asked
anxiously. "Truly, I think you should rest—"

"I have been resting for quite long enough," she
said firmly. "I have been thinking about this," she
continued, grabbing another piece of parchment. She
chose an item on the list at random, pointed at it—
then stared disbelieving at the word and the number
written next to it, and not just because she could actually decipher the word.

"Oh, the new napkins," Herbert confirmed, and she
fought to keep the surprise from her face. She glanced
at Herbert and he colored immediately as he drew back
slightly, panic in his eyes. "We had not nearly
enough. We needed fifty more."

"To make a total of...?"

"Two hundred."

"When did these new napkins arrive?" she asked.

"Before your wedding, my lady. We needed them
for that happy occasion," he added with a smile that
only increased Aileas's uneasiness.

For she well recalled the total number of napkins in

the linen cupboard the day Lady Margot had insisted they count them: one hundred and seventy-five.

Twenty-five had disappeared in a month. Either a servant was stealing them—unlikely, considering that the linen stores were locked in a cupboard and there were but two keys, one in the possession of the household steward and the other on the chatelaine's ring— or else some other criminal activity was afoot. Judging by Herbert's reaction, she could well believe the household steward was involved, whatever was going on.

"That seems to be quite a sum to be spent on linen," she remarked.

"Well, my lady, they are very fine ones."

"Yes, they are," she replied calmly, although inwardly, she was anything but calm. Her instincts had been right, after all!

Caution, her mind urged. It could be that she was eager to see dishonesty to prove her doubts to George when he returned. And if the steward was untrustworthy, it would not be wise to allow him to know of her mistrust while George was not here.

Then she recalled that Lady Margot had possession of the chatelaine's keys while she had been ill.

Could Lady Margot be a thief? Why would she steal?

All at once Aileas realized that she had come to trust Lady Margot. Aileas had seen rivalries and competition of many kinds, both subtle and blatant, and when she thought of how Margot had treated her, especially during her illness, she colored at the remembrance of her own petty jealousy. No, she could not believe Lady Margot would steal.

Herbert and Richard Jolliet were another matter,

however, especially in view of Herbert's guilty reactions. It was possible they had been hoodwinking George and his father for years, although if they had, they would surely have a very good explanation.

She would have to have more proof of dishonesty or the identity of the thief. At least she knew the kind of thing to look for now, and if her reading continued to improve, more evidence might yet be found.

"I would like to see what other wares this linen merchant might have," she remarked. "Does he live nearby?"

"No, no, my lady, he does not," Herbert replied quickly. "He comes from London. He happened to be passing through the village. Most conveniently, too, for us."

He smiled, but the panic had not left his eyes.

"A pity," she said. "Perhaps the next time Sir Richard goes to London on business for Sir George, he can ask the merchant to come our way again."

"Of course, my lady. I shall tell my brother of your request when he returns."

"Good. Is that everything, then, Herbert?" she asked.

Suddenly she heard a slight commotion from the vicinity of the gate, and for a moment, her heart seemed to stop beating. "Is that...is Sir George come home?" she asked, powerless to move, or so it seemed, as if she were a deer who had just heard the snap of a twig beneath a hunter's foot.

The steward went to the window. "No, my lady. It is someone else. A visitor, I believe, although we are not expecting—"

Now they could distinguish the voices of the arrivals as they entered the courtyard.

"Rufus!" Lady Aileas cried, leaping up from the chair as if she were as healthy as the proverbial horse. She ran to the window, roughly pushing Herbert out of the way. "Rufus!" she called, waving wildly.

Then she dashed out of the room as if pursued by a gang of cutthroats.

Herbert turned back to regard the group of men gathered in the yard, led by a fellow with the reddest hair he had ever seen.

One of the lady's brothers, Herbert speculated, judging by her joyous reaction. Perhaps this unexpected visit would make her forget all thoughts of napkins and their number.

The household steward turned away and wiped his sweating upper lip with his hand. God's wounds, why had she lit on that item, of all things? What if she had counted the napkins? She had been nosing about the stores that day a while ago, with Lady Margot.

What if she found out he had not ordered the number recorded? She might suspect—

Napkins were simple things to steal. He could blame the servants. That was what Richard always said they would do if they were caught. He had tried to tell Richard it was too risky, that instead of perishables, they were talking about goods carefully stored.

Herbert slumped down into the chair Lady Aileas had recently vacated. Perhaps he was getting all worked up over nothing. After all, Lady Aileas had not looked suspicious or said anything truly alarming. Perhaps it was only his own imagination running away with him. He was just getting fearful because she had happened upon that one item.

Nevertheless, it would be wise to send a messenger to Richard, informing him that there was some busi-

ness at Ravensloft that required his attention. Yes, that
was the best thing—send for Richard and let him deal
with this crisis, if crisis it were.

Herbert heaved himself out of the chair and went to
dispatch a messenger to his brother, occasionally
glancing over his shoulder as if he expected to see his
lord's men bearing down on him.

While down in the courtyard, Aileas joyfully
greeted Sir Rufus Hamerton.

Chapter Sixteen

"Rufus!"

The young man ceased his shrewd appraisal of the castle at the sound of the familiar female voice. "Aileas!" he cried happily, turning in the direction of the caller and crouching defensively, expecting her to try to knock him over, as was her usual method of greeting him after a prolonged absence.

Instead, he found himself slowly straightening and staring in amazement and dismay at the unexpectedly lovely woman, clad in a gown of rich golden brocade, who skittered to a stop several feet away from him. Smiling, she smoothed her garment and curtsied gracefully.

Rufus felt as if he had never seen Aileas Dugall before. Perhaps, in a way, he never had. He had never seen her in a gown that was so unabashedly designed to highlight its wearer's figure, cut with such care and clinging to her slender and astonishingly shapely frame. Much of the time, her features had been obscured by her unruly hair, so he had never noticed the perfection of her face, now outlined by the silk scarf and plain wimple, and the mind-numbing sensuality of her full lips. When she briefly lowered her eyelids in a demurely feminine manner, he wondered if this wasn't the Aileas he knew at all, but some changeling left by the fairies.

Rufus made a formally polite bow as she walked closer and gave him the kiss of greeting, her lips barely touching his cheek. She didn't even smell like Aileas, for she was wearing some kind of flowery scent that made him wrinkle his nose.

"Welcome to Ravensloft, Sir Rufus," she said, and when she drew back, he scrutinized her face—her tired, anxious eyes, the dark circles beneath them, the hint of worry in her brow, the unfamiliar hesitation in her smile.

God's wounds, what had George de Gramercie done to her to change her so? Where was the bold, fearless, teasing Aileas he had known for years? To be sure, she looked good in a dress, yet something infinitely more precious seemed to be lacking.

Rufus cleared his throat, suddenly aware of the several servants in the courtyard watching. "Lady Aileas, I must beg your forgiveness for arriving without an invitation," he said, carefully formal. "My father has summoned me home and I thought to break my journey here and spend some time with you, since I do not know when I might be able to return to this part of the country. I trust Sir George will not object?"

"He is not home at present," Aileas said, and something else flickered in her eyes that made his anger at her husband burn brighter. "He has gone to visit his other estates, but I'm sure he will not object. Allow me to offer you the hospitality of our hall." She made a wan little smile as she turned to lead the way into the largest building in the inner ward.

"This is a marvelous castle, Ail—Lady Aileas," he said, dutifully following her.

"Yes, it is, isn't it?" she replied flatly.

They reached the entrance to the hall and he paused on the threshold, his gaze moving from Aileas's slender back to the huge room. The first thing to strike him, beyond the sheer overwhelming size, was the ostentation and magnificence of the tapestries adorning the walls.

They were far too luxurious for his taste. A hall was not a cathedral, after all. A few tapestries for warmth were more than sufficient. The rest was wasteful extravagance, and he was rather surprised Aileas hadn't · removed them before they were ruined with smoke.

Her father certainly would have.

The rest of the hall seemed furnished with similar luxury, proving that Sir George was a man of wealth and taste—but that was completely unimportant, if he was not making Aileas happy.

Rufus realized Aileas had gone ahead and was waiting for him at the table on the dais. He quickened his pace and joined her, while an unabashedly curious maidservant poured them wine.

Because he was thirsty, he took a long drink of the fine wine, then wiped his mouth. Aileas lifted her goblet and took a dainty sip.

"Your father is in good health," he said. "And you?"

"I have had a slight illness recently. I am better now."

Her unnatural constraint troubled him more and more. Were they not old friends, at least? Rufus's grip tightened on his goblet. "Sir George did not return knowing you were unwell?"

"I did not send for him."

That, at least, sounded like something the Aileas he knew would do. She would never play the weakling, even when she was sick. "I should have guessed as much," he said quietly, smiling his approval.

She didn't answer, although a blush bloomed on her cheeks. His heart began to beat faster.

"You saw my father recently?"

"I stopped there on my way here. Snout is going to be knighted in the fall."

That brought a more familiar smile to her face, and a spark of her former liveliness to her eyes. "He has waited long enough."

Rufus took another drink as the silence between them stretched, and Aileas tried to maintain some kind of equanimity, although inwardly, she felt anything but calm.

Her first reaction to the sight of Rufus had been unallayed joy, because he was such a dear and old friend. In the first instant, too, there had been a touch of the old excitement that she had mistaken for love. That had disappeared quickly, to be replaced by affection, and memories of home and friendship.

That Rufus would be surprised to see her in a proper dress was not unexpected, but she had not foreseen the stunned shock on Rufus's face, which had turned to admiration and even awe. All at once she felt as if she were in the presence of a stranger. But she needed and wanted a friend.

As she sat beside Rufus in the hall of Ravensloft, she realized it was a good thing George was *not* at home, or he might have seen Rufus's reaction and taken it for confirmation of their illicit liaison.

"It must have been important business, to take him

away so soon after your marriage," Rufus noted, not looking at her.

"He thought it was," she replied.

A sudden clap of thunder made them both look at the windows, where they could see the first drops of rain. Rufus rose at once. "I had best see that my men attend to all the horses and baggage before everything gets soaked through," he said gruffly.

"Very well," Aileas said. "I will have a servant show you and your men to your quarters." He nodded, so like a stranger in that moment that she could hardly bear it. "It is so good to have you here, Rufus!" she said quietly, fervently and truthfully.

Rufus hurried away. His horses did not need his particular attention or care; it was simply that he could scarcely abide remaining with Aileas, who was so little like the happy, spirited woman he had known.

The woman Sir George de Gramercie was apparently slowly destroying.

George stared out the window of the hall in the manor house of his smallest estate. The rain had interrupted the hunting, and now he had nothing to do but look out at the water and mud and think about Aileas.

As well as the decision he had made regarding their future.

He had come to the conclusion that their marriage had been a foolhardy mistake, based on lust and loneliness and little else.

He might have been able to overlook her inability to act as a proper lady should, for there had been some improvement under Margot's tutelage. He might have been able to get used to her temper, or her suspicious nature.

But he simply could not overcome his anger at the thought that she had shared her bed with another man, or—even worse—men. He could not ignore the fact that she come to him under false pretenses, and that she was a dishonorable woman.

Nor could he risk the possible consequences of the anger she created in him. She made his temper ungovernable. Every emotion he experienced became magnified when he was with her, and he was without control. It was even conceivable that one day, he would get so enraged he would hurt her. He would act like the basest and weakest of tyrants.

He would never allow that to happen. Better he should end the marriage than behave so.

Once back at Ravensloft, he would tell Aileas of his decision and begin the process of having the marriage annulled. That would not be difficult in itself. He had many friends in the church, and he was sure one of them could find some obscure legal impediment to the marriage, such as a distant familial relationship. These things were done often enough.

He would say nothing more of his suspicions regarding Aileas's dishonor, not to Aileas or her father or anyone, in the same way that he would not reveal his own weakness. He owed her that for the time of blissful happiness he had shared with her.

She would be able to marry again, and so would he, if he had any inclination to take such a gamble a second time.

There would be some talk, but he was sure anyone who knew Aileas would think that she simply didn't suit his temperament, and he could easily imagine several gossips claiming they knew all along that his marriage to Aileas Dugall was a mistake. His expression became a sardonic smile. Aileas's next husband might even credit *him* with teaching Aileas her particular skills.

He should have acted on this resolution two days ago, when he had finally made it. Yet because of his feelings for her, the undeniable love he felt for her—for she made him feel that strongly, too—he had delayed his return.

A horseman appeared at the gate in the wooden wall that surrounded the small, muddy courtyard. The guard let him in, and the man quickly dismounted and hurried toward the manor hall.

Something was wrong. George's throat constricted as he wondered if Aileas had taken a turn for the worse. He had sent messengers every day to know how she fared, and the last had reported that she was much improved and certainly out of danger.

But that had been yesterday.

He anxiously hurried to the door, just ahead of Richard, who had been examining some ledgers as he sat beside the hearth.

"I have a message for Sir Richard," the young man panted, his cloak dripping water onto the packed earth of the floor as he handed over a pouch. "From your brother, sir."

George recognized the messenger as Derek, the fellow who had been rather the worse for drink the day after his wedding. "How is my wife today?" he asked, trying to sound calm.

"Better, I think, my lord," Derek replied humbly. "She was out of bed. I saw her myself, greeting a visitor."

"Come in and take off that cloak," George commanded in a friendly way, relieved. He saw the kitchen maid peering around the door and called out, "Some ale for this man, at once."

"Thank you, my lord," the young man said after he hung his soaking cloak on a peg beside the door and came farther inside the room. "It's not a good day for travel, I can tell you!"

George sat on a bench near the open hearth in the center of the room and gestured for Derek to join him. He glanced at Richard, who was reading the parchment he had taken from the pouch, his brow furrowed. "Not bad news, I hope, Richard?"

"Nothing urgent, my lord," the steward replied with a smile. "Still, I think I should return to Ravensloft tomorrow, unless you have something here you wish me to do?"

"No, you may go." George faced Derek. "So, we have a visitor at Ravensloft? Who is it?"

"Baldwin said his name is Sir Rufus Hamerton."

"I beg your pardon?" Sir George said, his voice very quiet and his gaze so intense Derek was sure he must have made a mistake.

"I thought Baldwin said the man's name was Sir Rufus Hamerton, my lord," he replied haltingly.

Sir George darted a swift glance over his shoulder at his steward. "I shall return to Ravensloft with you in the morning, Richard. We leave at dawn."

Derek regarded his lord with undisguised surprise at his sudden response, then surreptitiously shrugged his shoulders. Who could fathom the ways of the nobility?

"Lady Margot de Pontypoole, may I present Sir Rufus Hamerton," Aileas said as Rufus joined Aileas and another woman at the high table that evening. Aileas wore another gown, of a beautiful copper color that seemed to glow in the light of the flambeaux.

Rufus glanced at her companion, then swallowed hard, for she was easily the most beautiful woman he had ever seen. She was like a vision of loveliness, with a flawless, pale complexion, rosebud lips and eyes the color of the finest emeralds.

"Rufus, Lady Margot is my husband's cousin."

"Delighted to meet you, my lady," he mumbled, making a slight bow.

"I am happy to meet any friend of George's wife," the lady replied, in a voice as lovely as her face. Her smile warmed him as if it were the sun on a summer's day.

"Please, sit down, Rufus," Aileas said.

The meal proceeded, and for Rufus, it was a kind of exquisite torture. On one side, he had the distracting presence of Lady Margot, on the other, Aileas. Every protective impulse he possessed should have been focused on her, and he very much wanted to find out why her husband had gone away. Nevertheless, the hall during the evening meal was not the best place to have such a conversation.

Therefore, he was as free as he could be under the circumstances to converse with the beautiful, charming Lady Margot. In truth, he found that something of a relief, for the constraint between himself and Aileas was truly painful.

When the last of the meal had been cleared away, Lady Margot rose with what seemed genuine reluctance. "I must beg to be excused," she said. "I should speak to Father Adolphus about some special masses for my late husband. It will be the anniversary of his death shortly.''

She was a widow? Rufus found that interesting.

Aileas nodded her acquiescence, and Lady Margot walked gracefully away to speak with the priest seated near the dais.

''She's beautiful, isn't she?'' Aileas said softly, watching the lady's progress.

''Something is wrong, isn't it, Aileas?'' Rufus demanded quietly.

He realized she was still watching Lady Margot. In that instant, a very disturbing notion came to him.

''Has she no home of her own to tend to?'' he asked bluntly.

''Yes, she does,'' Aileas answered in a tone so soft and low, Rufus had to strain to hear her.

''Why is she still here? Your wedding was over a month ago.''

''Rufus, I—'' She glanced at a black-robed, sallow-faced individual sitting near the priest and grew silent.

''What is going on here, Aileas?'' Rufus demanded, even more upset when she raised her haunted eyes to look at him.

''Rufus, hush!'' she cautioned. ''Later. We will talk about everything later. Tomorrow. Meet me in the solar after the noon meal. We can be alone there.''

Rufus nodded his agreement, then abruptly left the hall.

The next day, Aileas paced anxiously in the solar, afraid Herbert or even Elma would come before Rufus did.

If he did.

Oh, but he must, she thought, her gaze lighting on

the piles of parchment laid out on the table. She had to tell someone her suspicions, and Rufus would listen. He would understand.

What was taking him so long?

At last there was a soft knock at the door, and Aileas breathed a sigh of relief when she opened it and found Rufus there.

"Come in," she whispered, glancing about to make certain no servant observed his entry as she closed the door behind him.

"Aileas," he breathed—and then he pulled her into his arms and kissed her passionately.

Alarmed, she drew back, wrenching herself out of his arms. "Rufus! Please!" she cried, hurrying behind the table to stare at him. "I...things are different now, Rufus!"

"I know, and I curse myself! Aileas, can you ever forgive me?" he pleaded, kneeling and holding out his hands in a gesture of supplication. "I was an idiot to let you go! I should have been begging you to marry me."

"Rufus, please! You don't understand!"

"Of course I do," he cried, getting to his feet. "I was a fool and I lost you. Once." He strode toward the table, his expression determined. "Come away with me!"

"No!"

He halted abruptly and his eyes filled with sorrow. "It is what I should have known an honorable woman would say. But you cannot stay here. At least let me take you back to your father."

She gazed at him steadily, willing him to recognize her sincerity. "I know what you say comes from the goodness of your heart and your feelings for me, Rufus. But I will not. I...I care very much for my husband, Rufus. We have had a misunderstanding. That's all, I assure you.''

"A simple misunderstanding? No, it is worse than that. Look at what he has done to you—what I allowed to happen. You are like a shadow of yourself, Aileas! Can you not see where this will end? He is *killing* you!''

"I have been ill," she explained ardently. "I am still a little unwell.''

"Why does that woman watch over you?" he demanded.

"I used the wrong words last night," Aileas said.

"Come away with me, Aileas," he said in a tone that was a command, not a request.

"I will not," she said firmly. "I love my husband.''

"You love a man being unfaithful to you, right under your own roof and with his own cousin?" he charged angrily. "Has he made you blind and stupid, too?''

Aileas regarded him steadily. "I am neither—and what you say is not true.''

"Why else would he have that woman here?''

"He wanted her to teach me how to be a lady.''

"What?" he scoffed.

"Have you not seen an improvement in my manners?" she asked as she went around the table, fearing little good could come of this meeting. It would be better to get away and go to George with her suspicions. She would have to make him see that something was seriously amiss in his household.

Rufus blocked her way and grabbed hold of her shoulders as he gazed at her intently. "Perhaps, but you are not happy here—and don't tell me otherwise, Aileas. I know you too well.''

Suddenly the door to the solar crashed open. Aileas and Rufus sprang apart as George strode into the room.

"George!" Aileas cried, flushing guiltily, even though she knew she had done nothing wrong, as she curtsied toward her husband.

"Welcome to Ravensloft, Sir Rufus," George said in a cold and measured tone, regarding her with all the curiosity he might bestow upon the humblest servant in his household.

Disappointment and dismay flooded through her. She had wanted him to return the same person he was on their wedding day: charming, exciting, interested in her.

Instead, he was even more the stranger. "I am glad you have come back," she said, willing him to believe her truthful words.

"Are you, indeed?" he replied lightly. "I am glad to be here." He strolled past her. "What brings you here, Sir Rufus?" he asked evenly as he sat in the chair behind the table.

"I am on my way to my father's in the north country," Rufus replied with some measure of calm, although Aileas felt as if she were watching two dogs circle each other. "Since I'll be gone some time, like as not, I thought I'd pay a visit. If I'm not welcome—"

"Oh, but you are!" George replied smoothly. "Isn't he, Aileas? Please sit and have some wine. Aileas, you should have offered him some wine. No matter, we can have wine later—or do you intend to go away today? It is an excellent day for traveling.''

His expression rather stunned, Rufus threw himself into a chair on the opposite side of the table while Aileas slowly slid back into the other one. She longed to tell George that she was truly happy he was home, that she had missed him, and explain the reason for Rufus's presence in his solar—but she was absolutely speechless as she mustered every ounce of determination she possessed.

As Aileas took her seat, George could not help watching her, once again filled with that incredible, passionate desire that she inspired. In her presence, he could seemingly remember every moment of their intimacy, and if Rufus had not been there, he would have taken her in his arms right then and there.

But Rufus *was* there, all six feet and more of him, with his ugly red hair and brawny body.

"Well, Aileas, why so secret that you meet in my solar? I must assume you want no witnesses to your rendezvous."

"I did want it to be secret," she said firmly, apparently none the whit ashamed, "because I wanted to tell him what I suspected about the Jolliets. They are cheating you, I'm sure of it."

She sounded so sure of herself, it gave him a moment's pause, until Rufus shifted in his seat. "Are you? Unfortunately, I am not. I have checked and rechecked the accounts at the other estates and found nothing amiss. Besides, if you had proof enough to speak to your dear friend about what you suspect, why did you not come to me?"

"I wanted to be sure."

"I would have made sure."

"Would you?" she charged. "Would you have believed me? Would you have taken me at my word?"

"Your word alone, against the men who have been in my family's employ for years?" he mused. "I agree, it is a precarious business. Is that why you preferred to present your case to Sir Rufus—because you would be sure of a *sympathetic* ear?"

"I would believe whatever Aileas says," Rufus said staunchly. "As you should."

"George, you were not here," she reminded him. "And I think there is proof."

"Think? A court of law demands more than speculation."

"I have evidence," she declared.

"Where?"

"There!" she said, pointing at the parchments he had barely noticed spread before him on the table. "In the lists. I'm sure things have been stolen. I even believe prices and amounts on the lists have been adjusted, when there should be no change, and the difference pocketed, probably by these stewards you trust so much. Who else would be able to steal from you without detection?"

George lifted one of the parchments and quickly scanned it. He saw nothing amiss. "Show me where, exactly."

His wife's eyes flashed with defiant anger. "I can't, exactly."

"Why not?"

"Because I cannot read," she announced defiantly.

George simply could not believe it. "You have been attending to the household accounts and you cannot read?" he asked incredulously. "Why is it you cannot?"

"My father didn't think it important enough to teach me," she answered.

God's wounds, that made sense. But she should have told him. What did she think he would do, make fun of her? Chastise her? He would behave better, as she should know.

"But there *are* discrepancies, of that I am certain," she finished, her tone as frustrated as a tutor with a slow pupil.

"What do you mean, questioning your wife as if she were the guilty one?" Rufus demanded. "She tells you what she suspects—you should trust her word alone!"

How dare this man criticize me, George thought as the anger built inside him. "As I should trust her word that she was a virgin when she came to my bed," he replied, fighting to keep his tone even, "despite the lack of evidence there, too?"

Rufus stared at him and Aileas rose abruptly, splaying her hands on the table before him. "Yes, you should—and you should have given me a chance to explain."

"I'm sure your explanation would have been very entertaining," George replied, unable to keep the scowl from his face. "Tell me, were you so confident in this explanation that you could invite your lover to cuckold me under my own roof?"

"Rufus is not my lover!" Her angry denunciation and the sincerity in her rebellious eyes told him more than her words did, and for the first time in many a day, he began to hope that it might be so.

Rufus jumped to his feet. "How dare you accuse Aileas of being unfaithful, you black-hearted, disgusting worm? She's the most loyal woman in England, and if you think—"

"I learned what to do by listening to my brothers

and the other men when they talked about their women!'' she cried.

George stared at her. He could believe that. He could see Aileas sitting amongst them, listening and learning. And yet... ''Your father allowed this?''

''He didn't *allow* it,'' she answered. ''He didn't know. Neither did they, most of the time. I can be as quiet as a mouse when I want to be.''

''Aileas!'' Rufus growled. ''You don't have to explain anything. If he thinks you capable of such base actions, he doesn't deserve you.''

Aileas turned toward her redheaded friend. ''You don't understand, either.''

''I do!'' Rufus shouted angrily. ''I understand that he set his cousin to watch over you, like some kind of guard.''

''She was to be my teacher!''

Rufus glared at George. ''Do you think Aileas so flawed, you blackguard? Or was that only your excuse to have your cousin come—so that you could have your mistress in your household! How cozy and convenient!''

''She's not my lover!'' George denied angrily. ''She is my cousin—and nothing more.''

''And a very lovely cousin, too!''

There was a gasp in the doorway, and they all turned to see Margot there, her hand covering her mouth.

''Margot!'' George cried, half rising from his chair—but she put out her hand as if to hold him there.

''It's...that's not true,'' she said haltingly, her expression as determined as Aileas's had been. ''George does not love me that way. He never has. He never will. I...I...'' Her voice broke, and a pitiful anguish appeared in her eyes before she spun on her heel and ran from the room.

Suddenly George realized how blind he had been, and how selfish, both toward his wife and Margot. Despite his very real regret for Margot's feelings, George forgot all about her when Rufus grabbed Aileas's hand as if he would drag her away by force. "Come away and leave this scoundrel!" he ordered.

"Let go of my wife!"

At the harsh command, Rufus froze. Aileas broke free and stared at George, for on his face was an expression of such blatant, naked rage that she could scarcely recognize him.

She took a step toward her husband—until, with a growl of primitive anger, Rufus leapt past her. He got hold of George and brought him down as if George were a stag and he the hound hunting it.

"Rufus!" Aileas shouted. "Stop!"

Rufus ignored her. He brought up his fist to smash George's face. Her husband rolled away and lashed out with his feet. Not fast enough, though, for Rufus could move quickly for a man of his size.

He glared at George and crouched, ready to spring or meet another attack, as George got to his feet. "You don't deserve her," Rufus snarled. "She couldn't love you. She loves me!"

"Rufus!" Aileas cried, aghast at his presumption, ashamed that she had once given him cause to think so. She looked intently at her husband. "George, please," she began, hesitating when she saw the wrath burning in his eyes. Then he suddenly ran toward Rufus with a bellow of equally primitive, impassioned fury.

When she moved to intercept, certain George would

kill Rufus, George knocked her out of his way with such force that she stumbled and struck her head on the corner of the table.

The room swirled about her, and Aileas knew no more.

Chapter Seventeen

"Oh, God help me!" George moaned as he stared in disbelief. "What have I done?"

Quickly he knelt beside his wife's crumpled body and took her in his arms, gently turning her over. He gasped when he saw the cut on her forehead and the blood. "Aileas, Aileas!" he whispered, gingerly brushing back the bloodstained scarf.

"Get away from her!" Rufus snarled.

"She is my wife!" George bellowed, glancing over his shoulder at his opponent with a look that halted Rufus in his tracks and silenced him.

George became aware that someone else had come into the room. "Margot?"

"No, my lord," a frightened female voice responded. "It's me, Elma."

"Get the apothecary," he ordered, rising slowly with Aileas in his arms. She groaned softly and the sound tore at his heart. "Quick!"

Elma ran out of the room.

George slowly turned and walked to the door, seeing nothing but Aileas, studying her face, pale beneath the blood oozing from the wound in her temple. Feeling nothing but the relaxed weight in his arms. Like the dog he had killed.

Oh, God, if he had hurt her...if she died...he would never forgive himself.

Never.

Standing in his bedchamber, Richard glared at his brother, his dark brows furrowed into one line of anger. He had parted from Sir George on the road, claiming that he needed to see to the mill weights, but instead had ridden straight to his own home. "What has happened that you sent for me to come at once?" he demanded.

"It's Lady Aileas. She suspects us."

Richard's eyes widened and his heartbeat quickened as a perplexing observation suddenly made complete sense. Sir George had acted rather oddly during their sojourn at his far estates, more circumspect and careful. At the time, the steward had wanted to ascribe it to the problems between the newly married couple. Now he was sure there was another reason. "Who does she suspect? Of what?"

Herbert swallowed hard, his Adam's apple bobbing unattractively. "I...I'm not sure. She asked about the napkins."

"What about them?"

"She questioned the number, and when we received them. She and Lady Margot did go through the linen cupboard a while ago. Maybe she counted them. Maybe she realized they've paid for more than they received."

"Didn't you alter the number of napkins in the list of linen?"

"I...I forgot. And who would have thought she would notice the discrepancy, if she can't read?"

"I would," Richard lied, although he had not thought many precautions necessary, given the circumstances. "Did she actually accuse you of anything?"

"Me?" Herbert asked in a strangled voice. "No." Then he regarded his brother with dread. "I will not be held solely responsible for any discrepancies."

"I haven't asked you to, have I?" Richard demanded. Inwardly, however, he thought assigning guilt to anyone other than himself no bad thing. "We can blame the servants, remember? You didn't let Lady Margot near the lists, did you? She might notice altered figures."

"She never came near the books."

"You're certain?"

"Yes. They have always been in my possession."

"Could the miller have said something to Lady Aileas that would raise her suspicions?"

"I doubt it," Herbert said. "Your men were very...thorough."

Richard regarded his brother thoughtfully. If there were a weak link in the chain of his schemes at present, it was Herbert. He would have done better to leave his brother out of it.

Too late for that now.

And it appeared that there was a new cause for concern, in the person of Lady Aileas. "So let me understand you. You think Lady Aileas suspects you of dishonest dealing, but of exactly what, you are not sure. She must have no proof, or she would have gone to her husband about it."

"Yes. That sounds likely."

Richard breathed a sigh of relief. "You've just panicked for no good reason," he said, as much to himself as to his brother. "If Sir George believed her or she had any kind of proof, we would already be arrested."

Herbert nodded, and Richard saw the fear in the man's eyes.

"Listen to me, brother," he said staunchly. "As long as our lord and his wife do not agree with each other, there is no cause to fear. Even if she does accuse us, he will not believe her allegations if it is simply her word—not against us, men chosen by his father. Still, we must ensure that there is no verification to be found."

Elma burst into the estate steward's bedchamber without so much as a knock. "Come quick, both of you, to the castle. Sir George—I think he's killed her! And Lady Margot is packing her bags and saying she's leaving as soon as she can! The whole castle is in an uproar!"

"Who's Sir George killed?" Richard demanded.

"Lady Aileas," Elma answered.

"His wife?" Herbert squeaked. "He's killed his wife?"

"I don't know!" Elma cried in frustration. "But you two had better get up there right away. I've just come from the apothecary's."

Herbert hurried to the door, then paused when Richard called him back. "Not so fast. Not yet." He gave Elma a significant look. "It might be a good thing for us if he has killed her," he said quietly. "Herbert tells me she was asking about the linen."

Elma cursed crudely. "I knew that was a mistake. We should have kept to the food and drink! But he's right. They had an argument. I heard part of it—she was talking about you."

"Who?"

"Both of you. The stewards."

Richard gasped.

"What are we going to do now?" Herbert whined, twisting the edge of his tunic in his hands.

"Keep quiet till we know for sure if we need to worry," Richard snapped.

"If we can find those men, the ones you set upon the miller…" Herbert began hopefully.

"You think to do the same to the linen merchant?"

Herbert nodded eagerly. "He is the only one who might be able to prove anything."

"If he won't cooperate, we'll need a scapegoat," Elma observed.

"Who? One of the other maids?" Herbert suggested.

Then he realized Elma and Richard were both regarding him steadily, with expressions as cold and unsmiling as stone effigies in a chapel. "Not me! I only did what you told me!"

"You don't understand, do you, you fool?" Richard said, walking slowly toward his brother, who stumbled back away from him. "You have raised their suspicions. Even if we make the linen draper see the wisdom of silence, the seeds have been planted. Sir George was easy to dupe when we had his trust. That is probably finished now—and it's all your doing!" He shoved his brother hard against the wall.

"Richard, please!" Herbert pleaded, cowering.

"Elma, would you leave us?" Richard asked evenly, turning away. Before she had moved, he suddenly spun on his heel and plunged his dagger into his brother's chest.

"Richard!" Herbert gasped, grasping at the knife protruding from his body.

"I should have done this years ago," Richard muttered, pulled the dagger out and let his brother's body fall to the floor. "Don't worry, Herbert. I'll see that Lisette isn't lonely."

Elma stared, aghast. "What did you do that for? There was no need—" Then her expression hardened. "You want Lisette for yourself?"

"I don't give a tinker's dam about Lisette," Richard said scornfully as he wiped his dagger on his brother's tunic. "He was too much of a liability. He always has been. God knows what he might have told that wench already. We can deny any part of it now, should anything be discovered amiss with the accounts, and Herbert can take the blame. Sir George will find it hard enough to discover he has been harboring one cheat. He won't believe there could be another." He put on a mournful face. "Alas, Sir George, how could I know that the brother I trusted was such a thief?" Then he laughed scornfully. "Now, help me move the body under the bed." Reluctantly, Elma came closer as he gripped his brother by the arms. "Take his legs," he ordered.

Together they dragged the body to the bed. Richard shoved it underneath. "I'll get rid of him tonight, when it's dark."

She nodded slowly, her face pale. "We'd both best get to the castle."

George had never endured such agony as he did when he carried Aileas up those stairs.

Carefully he brought her inside their bedchamber and laid her on their bed. Watching her intently, he pressed her cool hand against his damp cheek.

What kind of brute was he, after all? he thought helplessly. He should have stayed away. "Aileas," he whispered. "Forgive me, Aileas! You can wear what you like, and eat any way you like, only do not leave me. I was a fool to try and change you. Come back to me, Aileas."

Her eyelids moved. They fluttered like the wings of a butterfly and he let out a cry of relieved joy when she opened her eyes.

"George?" she whispered, gazing up at him with furrowed brow as she lifted her hand to her head. "What...what happened?" She gasped and grew a little paler. "You were fighting and I—"

"I knocked you down. Oh, sweet Savior, Aileas, I thought I'd killed you," he moaned as he took hold of her hand, clutching it tightly.

She smiled wanly and reached up to gently brush his hair from his forehead. "My father would tell you it would take more than a bump on my thick skull to kill me."

He managed a weak smile of his own. "Nevertheless, I must beg your forgiveness. And I believe every word you said. You've never had a lover. Richard and Herbert are scoundrels—anything, anything! But don't hate me."

"How could I?" she whispered. "I love you too much."

"You do?"

She nodded slowly. "I do." Then—oh, marvelous sight!—he caught a glimmer of laughter in her eyes. "I wouldn't have tried so hard to change if I did not."

"I was wrong to ask it of you, Aileas."

"My lord!" Paracus, the apothecary, stood in the doorway.

George moved away from the bed to let him near. "She's awake."

The middle-aged man bent down and stared at Aileas, then gingerly fingered the bump rising on her forehead, making Aileas wince.

"She's fine now, isn't she?" George demanded anxiously.

"I don't—" the apothecary began.

"Of course I am," Aileas interrupted defiantly. However, when she tried to sit up, her hand went swiftly to her head and she dropped back to the pillow. "Just a little dizzy, that's all."

Paracus continued to stare at her with narrowed eyes and pursed lips. "A cold compress on the bump, and do not let her sleep until after vespers. Then wake her several times in the night. If you cannot wake her, my lord, come for me at once."

"Very well, Paracus," George replied gravely.

"Now she should rest," the apothecary ordered. "Do not leave her alone, in case…"

He left his sentence unfinished, but George knew what he meant, and some of his joy left him. "I will stay," he said. "You may go."

"She needs to have that wound washed—"

"I am quite capable of doing that," Aileas replied. "My father would say you are treating me like a baby."

"You look as if you need rest yourself, my lord," Paracus noted.

George nodded his agreement. "I will take care of my wife."

The apothecary went to the door, and George saw Rufus anxiously waiting there.

He went toward him and spoke with sincerity. "Rufus, I apologize. I behaved—"

"God's wounds, man," Rufus said gruffly, "you behaved like a man in love with his wife." His gaze faltered. "God knows, she's in love with you."

George's heart rejoiced to hear it. "Forgive me for thinking ill of you, Rufus."

The red-haired man raised his eyes and regarded his opponent steadily. "It seems to me that you should be making your apologies to your wife. Now, if you will excuse me, I am leaving."

"Rufus?" Aileas called out, raising herself slowly. "Thank you for defending me."

Rufus colored and looked away. "I meant what I said, Aileas," he muttered. "I should have married you when I had the chance." With that, he made a brief bow and departed.

George sighed and closed the door. "He's right. I should be apologizing to you, Aileas." He went to the bed and knelt beside it, taking her hand in his. "Can you ever forgive me for what I said, what I thought? I should have trusted you."

Aileas smiled gloriously. "You trust me now, do you not?"

"Absolutely."

"I should have trusted you, too," she confessed. "Can you forgive me?"

He returned her smile. "Absolutely. And I have to explain, or try to. I want you to understand why I acted the way I did." His voice softened. "I was so afraid."

"Afraid? Of me? Of my father?"

"Of myself." Briefly, he told her about the puppy.

"And so you see, my love, I was terrified I was going to hurt you. Do you remember that day in the orchard when I chased you?"

She reached out and brushed his cheek with her fingertips. "Yes. I was afraid of you, but later you seemed so placid...I underestimated you, even then. I took that for a weakness, not a strength."

"My temper is a weakness," he insisted. "I would have killed Rufus today if you had not stopped us."

"You have the most amazing self-control of any man I have ever met. Besides, it wasn't you who struck first today," she pointed out. "It was Rufus."

"You're right!" he said, apparently realizing that for the first time.

"So while I am delighted to think that I could make you feel such passion, I believe your silence did the most harm."

George laid his forehead against the bed, the truth of her words touching him deeply, and sighed wearily. "I have been such a selfish creature! I didn't want to see how I was destroying the very things about you that made me love you, and I certainly didn't realize how Margot felt."

"I know," she replied softly. She tousled his hair. "For all my suspicions, I didn't understand Margot at all."

He raised his head. "Let us not talk of suspicions anymore today. I promise you, Aileas, that I will have complete faith in you from now on."

"And Margot?"

"Oh, sweet Savior," he sighed. "I have no idea what I shall say to her."

"Perhaps nothing need be said," Aileas suggested. "It might be too humiliating for her." Then she eyed him critically. "All this talk of Margot and me when you're hurt, too."

With a weary sigh, he raised himself to sit on the side of the bed. "A little, but it is nothing compared to what I felt here—" he touched his chest "—when I feared I was going to lose you."

"I've missed you, husband," she whispered, putting her arms around him and pulling him close.

"Paracus said you should rest—and I haven't even helped wash away the blood on your face."

"Then we shall be restful. In a little while. And you should know by now that I am not the most fastidious of women."

Several hours later, Elma counted all the coins hidden behind a loose brick in the back of the wall surrounding Richard's house.

She had been too clever to keep hers in the maidservants' quarters of Ravensloft, where it might be discovered. Instead, she had buried her share of their ill-gotten gains in the wood outside the castle.

Now she was stealing Richard's money. She had seen where he hid his share. Whatever she stole from him, she richly deserved, she told herself, recalling the night he had grabbed her and pulled her into the storeroom. When he was finished with her, never questioning why she struggled so fiercely or heeding her cries to stop, she had risen from the floor and demanded money.

How shocked he had been, until she lied and told him all her customers paid, convincing herself she should have some compensation for her dishonor.

Then she had watched him, and his brother, too, until she realized what they were up to. He had been shocked again when she told him what she knew, and what it would take to keep her silent.

Although no amount he ever paid her would truly compensate for her lost innocence that terrible day, causing him the pain of lost money while enriching herself was a good sort of revenge, and the time had clearly come for her to exact it.

She smiled at the bags of coins, the leather pouches shiny in the moonlight. There was more than enough to leave this place forever and go somewhere where she was not known. She could claim to be the widow of a wealthy merchant. She was young and pretty. She could win an even richer husband, perhaps even a knight.

Wouldn't that be a pretty trick, the serving maid turned into a lady? But if Lady Aileas could change, so could she. And wouldn't it be something to see the faces of everyone here if she returned in such a state?

Such speculation was mere daydreaming, for she would never come back here again. She loathed this place and everyone in it.

Especially Sir George, who had never looked at her twice, except as she could fetch him something. Who was so oblivious to the knaves running his affairs, and who therefore deserved to be robbed.

She moved back into the shadow of Richard's house, shivering as she recalled the cold-blooded way he had stabbed his own brother. What would he do to *her,* if he felt it necessary?

Glancing over her shoulder at the massive structure of Ravensloft Castle, she thought she couldn't have asked for better circumstances under which to leave. The whole place was in confusion, with Sir George's sudden return, the injury to his wife, the hasty depar-

ture of a sobbing Lady Margot, followed by the
equally abrupt departure of Sir Rufus Hamerton.

She pulled out the pouches she had tucked into her
skirt, special pouches she had prepared for the day she
would leave. She had sewn a thick lining inside tat-
tered old leather bags, and into that lining, she carefully began to put the coins.

No curious onlooker or thief would realize such
pouches would be holding a small fortune in gold and
silver.

When she was finished, she lifted the pouches,
which were heavier than she had expected. Fortunately, being a maidservant had made her arms strong,
as well as her will, she thought as she crept out of the
steward's enclosure. Waiting in the shadows of an
alley was a donkey she had taken from the stable of
Ravensloft. It was not a swift beast, but one less likely
to be missed.

Moving slowly so not to make any unnecessary
noise, she lifted the pouches onto the donkey, and for
extra precaution, covered them with bundles of linen.

She looked again at Richard Jolliet's house—and as
she did, she saw a light kindled in the upper window.

He must have returned, perhaps to dispose of Herbert's body. With another shiver and a greater sense
of urgency, Elma climbed onto the donkey and swat-
ted it on the rear.

The beast lurched into motion and Elma rode away
from Ravensloft.

"Ow!" George gasped sharply, his features illuminated by dawn's faint rays as he lay propped up on
the disheveled cushions. The rosy light also shone on
the naked Aileas, who was sitting on his chest.

"Lie still, then, and let me wash you properly," Aileas chided. "We should have done this last night, after you washed my face."

"I was distracted," George muttered. Then he fastened his keen gaze on her face. "Am I that dirty?"

"You *were* rolling about the floor."

"I would do it again in an instant if you would wash me like this again." He twisted to kiss her hand.

Aileas shifted, nearly upsetting the basin of water precariously perched on the bed. "George! Keep still!"

"How can I help but lie still when you are sitting on my chest. Did I mention that I think my ribs are cracked?"

"Really?" She started to lift her leg to get off.

He quickly grabbed her arms to still her. "It's not serious," he said with a low chuckle.

His wife playfully struck his arm. "Tease me like that again, and you *will* have cracked ribs."

"Well, they are a little tender on my left side," he confessed.

This time, somewhat to his regret, she moved and knelt beside him. He put his hands behind his head and gazed admiringly at Aileas. "Somehow, I don't think Paracus would approve of your version of resting."

"*My* version was fine. I scarcely had to move. It was *yours*—"

"Mine?"

"I didn't know it would fit that way."

He smiled at the memory. "I wasn't sure myself, but I thought it was worth the attempt."

"Oh, it was," she sighed. "It was. I do believe you have even cured my aching head."

"Perhaps I should forgo my noble duties and become an alchemist."

She lay beside him and stroked his chest lightly. "In some things, I believe you already are."

"Nevertheless, I think it might be wise not to bother Paracus with a report on how we 'rested.'"

Aileas laughed her agreement and nestled close to him. "And I think that perhaps for this one day, I might be persuaded to stay in bed with you."

"Excellent notion!" He chuckled softly. "Now, what else has been going on in my absence?" He gave her a curious, sidelong glance. "Other than vast improvements in my wife's deportment, all of which she will now forget—with my approval."

She toyed with a lock of his hair. "After all my efforts to make them? I think not." She frowned slightly. "Will you investigate the accounts? I truly believe that the stewards are not completely honest."

"I shall begin tomorrow," he affirmed.

She smiled, then sighed. "I wish I had learned to read."

"It is not too late."

She raised herself on her elbow to look at him, and he was surprised by the serious expression on her face. "I don't think I'm going to have time."

"You find the chatelaine's duties that interesting that you can spare no time from them?" he teased. "Or is it your intention to do all the hunting for the castle, too?"

She shook her head, suddenly as shy as he had ever seen a woman. "I'll be too busy."

"With what?" he asked, genuinely puzzled.

"With...with our baby."

"Our what?" George asked, astonished.

"Our baby. At least, I think I'm with child." She blushed prettily and shrugged her slender shoulders. "I'm not absolutely sure, but I'm late."

George threw back his head and laughed, then embraced her fiercely. "This is marvelous, Aileas! Wonderful! I am the happiest man in England!"

She regarded him with trepidation. "You don't think…"

He grew serious immediately. "I don't doubt that I'm the father, if that's what's troubling you," he said gently.

"No," she said, shaking her head as very real dread filled her eyes. "Do you think I'll be a good mother?"

George took her to him tenderly. "You will be a wonderful mother." His voice took on a teasing tone. "Especially if it's a boy. Why, I can think of no other women of my acquaintance who can teach their sons the finer points of archery."

"But I don't know anything about babies," she protested. "I've never even held one."

He held her away from him, and his expression was as serious as his tone. "Aileas, you will be a fine mother. I have absolute faith in that." Then, because he was George de Gramercie, he couldn't help grinning mischievously and saying, "Granted, you will not be the usual type of mother, but I think that will be wonderful."

She smiled with relief before they both became aware of a very low and tentative knocking on the bedchamber door.

"It must be Elma," Aileas said.

She began to get out of bed, but George held her back. "You are supposed to be resting, wife," he chided playfully as he rose from the bed. "I will have Elma bring us some bread and cheese and wine."

"You had better put on some clothes before you open the door," Aileas suggested, pulling the coverlet and sheet up to her chin.

He gave her a devilish grin as he drew on his shirt and breeches.

Then he stepped to the door and flung it open, to reveal a young maidservant trembling on the doorstep. She was one of the hall servants whose duties should not have extended to the upper chambers, as she seemed well aware, for her eyes widened with fear as she made a little curtsy. "If you please, my lord, I've been sent to wake you."

"Is something the matter?" George demanded, certain there was by the maid's appearance and manner. "Where is Elma?"

"If you please, my lord," the girl stammered, "she's…she's gone, nobody knows where. And nobody can find Herbert Jolliet, either."

"Herbert?" George repeated, puzzled.

"Herbert and Elma are both missing?" Aileas asked from the bed.

The maidservant nodded nervously.

"Did either of them say anything yesterday? Is it possible they've gone off together?" George demanded, realizing that stranger things had happened.

"No, my lord, my lady, they never said nothing—but yesterday, we was all in a muddle, what with the lady's head and Lady Margot and the other gentleman leaving."

George gave Aileas a surprised look, then turned back to the timorous maid. "Lady Margot has left?"

"Yes, my lord, yesterday afternoon, and Sir Rufus

after her. We were all in a bustle getting their things ready. Nobody had time to say much to anyone.''

"It seems my hospitality leaves something to be desired,'' George said ruefully, turning toward his wife.

"Margot must have been too upset to stay. And Rufus, too. He said he was going,'' she reminded him.

George nodded his concurrence. "What about Sir Richard?'' he asked the servant. "Does he have any idea where his brother might be?''

She shook her head. "No, my lord. He's waiting for you in the hall. It was him ordered me to fetch you.''

"Tell Sir Richard I shall be down at once,'' George said briskly. The maid nodded, dropped another curtsy and hurried away.

George closed the door and reached for his boots, pausing when he realized Aileas was getting out of bed. "No, you don't!'' he cried softly. "You have to rest.''

"But, George!''

"Paracus said you should rest. And there's nothing you can do, anyway.''

"I won't stay in bed another minute,'' she said, pulling her shift over her head. "I want to know what's going on.''

George opened his mouth to protest, then stopped. "You have every right to do so,'' he agreed. "Just promise me you will not overtax your strength.''

"I won't.''

Chapter Eighteen

Sir Richard Jolliet stood before the dais, his brow furrowed, his expression concerned, shivering with barely suppressed and genuine rage as he faced his lord.

How dare that wench steal his money? he thought angrily. When he got his hands on her, she would rue the day.

He would blame her for the murder of his brother, too. He would accuse her of thievery. He would see her imprisoned and then hung, and on that day, he would be a happy man.

"Disappeared, you say?" Sir George repeated slowly.

"Yes, my lord," Richard said respectfully, although it was all he could do to keep a sneer from his face. George de Gramercie was a fool, and so was his wife, who came dashing down the stairs like a boy chasing a ball, her bow and quiver slung over her body as if she were off on a hunt. He wished more than ever that she had broken her head yesterday. "I regret to say that it appears both he and Elma have been up to no good."

"Theft?" Sir George proposed.

"At the very least, my lord," he replied. "I am truly sorry to have to tell you that I fear Herbert has abused your trust and the responsibility you have placed in him." He lowered his head with the appropriate show of shame. "Indeed, my lord, I fear he has disgraced himself, and his whole family, by his actions."

He glanced first at Sir George, who was regarding him gravely, then at Lady Aileas. She frowned when he caught her eye, and the look on her face suddenly chilled him to the marrow of his bones.

Nevertheless, he swallowed hard and continued. "More than that, my lord, my house was burgled in the night. A dishonest brother missing, a maidservant absconded—perhaps together—my own money gone. This is truly a terrible business."

"What happened to the miller, Richard?" Lady Aileas asked very slowly and deliberately.

"He...he was beaten by some ruffians, my lady," Richard answered, startled by her question.

"You know no more of it than that?" she demanded.

"Absolutely not, my lady." She was fishing for answers. Surely if she had any, she would be accusing him now. "Sir George himself investigated the matter," he reminded her.

"Yes, I did," Sir George remarked, "but I may have been too hasty, in view of these...developments. Why do you think Herbert has gone away with Elma? Perhaps he is only visiting Lisette."

"Lisette, my lord?" Richard asked, apparently mystified.

"Who is Lisette?" Lady Aileas asked.

"His mistress," Sir George revealed. "Or was he dallying with Elma, too?"

"I don't know, my lord. Perhaps." *Yes. Let that be the story. Then, if Elma denied Herbert's companionship on her journey, or should someone somehow discover Herbert's body—although he had hidden it very carefully in the woods—either one could be blamed on a lover's quarrel.*

"We shall have to find them," Sir George said briskly. "The sooner the better. Some men should be dispatched to Lisette, and ten to accompany me. That includes you, Richard. Aileas, you should..." He paused and regarded his wife with a wry look. "You should come with me, too."

Then he marched toward the door, Lady Aileas right behind him, leaving Richard to hurry along after them.

Elma heard the mounted soldiers before she saw them, for the horses' hooves were like a hundred drums behind her on the road.

"Holy Mother!" she breathed as she quickly dismounted. It would be like Richard to come after her with an armed guard. She should have stolen a horse.

She yanked on the donkey's harness, dragging it off the road into the underbrush and through the trees, out of sight of anyone on the road as she had during the night when she had heard a lone horseman passing. Branches scratched her arms, and the ground beneath her feet was slick and muddy, but she persisted, knowing that she dared not be caught. This time, in the daylight, she had better go further into the woods.

To be sure, the money was well hidden and she could accuse Richard of far more serious crimes than she was guilty of, for his abuse of his position of trust was a far more serious matter than the petty thievery of a maidservant. Nevertheless, she would not risk hanging, the punishment for any and all theft.

She looked about her. She could still make out the road. The donkey, however, had apparently decided it had gone far enough and refused to move.

The riders were closer now. She could hear the jingle of their harness and realized it must be a large company, too large to simply be chasing a runaway servant. They must know about the theft.

Swiftly, she tugged the pouches off the donkey and abandoned the beast. There was a cave nearby, so small it could barely hold one person, but it was across a narrow stream that would throw any hounds off her scent.

She started to run in that direction, cursing the heavy weight of her burden. Then Elma stumbled over something and fell back, landing hard on the ground. Panting, she slowly rolled on her side to get up, still clutching the pouches—and came face-to-face with Herbert's dull, lifeless eyes.

She let out a cry, then clapped her hand over her mouth as bevies of startled birds soared upward.

George heard the cry and pulled his horse to a stop. Then all the men saw the birds, rising in the air like smoke.

George ordered them into the forest.

Panicked, Elma felt the sweat trickle down her back as she struggled through the bushes looking for the stream. It had been months since she had been in this wood, and years since she had last seen the cave.

But it was her only hope, so she continued, biting

back curses and trying to stay upright. It was tempting to drop the pouches, so that she could run with more ease, but in those pouches was her future, and she would not leave them.

Until she knew it was that, or be caught. With desperate, trembling hands she laid the pouches in the roots of a large oak, then covered them with dirt and leaves as quickly as she could.

It would have to do, she thought frantically, straightening. Glancing about, she neither saw nor heard any pursuers and for an instant dared to hope they had abandoned the chase. Snatching up her skirts, she began to run through the underbrush, shoving branches aside with her shoulders and ignoring the wet slaps on her face and arms.

She was wrong. George and the others had not given up. They had encircled her, as she discovered when she reached a small clearing to find dismounted soldiers in front of her and to the sides. She turned on her heel, only to see Sir George riding toward her, his expression grave.

Richard Jolliet was behind him.

Her chest heaved as she bent over and drew in heavy, rasping breaths, staring at the ground and desperately trying to think.

"Good morning, Elma," Sir George said, and she raised her eyes to see her lord sitting calmly on his stallion, eyeing her as blandly as if they were meeting in the chapel for mass.

Her only chance was to act a runaway servant, and nothing more. "Forgive me, Sir George," she panted. "I know I shouldn't have done—"

"She's a thief!"

Elma glared at Richard Jolliet. She clenched her

fists and would have screamed with rage if she thought it would help. "I am not!" she cried, facing Sir George again, even as she realized Richard had just made a mistake. "Of what am I accused of stealing?"

Richard opened his mouth to speak—then Elma saw the flicker of doubt in his eyes. "She robbed me of coin, my lord, you of linen—and who knows what else?"

"Don't you?" Sir George asked evenly as he dismounted. "It is a pity we cannot ask Herbert what else has gone astray, isn't it, Elma?"

"My lord, I...I ran away, it is true, because...because Sir Richard was abusing me!"

"Abusing you? What do you mean?"

"He...he attacked me. Several times."

"She is a base, deceitful liar, my lord!" Richard cried.

"She is certainly something," George remarked. He glanced back at one of his soldiers, who came forward carrying two pouches. "A thief, for one thing, I suspect. Let us see what she has made off with."

Elma could scarcely breathe as Baldwin opened the pouch. He lifted it, and clothes fell to the ground. "There is nothing else here, my lord," he said, hefting the pouch, a puzzled look on his face.

"Why is that empty pouch so heavy?" Sir George asked meditatively. "And what might you know about Herbert?"

"I know nothing about Herbert, my lord," Elma declared. "I daresay his brother does, though."

"Really? Is that so, Richard?" Sir George regarded his estate steward a moment, then in one swift motion, he drew his sword and jabbed at the supposedly empty pouch, pulling the weapon through the leather to make a jagged tear.

A rain of gold and silver coins began to fall upon the ground.

"You see, my lord!" Richard declared. "She has stolen from me!"

"I see, indeed," Sir George replied, and Elma knew she was as good as condemned.

"That isn't his money!" she cried desperately. "Sir Richard has been stealing from you for years. How else could he have so much money for anyone to steal?"

"An interesting point," George noted as he faced his estate steward, his tone still reasonably calm, although inwardly he was seething with anger at both his steward and himself. He should have listened to Aileas, who had not been lulled into a false sense of security regarding his household. Even if she had been wrong, he should have paid her more heed. "There would appear to be rather a large sum here."

"Well...well, my lord," Richard stammered, more nonplussed than George had ever seen. "Some of it is your money. I was keeping it—"

"For what?" George demanded. "A sudden, unexpected raise in our taxes? More napkins?"

Richard stared at his lord, his mouth gaping.

"Tell me, Richard, where is your brother?" George asked, his drawn sword in his hand as he strolled closer to the man. "Has he already escaped with his share of the money you have stolen from me and my father?"

Suddenly he grabbed Richard by the collar of his tunic and dragged him from his horse. "How much money?'' he demanded through clenched teeth. "How much have you stolen over the years?''

"My...my lord!''

"I trusted you,'' George said, his tone full of bitter reproach. "My father trusted you.''

"He killed Herbert, too!'' Elma announced. "I saw him do it.''

George continued to hold Richard as he glanced at Elma over his shoulder. "Herbert is dead? You saw it?'' His gaze shifted to Richard. "Richard, Richard, Richard, you are an evil creature.''

"As God is my witness, my lord—''

"I think I will let the account books be a witness. I will have them examined. Carefully.''

"My lord, please!'' Richard pleaded. "I am innocent.''

"Of course I shall have to summon in the linen merchant to question. And the miller will have to be reexamined to see if he has remembered anything more about the men who attacked him. Then I will find those men—''

"George!'' It was Aileas, calling from within the woods. "I have found Herbert. I have found his body.''

George shoved the estate steward so hard he fell to the muddy ground. "You killed your own brother?''

"No, I didn't!'' Richard screamed. "*She* did!'' He pointed at Elma. "She did it! Please, my lord, you must believe me! I am innocent.''

But George could see the confirmation of the accusations in the man's eyes.

Once more, George looked at Elma. "Did you kill Herbert?''

Before she could answer, Richard suddenly jumped

to his feet and knocked George's sword from his hand. In the next instant, he had grabbed George's arm, yanking it behind his back, and he put a dagger to his lord's throat. "Nobody make any sudden movements," he warned, "or I'll slit this fool's throat like a chicken's!"

Aileas, leading her horse toward the soldiers, halted the moment the scuffle broke out. Quickly she grabbed her bow and quiver, then crouched down and crept slowly toward the circle of men.

To see Richard inching backward, his dagger at George's throat. Aileas drew her breath in sharply, for there was a trickle of blood on her husband's neck.

"Don't you move!" Richard warned the men in the clearing as he took another step toward his own horse. "Stay back!"

Aileas drew an arrow from her quiver and willed her hands to be steady as she lay the arrow's notch in the bowstring. "Keep still, George," she whispered, hoping his incredible sangfroid would not desert him at this crucial moment.

She rose slowly, lifted her bow and drew it back steadily, taking careful aim.

Then she let the arrow fly.

Richard cried out as an arrow pierced his shoulder. His dagger fell to the ground from his now useless hand. At nearly the same time, George whirled around and punched him, sending him staggering backward. The other men quickly grabbed the steward and pulled him to his feet, oblivious to his curses.

"Take that miscreant back to Ravensloft," George

ordered, and some of his men dragged Richard Jolliet away.

From her place in the woods, Aileas sighed with relief, until a sudden movement caught her eye. Elma, seeing that the men were all watching George and Richard, had started to run away. Again, Aileas selected an arrow and drew her bow, then let fly. She aimed low, wanting only to wound Elma to stop her flight.

Elma screamed and fell before any of the men had realized she had fled. Baldwin and Derek went to her, while Aileas hurried toward the others, pushing her way through them. She threw herself into George's arms. "I thought he was going to kill you," she murmured, holding him tightly.

"I thought he was, too," George confessed. "I must say, this is far too exciting a way to begin my day."

"I heartily agree," Aileas said, drawing in a long, quavering breath.

"My lord!" It was Derek, standing near Elma.

"I shot her," Aileas said as she accompanied her husband toward the fallen servant, "to prevent her running away."

"I'll say you did," Derek remarked. "She's dead."

Aileas gasped and stared at the young woman's body lying facedown on the ground, her arms outflung and Aileas's arrow protruding from her blood-soaked back.

"I...I didn't mean to kill her," she whispered, stunned and horrified by what she had done. For all her practice in the arts of war, she had never actually caused a death, and it was ugly beyond imagining. She looked away, burying her face in her hands. "I didn't want..."

She felt George's warm, strong arms go around her. "I know," he said softly as he pulled her into the comfort of his embrace. "Believe me, Aileas, I know."

Two months later, Aileas found George glumly sitting alone in his solar, staring at parchments that covered his table, some open, others still rolled. Yet more parchments lay on a smaller table behind him.

He raised his eyes and managed a small, self-mocking smile. "It seems, my dearest," he said wryly, "that I have been the dupe of all dupes. Richard and Herbert Jolliet have been stealing from my father for years, and me, too. We may never know exactly how much."

Aileas came behind the table and laid her hands on his shoulders. "Never mind," she said quietly. "We have plenty."

Richard had been convicted of theft and murder and sentenced to hang. That judgment had been carried out a fortnight ago. In deference to their past friendship, George had commanded that the body be cut down immediately. The steward's body was denied Christian burial and had been buried somewhere in the forest, beside the body of his brother. They were together in death as they had been in life, but Aileas doubted either slept easy. Elma lay in a paupers' grave outside the village walls.

"This must be Sir Thomas's frugal daughter talking," he said, twisting to grin at her.

"Are you sorry I am not a spendthrift?" she charged gravely.

"We are far from ruined, I'm happy to say." He looked back at the table. "But it is truly embarrassing to realize one has been as blind as a bat for years. I suppose I should be happy that they were too smart to be overly greedy.''

Aileas lightly kissed the top of his head and came around beside him, gently caressing his arm. "You were too trusting, that's all," she said comfortingly. "The minstrels all say that love is blind. Trust is, as well.

"Indeed, you saw so many faults in me, I was beginning to fear you would never love me. Either I have been improving, or else you have truly fallen in love with me and become blind to my shortcomings.''

George reached out and pulled her onto his lap. "To be perfectly honest, Aileas, I think it is both. You are improving—in the nonessentials. In the essentials, you were always perfect—and I am so completely in love with you, you could easily hoodwink me." He frowned again. "Perhaps that is not a wise thing for a husband to admit.''

Aileas laughed softly. "I fear I have become blind to your faults, too.''

"Perhaps I don't have any," he suggested.

"Margot thought you did.''

"I wish she hadn't left under such circumstances," he confessed. "I have invited her again but—" he pointed to a small piece of parchment "—she declines. It seems she is to be married, to a man of the king's choosing.''

"The king's choosing?''

"Margot is quite wealthy, with a large estate. She is also the daughter of a very powerful lord. The king—and his courtiers—take a vast deal of interest in such widows.''

"I hope she'll be happy.''

"She deserves to be."

"I wouldn't want my husband chosen for me," Aileas said firmly. "And..." She blushed and hesitated.

"And?"

"And I was hoping Rufus..."

"Rufus and Margot?"

Aileas shrugged her shoulders and began to play with a lock of George's fair hair. "He thought she was very beautiful, and he is a good man. He comes from a noble family, too, although not a rich one. I know he's rather rough in his ways, perhaps, but—" her tone grew less serious "—I'm sure she could improve him."

"Maybe I should send a message to the king with a helpful suggestion concerning my widowed cousin."

Aileas's eyes widened. "The king would listen to you on such business?"

George's eyes twinkled merrily. "Does it surprise you to learn that your husband is an influential man? The king thinks me a most amusing fellow."

Aileas laughed gaily. "Again, I've underestimated you! But I must agree that you are amusing. And charming and wonderful and very, very desirable." She kissed him lightly.

"Aileas," George murmured, pressing an answering kiss on her delectable lips, "I am supposed to be attending to my accounts."

"I fear, my lord, that I have grown terribly dissolute living in your household," she replied without a hint of contrition, "because I must insist that you forget your accounts for a little while."

"Only if you promise you will learn to read so that you can take this onerous task from me."

"Gladly," she said, twisting a lock of his fair hair in her fingers, "for I have found being a student is not intolerable."

George's arms tightened about her. "Then, my love," he whispered huskily, "let us be dissolute together…"

* * * * * *

Can the scholarly
Geoffrey de Burgh tame
the "wicked" Lady Elene,
who must become his wife?

Find out in Deborah Simmons's
terrific new medieval novel

Coming in January
to your favorite paperback book outlet.

The deBurgh Bride

THE deBURGH BRIDE (ISBN 28999-5)

WELCOME TO *Love Inspired* ™

A brand-new series of contemporary inspirational love stories.

Join men and women as they learn valuable lessons about facing the challenges of today's world and about life, love and faith.

Look for the following January 1998
Love Inspired™ titles:

Night Music
by Sara Mitchell

A Wife Worth Waiting For
by Arlene James

Faithfully Yours
by Lois Richer

Available in retail outlets
in December 1997.

LIFT YOUR SPIRITS AND GLADDEN YOUR HEART with *Love Inspired* ™!

Steeple
Hill™

LI198

Harlequin®
Historical

"One of the top five historical trilogies
of the nineties." —*Affaire de Coeur*

Bestselling Harlequin Historical author

THERESA MICHAELS

presents the story of the second widow
in her heartwarming series

THE MERRY WIDOWS
Catherine

"Sensitivity, sensuality and a sense of humor are
hallmarks of Theresa Michaels' captivating storytelling."
—*Romantic Times*

Don't miss reading about Catherine in the second book in the
Merry Widows trilogy, coming to you in February 1998.

Unlock the secrets of romance just in time for the most romantic day of the year—Valentine's Day!

Key to My Heart
features three of your favorite authors,

**Kasey Michaels,
Rebecca York
and Muriel Jensen,**

to bring you wonderful tales of romance and Valentine's Day dreams come true.

As an added bonus you can receive Harlequin's special Valentine's Day necklace. FREE with the purchase of every *Key to My Heart* collection.

Available in January,
wherever Harlequin books are sold.

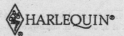

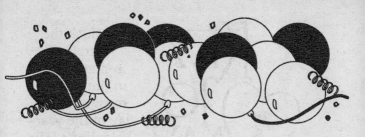

Ring in the New Year with

New Year's Resolution:

FAMILY

**This heartwarming collection of three
contemporary stories rings in the
New Year with babies, families and
the best of holiday romance.**

Add a dash of romance to your holiday celebrations
with this exciting new collection, featuring bestselling
authors **Barbara Bretton, Anne McAllister** and
Leandra Logan.

Available in December,
wherever Harlequin books are sold.

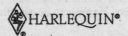

HARLEQUIN®

HARLEQUIN WOMEN KNOW ROMANCE WHEN THEY SEE IT.

And they'll see it on **ROMANCE CLASSICS**, the new 24-hour TV channel devoted to romantic movies and original programs like the special **Romantically Speaking—Harlequin™ Goes Prime Time.**

Romantically Speaking—Harlequin™ Goes Prime Time introduces you to many of your favorite romance authors in a program developed exclusively for Harlequin® readers.

Watch for **Romantically Speaking—Harlequin™ Goes Prime Time** beginning in the summer of 1997.

If you're not receiving ROMANCE CLASSICS, call your local cable operator or satellite provider and ask for it today!

ROMANCE CLASSICS

Escape to the network of your dreams.

See Ingrid Bergman and Gregory Peck in *Spellbound* on Romance Classics.

**Look for these titles—
available at your favorite retail outlet!**

January 1998
Renegade Son by Lisa Jackson
Danielle Summers had problems: a rebellious child
and unscrupulous enemies. In addition, her Montana
ranch was slowly being sabotaged. And then there was
Chase McEnroe—who admired her land and desired her
body. But Danielle feared he would invade more than just
her property—he'd trespass on her heart.

February 1998
The Heart's Yearning by Ginna Gray
Fourteen years ago Laura gave her baby up for adoption,
and not one day had passed that she didn't think about
him and agonize over her choice—so she finally followed
her heart to Texas to see her child. But the plan to watch
her son from afar doesn't quite happen that way, once the
boy's sexy—*single*—father takes a decided interest in *her.*

March 1998
First Things Last by Dixie Browning
One look into Chandler Harrington's dark eyes and
Belinda Massey could refuse the Virginia millionaire nothing.
So how could the no-nonsense nanny believe the rumors that
he had kidnapped his nephew—an adorable, healthy little boy
who crawled as easily into her heart as he did into her lap?

**BORN IN THE USA: Love, marriage—
and the pursuit of family!**